Beautifully Damaged

Beautifully Damaged Series Book One

J.A. Owenby

Beautifully Damaged

J.A. OWENBY

Edited by: Hot Tree

Cover Art by: iheartcoverdesigns

Photographer: CJC Photography

Model: Eric Guilmette

First Edition ISBN-13: 978-1-949414-41-7

For Susan, Vicki, David, and Alida. I couldn't do this without you.

Trigger Warning

Beautifully Damaged is recommended for readers 17+.
Due to dark and mature content, graphic sex scenes, and sensitive topics, please consider this your *trigger warning*!

Download your FREE Book!

SIGN UP FOR J.A. OWENBY'S NEWSLETTER and download your FREE book, Love & Sins. Stay up to date concerning exclusive bonus scenes, updates on upcoming releases, and more. https://authorjaowenby.com/newsletter/

Prologue ~ Present Day

My lungs burned and fire licked up my chest as I held my breath, struggling not to open my mouth to gasp for air that was just out of my reach. Every crazy moment of my nineteen years played before me as I clawed at the powerful hands that held me under the murky water. Fear ripped through me as I stared into savage eyes. The tip of my nose broke through the surface, and I attempted to push my head upward. *If I could only suck in a lifesaving ...* Before I was able to complete the thought, I was shoved under again. How had I gotten here, suddenly fighting for my life?

Holden's beautiful smile flashed across my mind and fueled a flicker of optimism that I could survive. I had to. Holden had to know the truth.

With an extra boost of adrenaline, I wedged my thumb between the two ligaments of my attacker's wrist, then pushed into the soft flesh as hard as I could. This had to work. My energy was dwindling, and fast.

Suddenly, my head popped up, and I gulped in much-needed air as I gazed into the twisted and depraved face of the monster that wanted me dead.

Whack. A scream tore from my throat as the impact against my skull rendered me helpless. Stars danced in front of my eyes as I slipped from reality. If this was it, I had one thing to say to my captor before I left this screwed-up world.

"Fuck ... you ..." The darkness beckoned to me, urging me to give in as she welcomed me into her arms.

Chapter 1

Five months earlier

The voices in my head whispered that I should end it all. There was no other choice.

My heart and mind were in a constant push and pull, like the moon and ocean—a consistent dance between life and death. Once again, I'd struggled to claw my way out of hell, clinging to a tiny thread of hope that one day I would finally succeed.

I flopped over in my bed, pulling the thin sheet under my chin and shuddering against the frigid air seeping through the cracks of my bedroom walls. The stupid mobile home was on its last leg, threatening to fall over on its disgruntled and weather-beaten side at any given moment. If a wind gusted through the trailer park and knocked my house over, I wondered if I'd survive, or if I would be trapped beneath it. If Dan, my sorry excuse for a guardian, died, I wouldn't shed one single tear.

Gently, I massaged my right bicep and peered at the blue-and-purple bruises that were forming. Yesterday, Dan had jerked my arm so hard it had nearly popped out of the socket. The piece of shit had staggered in through the front door, drunk and smelling like a skunk. It was bad enough when he drank, but when he lost himself in a fifth of whiskey *and* smoked weed, it was a recipe for disaster. Unfortunately, I was the one that caught the raw end of that deal.

Mom didn't have any actual family that she could count on, so she wrangled Dan into becoming my guardian if anything happened to her. Little did he know that Mom would disappear a few months after he signed all the legal documents. I was only three when Dan stepped in full time.

Life with him had been decent at first, until around eight years ago. Once my body had decided to grow boobs and curves, Dan had attempted to hide his sideways glances but failed. It didn't take me long to stop wearing tank tops and shorts around him. I hid my developing form the best I could in baggy jeans and sweatshirts, trying not to draw unwanted attention from him or anyone else. It hadn't worked well.

Dan was a lean and strong man for someone who had no idea what working even meant. He would hold a job for a few days, then stop showing up. At one stage in his life, he'd also been handsome, but his dark hair was unkempt, and he only trimmed his scraggly beard once a month. If he was on a nasty bender, it wasn't even that often. I'd forgotten the actual color of his eyes since they were always bloodshot.

For now, I had to bide my time until I could figure out how to escape this shit show and move out.

Most evenings, I would watch television and fall asleep on the couch until he came home from whatever cheap and grungy bar still allowed him to walk through their doors. Dan had been tossed out of so many that he'd lost count.

Earlier that night, I'd crawled into my twin bed and huddled beneath the sheet and the one threadbare blanket I owned. I'd just started my new job at Bob's Diner down the street last week, and quilts and a coat were on the top of my list to buy. At least the restaurant was only a few blocks away. Unless there was snow on the ground and ice on the sidewalks, I could run to and from work, so I didn't turn into an icicle. I'd been working measly jobs since I was ten, paying the water and food bills that Dan never took care of. Clothes and warm blankets weren't a priority, but so far, winter had been brutally cold. I would have to go straight to the secondhand store as soon as I got my first check. Now that I was earning tips, maybe even sooner.

The owner of the diner, Bob Davies, had lived in Havre, Montana, since before I was born. He'd also attended high school with Mom and Dan. Bob remembered Mom before ... I sank my teeth into my bottom lip until I winced, forcing the memories to stay locked away.

I tossed and turned, the springs on the mattress jabbing me in the back as the fragile metal frame creaked and groaned.

Slipping my hand between the bed and the wall, I felt around for the folded piece of paper. Carefully, I pulled it out of the hiding place I'd chosen and clutched it to my chest. The smooth sheet crinkled between my fingers, and for the first time that day, I smiled. I opened the letter I'd printed at the library, my attention landing on the PSU logo, then my name.

Dear River Collins,

We're happy to extend a full scholarship to Portland State University...

My pulse kicked up a notch. Freedom was right around the corner. My heart leaped inside my chest while I pondered what my new college life would look like in the fall. I'd missed the application deadlines my senior year of high school, but not this time. I'd spent long days at the library applying for scholarships and reaching out to my old school counselor, Mrs. Donaldson, for help. I hadn't even had the money to apply, but Mrs. Donaldson covered the fees, and I was paying her back a little each week now that I was working again. Since I didn't own a cell phone, we kept in touch through email.

Thank God for the library printer as well. Instead of paying for what I printed, I worked out a deal with the manager to volunteer. She agreed that my time would help solve the budget problem, and she happily let me use the computer and printer as often as I wanted.

What she didn't realize was that she'd given me a sanctuary. The staff wouldn't kick me out until 9:00 p.m., so when shit got bad at home, that was where I hid.

Mrs. Donaldson was the first person I'd messaged when I received the email that I'd been accepted to Portland State University with a full ride, plus enough money left to live on. The second person I told was my best friend, Addison.

Addison and I had been friends since grade school. She was already at PSU, and I was excited to join her soon.

Addison had an amazing family, but they also struggled financially. Her big blue eyes filled with tears when she told me about her college plans. She'd received scholarships, which had helped her escape this little hellhole of a town we lived in. When we were twelve, we pinky swore that we would make it out of here. I also promised myself I'd leave before I turned into my mom or Dan.

A tear burned my wind-chapped skin as it escaped my eye. I swiped at it, then tucked the email in its hiding place again. Not only did I miss Addison, but I was secretly afraid she'd moved on without me.

I was sick and tired of Dan, too. Lately, his drunken episodes had grown worse. I wasn't sure if he was popping pills or what was different, but he had recently turned into even more of a challenge.

The slam of a kitchen cabinet startled me, and I laid still, pretending to be asleep in case he staggered toward my room. My arm was already sore, and I didn't need any more attention from him.

"Georgia, you awake?" Dan's words were slurred.

I peeked at him and held my breath. He wore the same brown, long-sleeved shirt he had on yesterday, paired with dusty and worn cowboy boots. But why had he called me Georgia? It was my mom's name, and she'd been gone for years.

His footsteps grew closer as he entered my room, and my pulse kicked into overdrive. "Georgia, goddammit, wake the fuck up, you whore." Dan plunked down on the side of the bed, and his large hand palmed my ass through the blankets. *Holy shit, not again.*

I shot up, glaring at him. His shirt had a hole in the pocket, and his jeans were faded and grimy. My expression twisted with disgust. "I'm *not* Georgia. I'm her daughter River. You need to get out. *Now.*" I pointed to the door, my voice sounding more confident than I felt.

My nose scrunched up. The bastard reeked of cheap whiskey and stale cigarettes.

A harsh chuckle filled my tiny room. "You sure are pretty, Georgia." He touched my cheek with the back of his hand and dragged his knuckle down the side of my face. "Are you going to give me what I want, or am I going to take it again?"

"Dan," I whispered, my body trembling with fear when I realized he wasn't going to snap out of his drunken haze. I pulled the covers tighter around me, but I was well aware that it wasn't enough to protect me. He overpowered me all the time.

I drew my knees to my chest and backed away from him. Terror gripped me when I realized I was trapped between him and the wall. There was nowhere for me to go.

"Dan, it's River. You're drunk and think I'm Mom." Maybe I could break through to him before anything happened.

With a quick move, he placed his palm against my mouth and pulled on my ankle with his other hand, pulling me down onto the bed. I felt around on the top of my secondhand nightstand, frantically searching for anything that I might be able to use to hit or stab him with. Nothing. It was empty. Shit, I must have forgotten to return the letter opener. I usually kept it next to me for protection on nights like this.

I scratched and clawed at his arm as I struggled against him. Hot tears spilled down my face as he easily outmaneuvered me. With a quick jerk, he threw my sheet and blanket on the floor.

"Little bitch, how dare you hold out on me? You know this tight pussy is mine."

Bile rose in my throat, and I choked it down. I bit the inside of his palm as hard as I could. Dan snatched it away, and I swung my clenched hand at his jaw. Unfortunately, he was too close to me, and all my struggling and thrashing around were just pissing him off even more.

"Oh? You like it rough?" He sneered at me, and a harsh laugh escaped him.

I curled my arms over my head, but he pulled them away, then his fist met my cheek. Before I had time to scream, his fury landed on my nose. Blood spurted across my black sweatshirt.

"You stupid piece of shit. I hate you!" I kicked at him as he tried to pull my legs apart. Pain dimmed my vision as I continued to fight him with every last drop of strength.

Earlier that day, I'd spotted a cot in the cleaning closet at the diner. I shouldn't have come home. I should have slept at the restaurant.

I slammed my eyes closed. Time slowed to a crawl while my ears rang. Dan pinned me down and jerked my sweatpants and panties down to my ankles. A whimper escaped me as my entire world was turned inside out again in less than sixty seconds.

* * *

I was nineteen and only had sex willingly twice. Both occasions were with my almost boyfriend when I was sixteen. It was awkward, but we'd been friends for years, and he felt like a safe person for me to explore with. But Dan ... he'd overpowered me and stripped me of my choice more times than I could count over the years.

My head throbbed as I attempted to sit up on my bed. As soon as Dan had finished, he'd crawled off me and left my room. Hopefully he was passed out cold because I needed to leave. One thing I knew for sure was that I couldn't live here any longer. I thought I could lay low and stay off Dan's radar, but he'd made it clear that I was sadly mistaken. Trying to manage the situation was a losing battle. Plus, I wanted more than a measly life where all I did was pick up everyone else's scraps as they moved forward. The only reason I hadn't escaped sooner was due to lack of money. But I didn't care anymore. I would figure it out.

The diner was open twenty-four hours, so that would be my first stop. Although I wanted to shower and scrub that son of a bitch off me, it would have to wait. I was terrified he'd come in and hurt me again.

I quickly emptied my drawers and stuffed my clothes into my ratty pink-and-black backpack. A creak in the floor sent ice through my veins and I stood rooted in place. Holding my breath, I listened for Dan's movements. I counted to thirty in my head and when I hadn't heard any other noises, I decided it was the wind.

After removing my blood-streaked sweatshirt and pants, I changed into clean clothes and tossed on a hoodie over my long-sleeved black shirt. I slipped the backpack onto my shoulder and crept out of my room. Thankfully, I had a bathroom next to my bedroom, so I was able to grab my toothbrush and other toiletries. My gaze narrowed when I spotted the flashlight. Why it was in here, I had no idea, but it would have come in handy when Dan ... I blinked several times, trying to clear the memory of him on top of me just minutes ago. My skin prickled from his touch and the hair on the back of my neck stood on end. I had to hurry the hell up. I could feel sick later.

A part of me wanted to look at my reflection in the medicine cabinet mirror that hung over the sink and see the damage Dan had inflicted on my face, but I couldn't stop. If I saw my long, tangled brown hair along with the bruises blooming across my skin, I would lose it, and I had to keep going.

I shoved the flashlight and disposable razor into the front pocket, then tiptoed to the living room.

Dan was sprawled out on the floral velveteen couch that was older than I was, his mouth open and his leg hanging off the side. A soft snore told me he was passed out. Hopefully, he would stay that way.

I continued to the kitchen and loaded up my bag with food for the road. If I needed to, I could buy a hot meal at the diner while I planned my next move. Staying here with the son of a bitch was out of the question.

Eyeing Dan, I quietly opened the cabinet under the sink and removed the container of rat poison. I gently shook it, confirming there were still enough pellets in the box to get the job done. Since I always made the coffee in the morning, Dan wouldn't think twice if there was some in the pot for him. This time, though, there would be an added surprise for him. If he happened to die, no one would think too hard about it. He was an alcoholic and drug addict. Hell, I doubted that anyone would squeal on me if they did suspect foul play. What I did know was that Dan had to pay for raping me.

A few minutes later, the rat poison pellets were mixed with the coffee grounds, and it was ready for Dan to turn on and brew in the morning. I slipped my other arm through the strap of my backpack and glared at him. I prayed that bastard would suffer. I would have to rely on word of mouth to see if he lived or not, but after what he did, I hoped like hell he died.

My nostrils flared as I headed toward the door. I was almost home free when the floor creaked beneath my weight.

"River? Where the fuck do you think you're going?" Dan growled.

Chapter Two

Dan's callused fingers wrapped around my arm, and I slammed into him with my backpack, using his weight against him. The moment he landed on his butt, I hauled ass out of the trailer. My long legs propelled me forward, my arms falling into an easy rhythm. I'd been born with a body built for long-distance running and had excelled at track in school.

"You bitch! Get back here, River!" Dan yelled.

"Fuck you, asshole!" The cold air nipped at my exposed skin as my tennis shoes smacked the road and little clouds of dirt kicked up behind me. I chanced a look over my shoulder, and to my surprise, Dan was hot on my heels. How that bastard ran while he was wasted was beyond me. I'd anticipated he'd be slow, but I'd obviously miscalculated.

Suddenly grateful for the lights from the other mobile homes, I spotted the trail I loved to walk in the summer. I took a sharp right and started my descent down the steep hill. Hopefully, Dan wasn't familiar with the path, which would give me much-needed lead time since he'd have to run farther down the road to enter the heavily wooded area.

A yelp escaped me as my foot slid on a rock. I landed on my ass with a thud, but I had too much momentum built up to stop. Digging my heels into the hard ground, I attempted to halt myself before I was launched into the ditch, but it was too late. My body bounced, then rolled to a standstill when I smacked into a tree. The impact had knocked the wind out of me, and I clutched my chest, struggling to breathe.

Dead leaves crunched nearby, alerting me that Dan was gaining ground. I had to move, and fast. Fumbling around in a ditch in the middle of the night wasn't how this was supposed to have happened, but at least the moon was bright enough to light the path, and I didn't need to give myself away by using the flashlight.

Swearing under my breath, I gained my footing again and did my best to disappear behind the trees. Once I reached my favorite oak, I grabbed the lowest branch and shimmied up the side of it. I continued to crawl more than halfway up when I finally arrived at my spot. The rough bark cooled my clammy palms as I found my balance and plastered myself against the trunk. I steadied my breathing, grateful for my years of cross-country track in high school. Who knew that it would one day save my life?

"You think you can hide from me, River?" Dan stood near the oak, searching for me on the ground. "I know you're here. I can smell your fear." He lifted his nose in the air and sniffed like he was a dog on the hunt and laughed. In a way, he was, and I was the prey.

I tilted my head and peered through the darkness below when the sound of raindrops splattering against the dried-up leaves caught my attention. Plop ... plop.

Dan stared at the ground, then up at the inky black sky. He knelt and picked up something I couldn't see. "Oh, you're close, all right." He stood and glanced up, searching.

I jerked back and hoped that he hadn't spotted me. *Dammit.* Nausea swirled in my stomach as I tasted blood in the back of my throat. It wasn't raining. My nose was bleeding again. I cupped my hand beneath my nostrils while I focused on Dan. I doubted he could climb the tree, which is what I'd counted on. But even drunk, the asshole was resourceful.

"Haven't you figured this out yet, River? I'll always find you, and you *will* come home with me."

I wanted to open my mouth and remind him I was nineteen. I no longer had to live with him, but if I said anything it would give away my location. He already knew I was above him, but he hadn't spotted exactly where yet.

A low growl broke through my thoughts, and my eyes widened. Leaning over enough to see what was happening below, I stifled my laugh when I discovered our neighbor's Doberman Pinscher, Killer, advancing on Dan. He hated dogs, but especially Killer because he was trained to do just that. Kill. Good ol' Logan, who lived a few trailers over from us, was a known meth dealer, so having attack dogs around to warn him of strangers approaching was a necessity. No one messed with Logan, he was pure evil, and I wasn't stupid enough to poke my nose into his business.

Tension snaked down my neck and traveled between my shoulder blades as Killer began to snarl and bark at Dan. I wanted to encourage that monster to run just so he would understand what it felt like to be hunted, but I needed to let Killer deal with the situation instead. Mentally, I cheered for my neighbor's dog to shred Dan to pieces. He fucking deserved it. I was sick of the beatings, too. I swear, it seemed like I spent more of my paycheck on makeup to hide the bruises than I did groceries.

Dan backed away and talked to Killer in a soothing tone. It wasn't working on the dog any more than mine had worked on Dan. Trying to reason with insanity had gotten me nowhere. Killer bared his teeth, and then, with one powerful leap, the Doberman jumped on his chest and knocked him to the ground with a loud thud.

I sucked in a sharp breath as Killer tore into Dan's throat, muffling his screams. Tears welled in my eyes as the sounds from Dan became garbled, but Killer didn't stop. I reached above my head and clung to the branch above me. I couldn't fall, or my fate would be the same.

My heart ached as Killer backed away from Dan's body. It was one thing to put rat poison in his coffee and hope he died. Another to witness a violent death.

Blood dripped from Killer's jowls as he licked his snout. Forcing myself to look at the son of a bitch that had hurt me for years, I slapped my palm over my mouth, willing myself not to scream. I cringed as blood ran down his neck. His throat was ripped open, and his eyes stared into nothingness. Dan was gone. Dead. A wave of relief washed over me while a ball of puke lodged itself in my esophagus. I swallowed several times and tried to calm down, but my brain was struggling to process what I'd witnessed seconds ago.

I buried my face in my hands. The man who had beaten and raped me more times than I could count was lying on the ground, his blood soaking the leaves and brush beneath him.

Killer finished cleaning and ridding himself of any evidence, then trotted off as though killing a human being was all in a typical day's work for him.

A sudden chill traveled through me. I needed to move, or I'd wind up with hypothermia. If I descended the tree too soon, though, I'd end up dead along with Dan. Killer hadn't made it up the hill yet, which meant that if he heard me, he'd be back in seconds.

I forced myself to take deep, long breaths. The monster below me couldn't hurt me again. Ever. I allowed the truth to seep into my soul, setting me free from the abuse and danger I'd lived in for years. "No more. It's over, River," I whispered out loud, my throat parched.

I trained my focus on Killer until he was up the hill, then I stayed in the tree for another fifteen minutes. At least I could head back to the trailer and wash up without fear of Dan coming for me.

After what felt like an eternity, I left the safety of my hiding place and made my way back to the ground on the other side of Dan. I shivered beneath my worn hoodie and thin shirt. At least I could start moving and warm up.

Carefully, I began to walk home. My achy and weary legs mocked me as I climbed up the hill. A deep voice carried through the night, catching my attention before I reached our dirt road. My mouth gaped open as I spotted Killer, his owner Logan, and two other men in front of my house. Dan's name reached my ears, and I ducked behind the slope, hoping I'd stayed out of sight.

"That motherfucker owes me a lot of money. If he ran, I'll take River as my payment. Have you seen the tits on that girl? I bet they'd bounce nicely as I fucked her real hard." The skinny man thrust his hips forward as his laughter echoed through the trailer park.

The other men snickered and continued to talk about their plans for my body. Whatever Dan had done, I wasn't only in danger from him. I was in jeopardy from these guys as well. Killer and his owner only lived a few spots down from me, which meant he could easily keep an eye on my place. I gulped as the horrid realization settled in. There was no way I could go home. My fear was so intense I could taste it on my tongue. *Shit.* I was officially homeless.

I grabbed the strap of my backpack and quietly shimmied back down to the ditch. Hopefully those disgusting bastards wouldn't send Killer to search for me. But one of them had come to the diner earlier in the day and looked right at me, so they knew where I worked.

Goddammit. My hopes of living a quiet and peaceful life dimmed suddenly. Dan had managed to give me one last 'fuck you' before he'd died.

I wracked my memory, attempting to recall what server had the night shift. Not only was I in desperate need of washing Dan's stench off of me, but I needed a first aid kit for my face and as many Advil as it was safe to take at once.

I picked up my stride and headed toward the restaurant. I grimaced as I flew past my favorite oak tree that now marked Dan's place of death. My stomach soured as I recalled his greedy and intrusive touch from earlier. The son of a bitch had gotten off easy. Hatred for Dan pricked my skin, but I couldn't waste my energy on him. He was gone, and I had to figure out where the hell I would live and stay off the radar. The last thing I wanted was for those sick pieces of shit to get their grubby hands on me. Anger fueled me forward, the full moon lighting my way.

As the town lights grew brighter, I realized I was almost to my destination.

I slowed, inhaling deeply. My toes and fingers were numb from the cold, and my nose hurt like a son of a bitch. I suspected I would have a nice black eye soon, but I couldn't think about that yet. I desperately needed food and a hot shower, but I couldn't just waltz in through the front door of the diner without drawing attention. For all I knew, Killer's owner had hopped in his truck, and was eating dinner while waiting for me to show up.

Reaching the edge of the woods and the highway that ran through our small town, I pulled my hood over my head. The neon red sign flashed "Bob's," and I peered through the large windows. A bald man sat at the counter and another heavy-set bearded guy at a booth. Other than that, it wasn't busy. I looked both ways for any traffic, then hurried across the main road.

Gravel crunched beneath my shoes as I cut through the parking lot of the restaurant. Unfortunately, I hadn't been able to get close enough to see if either of the men inside were friends of Logan's.

Ducking around the back of the building, I noticed the employee entrance door was wedged open with a large rock. I quietly approached and opened it enough to slip inside. Hopefully I wouldn't scare the shit out of the cook, but I would have to take my chances.

I tiptoed down the hall, but before I could peek into the kitchen, a body came barreling at me. My back slammed against the wall, and the air whooshed from my lungs. Dammit. I'd forgotten to remove my hood.

I tossed my hands up as I stared into Ed's face. "It's me," I whispered. "It's River. Take my hood off, but please don't let anyone know I'm here." The tremble in my voice betrayed my attempt to sound brave.

"River?" Ed's meaty fingers tugged on my hoodie, and my thick brown hair spilled across my shoulders. He swiped the corner of my mouth with his thumb, then a horrified expression twisted his features. "What the hell? I'm calling the cops."

I shook my head adamantly. "If you do, they'll kill me. Please. I'm begging you." A nervous knot of hysteria formed in my throat. If Ed didn't help me, I could kiss my freedom and, most likely, my very existence goodbye. Once again, my life hung in the balance of someone else's decision.

Chapter Three

"What did you do, kid?" Ed asked, his deep voice hovering above a whisper.

"Are you calling the cops or giving me up?" My heart knocked so hard against my ribs I thought it might leap right out of my chest.

"I don't know yet. What the hell happened to your face?"

I gulped, unsure if I could trust him. I had no idea if he was mixed up with Logan and the group of guys that wanted to find me or not. I gathered up my courage and gave him a quick and dirty rundown of what had taken place, including the rape, Dan's death, and the men that were looking for me. I waited for his response and silently counted the beats of my pulse.

Ed folded his arms over his massive chest, his dingy white T-shirt stretching across his muscular biceps. Ed was in excellent shape and handsome for an older guy in a rough-around-the-edges kind of way. He also had a no-nonsense air about him.

His blue-gray eyes pinned mine. "He's dead?"

I nodded, the gravity of the situation fully dawning on me.

"And you overheard Logan and a group of men talking about hurting you?" Ed rubbed his chin, the thick, black stubble scraping beneath his fingers.

Again, I nodded as tears welled in my eyes.

"Let's get you cleaned up, kid." Ed stepped back, his gaze filling with protectiveness. "You got somewhere safe to go?"

"No. Dan was the only family I had left." *Fuck.* "Is there any Advil around here? I feel like absolute crap."

"Yeah, you look like shit. You're sporting a shiner, and it looks like your nose is broken. I'll get you some pain reliever. Not much you can do about your snout unless you go to the hospital, but they'll also want a rape kit and full exam."

"No thanks. I'll deal with it on my own." I heaved a sigh. "Every time I see my crooked nose, I'll think about what Dan did to me."

A frown furrowed his brow as he raked his gaze over me. "It's a good thing he's dead. That's all I've gotta say about that." Ed offered me a kind smile, then led me to the employee break room, where he handed me four little round pills. I swallowed them with no water, hoping they would kick in fast.

Ed continued down the hall, and I walked silently beside him. He opened the boss's door and turned on the light. "There's a shower in the bathroom. Lock the door after I leave so no one accidentally walks in on you."

"Thank you." I slipped my backpack off my shoulders and watched as Ed disappeared down the hallway. I twisted the lock on the doorknob, then clutched my bag to my chest. It was weird being in Bob's office without him. I took a long breath, then made my way toward the bathroom and flipped on the light switch. I gasped when my deep blue eyes stared back at me in the mirror. "Jesus," I whispered. Dan had really fucked me up. Not only did I have a black eye, but I had a gash across my cheek. Ed was right. My nose looked broken. If I knew how, I would try to reset it, but having a slightly crooked sniffer was the least of my worries.

For the next half hour, I stood beneath the hot spray and scrubbed Dan off my skin. A muffled cry escaped me, and I finally allowed the grief and horror to flow out of me and down the drain.

After I rinsed the suds away and dried off, I dressed in clean clothes. My stomach growled loudly, and I wondered what Ed might have to eat in the kitchen. I had a little cash in my backpack to buy some food while I figured out what my next step was.

I unlocked the door and entered the employee break room.

"Oh, my Gawd. River?" Apparently, Shirley's East Coast accent was even thicker when she was upset. "Who did this to you, hon?" She waved me over to her, and I sat down across the white foldable table we took our breaks at if we weren't a smoker. The smokers stood outside where they shivered their asses off for as long as it took to get a hit of nicotine.

"Dan."

Tension hung thick in the air. "No one has a right to hurt another person like that." She pursed her lips. "Have you eaten?" she asked, changing the subject. Her dishwater blonde hair was piled on the top of her head in a tight bun. I was guessing that Shirley was in her late forties but possibly younger. She'd spent a lot of time in the sun, so it was difficult to tell.

"No. I was going to see if I could buy dinner. I have a few dollars." Weariness washed over me. The adrenaline rush that had kept me alive was fading, fast. I was exhausted, not to mention emotionally depleted.

"You're not paying for shit. I'll get you something to eat. Wanna hamburger and fries?" Shirley stood and smoothed her gold and white uniform with the palm of her hand.

"That would be awesome, thanks." I propped my elbows on the table.

Her large brown eyes narrowed as she assessed me. She chewed on a piece of gum loudly as she pinned me with her intense gaze. She held a slender finger in the air. "Stay put, doll." Shirley pointed at me for emphasis. "I'll get your dinner first, then you're going to explain to me what in the hell happened to you tonight."

I folded my arms on top of the table, then laid my head down. Maybe it was safe enough to doze while my food was being cooked. My eyes fluttered closed and popped open seconds later as images of Dan's bloody corpse flashed through my brain. I sat up quickly and winced as pain shot down my back. Dan might have only hit my face, but my entire body ached from fighting him.

"Here. We'll get your belly full." Shirley set down a bowl of vegetable soup and crackers in front of me. "Ed is making your meal, and Ginger is watching the front so I can stay with you."

I picked up the spoon and dunked it into the steaming tomato-based liquid. "Thank you. I didn't know where else to go. Hell, I don't even know you guys very well. We've only worked the same shift a few times. I'm not sure why you and Ed are helping me."

Shirley stared at me for a few heartbeats before she spoke again. "River, you seem like a good kid that's caught a bad break. Tell me what happened, and I'll see what I can do to help. I know every cop in this shitty town, so I promise you'll be safe."

My spoon clattered to the floor, and I could almost feel the color drain from my cheeks. "No cops."

Shirley crossed the tiny room and grabbed clean silverware for me. "Are you in trouble? Did you break the law?" She put her hands on her narrow hips while she looked straight into my soul.

"No, but I can't stay. If word gets out... the police will have everyone looking into the information, and I'll be forced to remain in town until the investigation is over. I can't. I'm not safe here."

I shoved a spoonful of soup in my mouth, the heat of the food traveling through me and warming me from the inside out.

"Here ya go, kid," Ed said as he strolled into the room with a giant hamburger and plate full of fries.

For the first time that night, I cracked a smile. "I really appreciate it." I snatched up a crunchy golden fry and popped it into my mouth.

I stuffed my face and relayed the events that had led me here to Shirley. She sat across from me, slack-jawed and furious while she listened. Finishing off the last bite of my dinner, I leaned back in my chair and sighed as I rubbed my flat stomach.

"You're right. You can't stay if those sons of bitches are looking for you. I know Logan and his friends, and they're up to no good. There are rumors that those good-for-nothing boys are involved in some other shady dealings besides selling meth." Shirley pursed her lips.

My mind spun with possibilities of what could be worse than dealing drugs, but I'd heard Logan's threats firsthand, so I had a pretty good idea. My heart skipped a beat, panic rose, and I thought I might be sick.

"It would be best if you headed on out of town first thing in the morning. There's a bus that will take you to Coeur d'Alene. I know a lady that works at the homeless shelter. Dottie is a doll. She'll help you get a job and back on your feet."

"Isn't Coeur d'Alene on the other side of the state? I'll probably stand out like a sore thumb." I smoothed my frayed sweatshirt, feeling sleep beckoning to me.

"It's actually in Idaho. It's a great place for people to get off the streets and start a new life. You tell Dottie I sent you."

I chewed on my bottom lip. "How much is a bus ticket?"

"Don't you worry about it, hon. I'll have that and a bit of cash for you. For now, curl up on Bob's sofa over there and get some sleep. I work until four in the morning. I'll wake you up, and we'll pack your bag with food. It's an all-day bus ride, so you'll need to have sand-wiches to eat."

I was too damned tired to argue with her. "I'll pay you back, Shirley. I promise."

Shirley waved me off. "River, get your life together and make it a good one. That's the only payback I need." She smiled at me and stood. "I have to get back to work. I'll wake you up in a few hours."

As soon as Shirley left the room, I dragged my feet across the tile floor to Bob's office. I didn't lock the door this time since Shirley would need to wake me, and I left the light on. I cured up on the couch and drifted off into a fitful sleep.

Chapter Four

I felt hands on my shoulders, shaking me. The touch was much gentler than I was used to.

I detected a soft voice. "River, wake up."

I bolted upright, nearly smacking Shirley on the head with mine.

"It's all right, doll. It's just me." Shirley sat down on the couch near my feet, her kind eyes assessing me. "How ya feelin'?"

"Like I got my ass beat last night." I stretched, my body creaking and groaning. I ran my fingers through my hair, making a half-assed attempt to manage the tangles.

"While you were sleeping, Ed and I gathered up a few necessities for you."

I frowned, not understanding what she was referring to.

"Here." Shirley handed me a plastic grocery bag.

I rifled through it, tears welling in my eyes. A brush, toothpaste, toothbrush, deodorant, tampons, an iPod, charger, headphones, and a disposable phone.

"Shirley," I whispered, my tone heavy with gratitude.

"And this." She took my hand and turned it palm up. Shirley placed a small wad of bills in it. "Now listen to me, young lady. You keep the phone and bills in your pocket, or better yet, your bra. That way, if you lose your bag, you still have a way to call me and money to eat with. Do you understand?"

I gulped, attempting to clear the lump in my throat. No one had ever been this kind, much less given a shit about what happened to me. Unable to form words, I threw my arms around Shirley's neck and clung to her.

"It's going to be all right, River." She patted my back.

I released her and nodded, even though I couldn't believe what she'd said.

"My number is programmed into the phone. You have an hour of prepaid minutes so use it wisely. Texts are cheaper than calling, so send me one and let me know when you're at the shelter."

"I will." Tears pricked my eyes. "I don't know how to thank you enough."

Shirley waved me off. "If I had a daughter, and she was in your shoes, I would hope a kindhearted person would help her out, too. Pay it forward. You got it?" Shirley tucked strands of my brown hair behind my ear and smiled as she patted my cheek gently.

"One more thing," Ed said as he strolled into the room. He approached me and held out his hand. "Keep this on your person, not in your bag."

I frowned and took the knife from him.

"Do you know how to open it safely?" Ed asked, compassion in his eyes.

"Yeah, Dan had a knife. Not like this one, but it folded." I carefully opened it, the blade locking into place. "This is ... wow."

"It's a Spyderco Matriarch 2 with a three-and-a-half inch and reverse S blade."

I arched an eyebrow at him.

"It will protect you." Ed smiled at me. "I need to know you'll have a chance if those fuckers come after you."

"Yeah, me too. I'll make sure I can easily reach it if needed." It wouldn't fit in my shoe, but I could put the money and knife in my bra. Even if it bulged a little, my sweatshirt was baggy enough to conceal it.

"Keep us updated, kid. And good luck." Ed gave me a brief salute, winked at Shirley, then left Bob's office.

I observed Shirley as she watched Ed walk away, not missing the longing in her eyes.

"You love him." I took her hand in mine.

Pink dusted Shirley's cheeks while she patted my arm. "He's a good man, River. Save yourself some pain and find a good one the first time around." Shirley stood and smoothed her uniform. "Are you ready? I'll drive you to the bus station and buy your ticket. I'll stay with you until you're safely seated and on the road."

"You don't have to go to all that trouble." I stood and hid the knife and money in my bra, then put the bag of other items in my backpack.

"Hon, you're worth going the extra mile for. I'm just sorry no one has treated you that way before."

I suppose you couldn't miss what you'd never had.

Slinging the bag over my shoulder, I followed Shirley out of Bob's office and into the kitchen.

"Here's your breakfast, ladies. River, you have lunch and dinner as well. I tossed in cookies, chips, and a few apples for you, too." Ed handed me a bulging brown paper bag.

"Thank you." I hugged him goodbye, then waited by the back door so Shirley and Ed could have a few minutes alone.

I took a quick peek over my shoulder at them. A small smile pulled at the corner of my mouth as Ed leaned down and gave Shirley a sweet kiss. It was nice to see people who were kind and loving to each other. It wasn't something I'd had the chance to see very often.

I leaned against the wall and waited for Shirley. My face wasn't as sore today, but I assumed I looked like a complete mess. Nibbling on my already too short thumbnail, I tried to calm my churning stomach. In less than twenty-four hours, my guardian had been killed, I was homeless, and I had several evil men searching for me. Time was a strange concept. For years my life had been the same. Nothing changed from day to day, year to year, then everything shifted in a blink of an eye.

"Ready, hon?" Shirley asked, pulling me out of my thoughts.

"Yeah." I pursed my lips together as Shirley pushed the back door open, and we stepped outside into the frosty morning. The woodsy scent of pine and tamarack burning in neighbors' wood-stoves filled the air. I'd always wanted a stove. Often on the freezing wintry nights in the trailer, I would close my eyes and imagine reading a good book next to a roaring fire. It had offered me a little peace.

Shirley walked to a newer silver-and-black Subaru and unlocked the doors. I settled into the passenger seat and clutched my bag in my lap.

"You've got tangles. Why don't you brush your hair while I drive? There should be a tube of concealer in the bag, too. It will help with the bruises." She buckled up, then leaned over and flipped my visor down. The light on the mirror blinked on.

"Yeah, I look like shit." I gently touched the tender skin around my eye and nose. "The concealer might not work since the bruising is so dark."

"That stuff will." Shirley nodded to my bag as she eased out of the employee parking lot behind the diner, the gravel crunching beneath her tires. "I got it from my neighbor who is with the theatre here in town. She has a ton of stage makeup. What she gave me even covers tattoos."

"Holy crap. I didn't realize they had stuff like that." I reached into the backpack and searched for the coverup.

"Right?" Shirley grinned, checked the main road for oncoming traffic, then turned left toward the edge of town.

Shirley kept the conversation light as I dabbed the miracle concealer on my nose and cheeks, then brushed my hair. By the time we reached the bus station, my appearance was almost back to normal. Too bad my face and head still hurt like a son of a bitch.

"Does there happen to be a small bottle of Advil in the bag? I can buy some if not."

Shirley parked the car and flashed me a pretty smile. "We've got you covered. Ed remembered to put Advil in there for you."

"You both are saints." I returned her smile as we climbed out of the car and headed inside the station.

An hour later, I boarded the bus and waved goodbye to Shirley. Dryness seized my throat, and I attempted to drown the sudden loneliness that cloaked me as I chose my seat and sat down near the window. Shirley waited until the bus lurched forward before she walked back to her car.

"Goodbye Havre, Montana," I whispered and dug around in my bag until I located the iPod and headphones. I slipped them in my ears as a young woman that appeared to be in her twenties sat next to me. She stared at me for a moment, then smiled.

It would be a long bus ride, and I hoped I would be able to get some rest. I wasn't actually sure what to expect when I reached Idaho. For now, I flipped through the tunes on the iPod and grinned when "Bed on Fire" by Teddy Swims started to play. I wondered if this was how Ed and Shirley felt about each other. Chewing on my bottom lip, I adjusted the volume so I could still hear what was going on around me. Then I blew out a soft sigh, the lyrics pulling at my heartstrings. Growing up, I'd never allowed myself to think that a good guy could want me, but after seeing Shirley and Ed, I was beginning to think that maybe love and happiness might actually be a possibility.

Chapter Five

"Next stop is Spokane, Washington," the bus driver announced through the speaker.

Fear consumed me as I bolted upright in my seat and jerked my headphones out of my ears. *Shit.* I'd slept through my stop.

I shoved the now dead iPod into my backpack and finally realized that the lady who had been sitting beside me was gone. Anxiety tugged at my insides while I stood and made my way to the front of the bus.

"Hi, excuse me," I said to the driver. "How far back is the bus station in Coeur d'Alene?"

"About an hour. You miss your stop?" he asked.

"Yeah," I mumbled, my cheeks flaming red over my stupidity.

"The next bus heading that way isn't scheduled until tomorrow at ten in the morning." He adjusted his sunglasses as the sun began its descent, painting the sky in brilliant pink and blue hues.

"Can I stay at the station tonight?" I held my breath and hoped his answer would be yes.

"Not allowed, miss. It closes in another five hours at nine. You can hang out until then and stay warm, though."

I mentally swore at myself for falling asleep and missing my stop. "Okay, thank you." Sinking back into the seat, I watched the city buildings pass by and tried to form a plan. Maybe Spokane had a shelter, too.

Tears threatened to spill over, but I refused to fall apart. I'd lived through worse. I could handle one night as a homeless person.

I tapped out a quick text to Shirley to let her know I'd arrived safely. I couldn't bother her anymore. She and Ed had helped me enough, and I was worried that she'd hop in her car and drive all the way here to rescue me. I refused to be a burden.

* * *

I shivered and rubbed my arms rapidly, hoping to generate some heat. Not only had I gotten lost from the bus driver's directions to the shelter, but I'd managed to find myself in a neighborhood. A really nice area where the people would think I was scoping out houses to break into if anyone spotted me. *Dammit.*

Growing up in a small town, I'd never needed directions anywhere. Shopping, restaurants, and gas stations were all off the main road, and with a population of less than ten thousand, it was easy to find my way around. What I did realize was that I couldn't stop moving or I would freeze to death. I'd survived too much shit in my life to die now.

I cupped my hands over my mouth and blew a warm breath on my fingers. A dog barked in the distance as my tennis shoes slapped against the sidewalk, echoing through the otherwise quiet night. Wherever I was, it was obvious the people here hadn't ever missed a meal or lived in a shitty trailer park. The houses were so large, I could probably live in one room and be happy.

My legs ached from walking around for hours. I reached a small tree and leaned against it while I emptied a rock from my shoe. I'd paid so much attention to my surroundings and who was near me that I hadn't noticed the sharp edge cutting into my heel.

Wearily, I slipped my shoe back on and scanned the area. Street-lights lit the neighborhood well, allowing me to see the mansions lined up next to each other. Most homes were dark inside, or they had a small amount of light from a room. An idea suddenly occurred to me, and I glanced around nervously, but there was no one else outside.

I rubbed my arms, willing the blood to keep flowing. I hurried to the other side of the street and up a hill between two large homes. As I suspected, they both had a fence around the backyard. I followed the pristine wood barrier until I located a door that was cracked open. Relief washed over me as I slipped into a massive backyard with a swimming pool and a covered outdoor kitchen. A small pool house that looked more like a shed would allow me a safe space to hide until the sun came up and I could be on my way.

I moved silently to the small building and tested the door. It opened with ease. Maybe people didn't feel the need to lock anything here, but they were stupid. I gawked at the number of boxes, outdoor furniture, and swimming toys that were piled to the ceiling. No way would I be able to fit inside and sleep. I chewed on my bottom lip, then my attention landed on what I thought might be a sleeping bag.

I slipped my backpack off, set it on the ground, then wedged my body between a small gap. My fingers were just short of reaching for what I hoped was a blanket or bag. Grunting, I shoved my upper body against the boxes and stood on my tiptoes. My boobs screamed at me for smashing them, but I didn't care. With one last try, I grabbed the soft material and I pulled it down, the blanket piling on top of my head. I gripped it tightly and buried my face in it.

I closed the door and scooped up my bag. Now I had to find a place to curl up and try to sleep. I crept toward the house, and my heart skidded to a stop as floodlights caught my movements and lit up the backyard. I stumbled backward and tripped over a nearly deflated ball. Although I tried to regain my footing, I landed against the unfor-giving ground with a thud, and my body scolded me. I scrambled around the corner of the house as the sliding glass door opened and a guy stepped outside, searching the area for the cause of the commotion.

"What is it, baby?" A girl that didn't look much older than me slid her arm around the guy's waist. Her platinum blonde hair grazed her back as she pushed her enormous chest against him.

"Probably just a cat. I don't see anything. These lights kick on all the time."

I strained to see him, but she was blocking my view.

"It's cold. Why don't we go inside, and you can warm me up?" she purred.

"Probably because your ass cheeks are hanging out of your see-through pajama shorts," I muttered to myself, wishing I could sneak inside and sit near the heat for a few hours. Blondie had no idea how good she had it. I chastised myself for being childish. At least I had a safe corner of the world to sleep in with a real blanket, not the thread-bare ones I had back home. Unfortunately, the covered patio offered no place for me to sleep without being seen.

The slider lock clicked into place, and the shade slowly lowered. I released a heavy sigh. At least I hadn't been caught. I stood at the edge of the patio and searched for a hiding place. A soft pitter-patter reached my ears, and I glanced around, then tilted my face up to the sky. Rain. It was warm enough to rain? I barked out a laugh, then smacked my hand over my mouth. Plump drops ran down my hair and onto my forehead, and I wiped the water off with my sweatshirt sleeve.

Frantically, I searched for a place to stay warm and dry. My nose wrinkled as my attention landed on a large container with the word *recycle* on the front in bold white letters. I hurried to it and gently laid it on its side, opening the lid to extend the length of the container. Poking my head in, I surveyed the space. I would easily fit. I shrugged off my backpack and placed it at the other end of the recy-cling container. It would have to work as a pillow. Before I crawled inside, I reached into my bra and removed my knife. If anyone found me, I would be ready to protect myself.

A few minutes later, I settled into my home for the night and covered up with the multi-colored blanket. At least I wasn't sleeping in an actual garbage can, and this one was pretty clean. At this point, I couldn't afford to be picky, though.

The sound of the rain bounced off the top, and I gazed up to search the opening, tucking my feet in. I hoped like hell I was hidden and safe. I stifled a yawn while my eyes fluttered closed, and exhaustion pulled me under.

* * *

I wasn't sure if the bright sunlight woke me or if it was the jerk to my leg. My body moved without my permission, and I immediately transitioned into fight mode. Pulling the knife blade out, I also kicked at the mysterious fingers that were wrapped around my ankle.

"Ow! What the hell?" a deep voice said without releasing me.

With a forceful pull of the stranger's hand, I slid out of the recycling bin and onto the ground. I held the knife to my chest with the tip pointed outward. What I hadn't counted on was the merry fucking sunshine being so bright I couldn't see shit. I waved the blade around, blinking rapidly, trying to clear my vision.

"Hey, hang on there. I won't hurt you. I promise." He stepped toward me, invading my personal space.

"Promises don't mean shit," I retorted as my sight finally cleared enough to see who was in front of me. I scrambled to my feet and shifted the knife in my hand, ready to swipe at him. I stood there as my cheeks blazed, eyes burned, and every sore muscle in my body was taut as a bowstring. An icy shiver traveled down my back.

"My word is good. I just want to know why you were sleeping in my garbage can." Concern captured his features.

My mouth gaped open as my attention landed on him. His deep chocolate-colored eyes peered into my soul, leaving me breathless. His dark brown hair was longer on top and shaved on the sides. His full lips and the tip of his nose were red from the cold. Even beneath his long-sleeved shirt, I could see his arm and chest muscles bulging against the white fabric. Gray sweats hung low on his hips, and my pulse kicked up as I savored the vision of him.

Dammit. Why was I checking this guy out when I needed to do some fast-talking and not get arrested for trespassing?

His expression morphed into shock and anger, then his gaze finally filled with compassion. "You've been hurt." His deep voice sent chills down my spine.

"I'll leave. I'm sorry. I got lost last night and—"

"You were walking around at night when it was only thirty-four degrees?" He ran his fingers through his hair, curiosity flickering over his gorgeous features.

"I'm from out of town." I gulped, still refusing to lower my blade.

"Why don't you come inside and shower? I'll make breakfast."

I backed away, nearly tripping over the recycling bin.

"Whoa." Before I could blink, he reached out and grabbed my arm, saving me from landing on my ass again.

My knife clattered to the ground. He bent over, scooped it up, and folded the blade closed. "Here." He gave it to me. "I swear you're safe, and I understand if you don't believe me, but I'm telling the truth. I don't want to hurt you. Keep your knife close if you want. But come in, warm up, and eat. My parents aren't home, so you won't have to answer a bunch of questions, either ... Well, just mine." He gave me a lopsided grin. My stomach growled and he held his palm out to me. "I won't bite. Come on. It's fucking freezing out here."

"My backpack is still in the container." My heart hammered against my chest. If I crawled inside the bin to get my bag, I would be a target again. He'd already caught me off guard once.

"I've got it." Before I could protest, he lowered to the frozen ground, then reached inside and produced my bag for me. He stood and offered me my stuff.

"Thanks." I clutched it to my chest with my free hand while holding my knife in tightly clenched fingers.

"I'm Holden, by the way. Holden Alastair." He took a few steps toward his house, then paused and waved me forward. "My sister is in Spain right now, but I'm pretty sure she wouldn't care if you borrowed some of her clothes. I can wash what you have on."

"I have clothes," I snapped.

My rude remark didn't seem to deter him.

"Okay. I was just trying to help. How does an omelet and sausage sound for breakfast?" He continued walking until he reached the slider.

Over the years of living with Dan, I had to learn to trust my intuition. Most of the time, it had served me well, but I wasn't sure that my fear of being raped again wouldn't overrule the kind offers Holden was giving me. My legs trembled as I stood rooted in place, and I contemplated whether I would be safe in his home, or if I should save myself now while I still could.

Chapter Six

Holden shoved his hands in the pockets of his sweats. "Listen, you've obviously been through a traumatic experience. I mean, you picked my recycling bin to sleep in over everyone else's in the area. Call me silly, but maybe fate brought you here. Maybe I'm the friend you've been praying for. Maybe not. Regardless, come in and eat. After that, you're free to go or shower. You can even eat breakfast right next to the slider. That way, if you feel the need to leave, you can."

The more he stared at me, the more I wanted to throw caution to the wind. Finally, my basic need for food and warmth won. "Okay. I'll stand there." I nodded nervously. At least I would be able to run if I felt that I was in danger.

Holden disappeared into the house, and I followed, closing the door behind me. My attention landed back on him, and I tracked him like he was a feral animal about to attack at any given moment. He strolled through the family room, then into the kitchen, completely relaxed that a stranger was in his home. With the open floor plan, it was easy for him to keep an eye on me as well.

"Holy shit," I said before I could stop myself.

Holden pulled out a skillet from the lower cabinet and twirled it in his hand, grinning. "What are you shitting about?" A deep chuckle rumbled from his chest.

"Your house is ... stunning. You have a water fountain in the middle of the room." I pointed and gawked as the sound soothed my frayed nerves. A blue-and-tan rug covered a large portion of the white marble floor.

I took in the triple crown molding and tray ceilings, buttery brown leather couches, dual-sided stone fireplace, and a television that would have taken up an entire side of the trailer I used to live in. Well, that was an exaggeration, but I had no idea they made TVs that big. I leaned against the wall and absorbed the beautiful kitchen: black-and-brown marble tops, dark cabinets, and the appliances all in stainless steel. I'd only dreamed of a kitchen as gorgeous as this one.

"Have you lived here long?" My voice cracked, and I was suddenly embarrassed that I was the poor girl in ratty clothes standing in his home.

"Yup, all my life. Mom wants to update the house, but Dad told her there's no need to since they're never here. Plus, there's nothing to really do unless she wants to change paint or countertop colors. It's kind of silly to me."

"Why aren't they ever around?" I hoped he would continue to divulge information. I didn't want to be caught off guard by someone walking through the door.

"Business. They travel all the time, which works for me because I get the place all to myself since Mallory is in Spain."

"Your sister?" My stomach growled again, the smell of eggs pulling me a little closer to Holden and the kitchen. I was still close enough to the door to run if I had to.

"Yeah. She's in Madrid for a year, *studying*." He used air quotes as he said studying. "I mean seriously, what would you do if you were in Spain for a year?" Without allowing me to answer, he kept on speaking. "Drink, fuck, and shop."

I sucked on my bottom lip, unsure of how to respond, but he continued and saved me from embarrassing myself.

"What's your name?" He picked up the spatula and focused on the skillet full of eggs. "Nope, let me guess." He grinned at me, his straight white teeth making me self-conscious of my own. Not that mine were bad, but my front lower ones were a little crooked.

"Okay." I shyly tucked my hair behind my ear, my eyes following his every move.

"Natalie?" He peeked up from our food, and I shook my head. "Donna? Nope, never mind you don't look like a Donna." He tapped his chin up, appearing deep in thought as he focused on me.

I sucked in a sharp breath, heat creeping up my neck and cheeks in reaction to his attention.

"Freya, Jackie, Novie, Cassie?"

"None of those," I said, fighting a smile.

"Alexa? Oh, you definitely look like an Alexa." He quirked an eyebrow at me.

"I look like a talking disc or round ball?"

Holden threw his head back and laughed. "Nope, and I'm guessing you have way more personality than she does too."

"I'll be sure to share your feedback with Amazon." I gave him a shy smile.

"Food's up." He loaded my plate with a fluffy omelet and sausage links. He placed it on the counter and whirled around, opened a drawer, and produced a fork. "Come get it."

My heart and mind still waged a silent war. Was this his trap? Was he being kind and funny to lure me farther into the house? I stepped backward instead.

"Hang on," Holden said gently, raising his hands in the air, but this time he backed out of the kitchen and a good distance down the hall. "If I brought you the food, I'd have a fork for you. I don't want you to feel threatened, so I'm walking away so you can feel better about getting something to eat."

I was so edgy that I hadn't considered his dilemma. "Okay." I cautiously approached the counter with a firm grip on my knife. Worst case scenario, I would throw my hot food in his face and bolt. I gathered my plate and silverware, then walked backward, my eyes never leaving his. My heel hit the slider, then my ass bumped the half-lowered blind, which clicked against the glass. I stood still, watching his next move. I hated being this wired, but Dan had left me broken. Over the years, he'd worn down my hopes and dreams that good people existed in this fucked up world. My one break had been college, and my goal was still to get there.

"Avery? Gemma? Lily?" He smiled and walked back to the kitchen.

"Nope." I shoved a forkful of egg in my mouth and nearly moaned. "Oh my God, these are amazing. What did you season them with?"

"I'm glad you like them. It's a recipe on my mom's side." He popped a sausage link into his mouth. "I'll tell you what's in the eggs if you tell me your name."

I shook my head. "It's a lot more fun hearing you guess. I do like Gemma, though. I mean if I changed my name, it would be on my list."

"Okay, good to know." He narrowed his eyes and continued to eat. "Haley? Linda? Eww, no. You're definitely not a Linda. It's such an ordinary name, and nothing about you is plain." His eyes widened. "Shit, is your name Linda? If so, I'm sorry! I take it back."

I giggled and pondered if I wanted to make him feel bad and tell him yes, but he'd been cool so far. "No, it's not."

Relief washed over his gorgeous features. "I would have felt like an ass if it were."

"It's River. River Collins," I said softly around a mouthful of eggs.

"River?" He didn't try to disguise his surprise, but most people didn't. "Wow. I love it. Deep, free-flowing, running ... exactly like the girl in my recycling bin." He lowered his empty plate to the counter and placed his silverware down.

My cheeks flamed red. I wasn't sure if he was making fun of me or if it was just how he saw me.

"My mom named me, but she's uhh ... I haven't seen her since I was three." I forced away the dark memories and focused on what was right in front of me.

"Well, River, your mom did well. It's a unique name. I like it." He leaned against the kitchen counter and folded his arms over his chest. "Are you still hungry? I can make pancakes if you'd like."

I nodded as the word no escaped my lips.

Holden laughed at the contradiction, then opened the cabinet above his head and pulled out a package of pancake mix.

"When you get more comfortable, feel free to have a seat."

I visibly flinched and sucked in a shaky breath.

"Or you can continue to stand where you are. Do what feels best. This is a no pressure zone."

"I'm good." I cringed at the wobble in my voice. Shit, he could probably smell the waves of fear rolling off me right now.

Holden busied himself making more food while I finished what I had. I inched forward when he wasn't looking, testing my instincts. At the moment, they weren't screaming at me to run like they had so many times with Dan. Flashes of him chasing me in the woods the other night flickered through my mind and a small cry escaped me. White-hot panic coursed through my veins, and I dropped the plate on the floor. A loud crash filled the room, and pieces flew across the tile.

"I'm so sorry." Without thinking, I knelt and began collecting the broken shards, my hands trembling.

"Hey, no. River, stop. I'll get the broom. It's only a plate. It's okay."

I immediately stood as it dawned on me that he could have taken the chance to hurt me, but he hadn't. I stepped away.

"I'm sorry. I should leave." I gripped the knife so hard pain shot through my arm as I backed up toward the door.

"River, it really isn't a big deal. Please, don't go." He rose slowly, his kind eyes pleading with me. "Whatever happened, whatever you're running from, I can help."

Before he could say another word, I opened the slider and flew out of the house.

"River, wait!"

I cleared the outdoor table and sailed through the air. I'd jumped hurdles in cross country track like they were nothing. A little outdoor furniture wouldn't stop me. But apparently my legs were still cold, and I misjudged the chair. My toe caught the back of it, and I tumbled to the ground. Swearing a blue streak, I scrambled to my feet and made a mad dash out of the fence and into the alley.

"River, I'm sorry."

Dammit, he's closing in. Panic propelled me forward. The last time I'd accidentally broken a dish, Dan had punched me in the stomach and side until he'd cracked a rib. The sorry son of a bitch never apologized either. No one would hurt me again. No one.

With another glance over my shoulder to see if Holden was still following me, I picked up my pace, pushing myself forward.

"River! Stop!"

Didn't this guy understand that I wasn't going to stay?

A loud horn blared at me, and I turned in time to see a red-and-black Mini Cooper headed straight for me.

Chapter Seven

My body rolled up onto the hood of the vehicle with a loud thud, then dropped off the car. I heard a crack and agonizing pain shot up my leg as I smacked the unforgiving pavement. Sobs shook me so hard I couldn't see, and nausea twisted my stomach into knots.

"Holy shit! I'm sorry! She ran right in front of me," the male driver explained.

"I saw what happened, Maxwell," Holden said as he knelt beside me. "River, you're going to have to trust me now. Let me look."

I clenched my jaw, admitting defeat while angry tears streamed down my cheeks. Unable to speak, I simply nodded at him.

Seconds seemed like an eternity as he pulled the dirty and torn jean leg up carefully.

"I'll cover the medical bill. Well, I'm sure my parents will. Maybe we can leave the insurance out of it?" Maxwell's light brown eyes pleaded with me, then Holden.

"Shit, I think you broke it. We need to get you checked out at the hospital." Without another word, Holden scooped me into his muscular arms. "Yeah, I'll call you later, man. I need to get her to the emergency room."

Holden hurried to the house. As he sat me on the kitchen counter, a scream tore from my throat. "Jesus, what did I break? It hurts so fucking bad." I was used to pain, but not like this.

"Your leg. Hang on." Holden darted to the freezer and removed an ice pack and applied it to my injury. "I'll be right back. And for shit's sake, do *not* try to leave again."

I whimpered as I held the cold compress against the throbbing area that pulsated with sharp stabbing pricks. Holden must have been running because he returned in seconds. "I had to grab my wallet, keys, and phone." He lifted me again, then took long strides up the wide stairs to what seemed like the main floor. I peeked at the living room to the left.

"Two houses?" I managed to squeak out, hoping to take my mind off my situation.

"Basically. This is the main house, we were in the basement, but it has its own door, three bedrooms, two bathrooms. So yeah, it's another house."

Holden hurried down the hall, his shoes slapping against the floors. "Marble?" I asked, suddenly praying I didn't stink while his grip tightened around me.

"Yeah, I'll give you a tour later. And River?"

"What?" I hiccupped.

"You need to eat more. You don't weigh shit."

"Holden?"

"Yeah?" he asked as he managed to open the front door with me still in his arms.

"I think I'm going to pass out. It hu..." I didn't have the opportunity to finish my sentence before my entire world went black.

* * *

After X-rays and pain meds, I must have dozed off. Strange voices pulled me from the darkness. Someone needed to dial their volume down. My head ached like a son of a bitch. I felt around for my knife as I waited for the bright lights in the room to stop blinding me, but I couldn't find it. I groaned softly and peeled an eye open, then closed it again.

"She's my cousin from out of town," Holden explained to the doctor.

"So, she's family?" he asked and nodded toward me.

I continued to pretend that I was asleep and eavesdropped, assessing the situation while watching them through slightly open eyelids. The doctor seemed young, maybe early thirties. His wavy brown hair was short, and he had a runner's build. Long and lean.

"Yeah, from Michigan. My mom's sister's daughter. They're not really close and this is the first time I've seen River in years," Holden explained.

"Wouldn't you know your cousin's last name?" The doctor arched an eyebrow at him.

"I do. I was just rattled, and it slipped my mind. As the X-rays showed, she broke her leg pretty badly. I heard it snap. Her last name is Collins."

"All right, son. I understand that it might have freaked you out a little bit. But you're a star quarterback. You've seen a lot of injuries, Holden. I wouldn't think you'd get shaken up over something as common as a broken bone."

"Yeah, but that's on the field. This ... this one was my fault."

"What do you mean?"

Shit, Holden. Hush already. You're digging a deeper hole for us.

"She was teasing me and took my phone. I chased her through the house, and she flew out the door, and jumped over a chair. I was right behind her and heard ..." Holden's face paled. "But she's going to be okay?"

The doctor smiled. "Why don't you ask her?" He nodded at me, and I gave them a sheepish wave.

"Hi, River. I'm Doctor Martin. How are you feeling, young lady?"

"A little nauseated, but other than that I'm okay. Better than earlier."

"I'll send you home with a prescription to settle your stomach and some pain pills, but your leg is broken. You took a really nasty tumble and now you have a stable fracture. It looks like your face is bruised as well." The doctor cleared his throat and pointed to my nose. "Those aren't fresh, though." He glared at Holden again.

Fuck. My makeup must have worn off. I raised a hand to the bruises. "Yeah," I whispered, refusing to look at either of them. I stared at my cast instead. No wonder Dr. Martin was grilling Holden hard.

"Let's get your nose reset since you're here. Holden promised me he'll look after you for the next six weeks while you heal. I better not see any more marks on you, though." He narrowed his gaze at Holden as he spoke.

"He didn't do it. I swear," I said, jumping to Holden's defense. This guy had fed me, driven me to the hospital, and stayed. He didn't deserve to be accused of hurting me. The least I could do was clear his name of any suspicions.

"I believe you, River, but I'm still going to keep an eye on the situation." He folded his hands in front of his waist.

I nodded, unable to speak for fear I'd let something slip about being on the run from those sick and twisted men in Montana.

"I'll see you in two weeks. If everything looks good, I'll see you at the six-week mark, then physical therapy."

I ground my molars together. Where was I going to stay while I healed?

"When are you going back to Michigan?" The doctor approached the computer and started typing.

"She's staying here for a while. She's considering college in the fall, so she's pretty much moved in since my sister is gone."

What? I sure as hell couldn't argue with him at the moment, but there was no way I was about to become his problem. I would figure shit out on my own.

"Excellent, then I'll see you in a few weeks." Dr. Martin patted me on the arm, then left the room.

After my nose had been reset, I was more than ready to leave the hospital.

"Let's go, Bambi."

I scowled at him. "You're not funny. If my legs hadn't been so damned cold, I would have cleared the chair without any issue."

"I wasn't referring to that. You're skittish like a baby deer. When they're spooked, they jump over shit and run their asses off."

"Lame. You need to work on better comparisons." I tilted my chin up at him as the pain meds began to seriously mess with my overstimulated brain.

"Well, regardless, you're stuck with me now. Let's get you home and your leg propped up. I have crutches from my own accidents. I'll adjust the height, and you can use them."

My emotions and logic were in a full-on tug-of-war. My head said no, but I was exhausted and tired of fighting. Tired of fighting to live, tired of fighting off men with shitty intentions, and tired of my dumbass luck. If I left Holden's house, I would be a hobbling target, begging for some stupid fuck to hurt me again. Maybe this time, I needed to trust Holden.

A nurse rolled a wheelchair over to my bed. Before I could protest, Holden lifted me off the uncomfortable mattress and gently placed me in the chair.

"At least you didn't have to change into a hospital gown." A wide grin played across Holden's lips.

"Ha! No way am I baring my ass to everyone." I lightly swatted at his hand. "I can ..." I was going to say walk, but I couldn't. The cast was wrapped up to my knee, so I could hardly bend it. There was no way in hell that I could put any pressure on it. I suppose I would have to learn to hop around with one foot when I was in a situation where I couldn't use the crutches.

The nurse pushed me down the hall and to the elevator.

"I'll bring the car around to the entrance," Holden said, looking down at me.

My heart slammed against my chest. He was the most beautiful guy I'd seen in my life. Absolutely mouthwatering. Angular jaw, light stubble across his chin, and muscles that I'd love to dig my fingernails into when ... I blinked rapidly, trying to steer my thoughts in another direction, but all I wanted was to touch him.

Holden laughed and gently patted my shoulder. "Those pain meds are treating you pretty well."

"Yup," I said, giggling. The sound was completely foreign to my ears. I hadn't giggled in years. Not even with Addison.

"I miss Addison," I sighed. "A lot." Holden had no idea how bad I missed her. Dammit. Addison didn't even have a fucking clue of where I was. I really needed to figure out how to email her.

"Best friend?" Holden asked.

"Yup." I popped my lips together for the sound effect and snickered.

The nurse grinned. "I gave your partner your prescription. You'll need those for a few days."

Neither of us corrected the nurse. Holden wasn't my boyfriend, but by the time my brain strung the words together to set her straight, I'd forgotten what the hell I was trying to say.

"Messing with your drug-addled head is going to be so much fun." Holden covered his mouth with his fist, attempting to hide his big-ass grin.

"You better be careful. I'll knock you out with my cast if you try to rape me. Damn shame I didn't have a weapon around when Dan did."

Time stood still in the elevator as it dawned on me what I'd said. Holden's smiled dropped off his face, and he balled his hands into fists, his nostrils flaring with anger.

Confused, I struggled to figure out if I'd pissed Holden off or if he was mad about something else. One thing I couldn't fucking afford to do was irritate him. For now, I needed to play it safe until I was healed. Dammit. I sure was tired of walking on eggshells around people. One day, I would get it right. One day, I'd tell the heavens to go fuck themselves as I took my life back and created a new one. *I would rewrite my story.*

The ding of the elevator pulled my attention away from him.

"I'll get the car." Holden darted out before I could say anything else.

The nurse hit the button, and the doors slid closed. "Hon, are you safe at home? Who is Dan?"

"I'm fine. It was a long time ago." I gulped, praying that I could clear my head enough to lie and cover up my slip. "I think I'm just feeling a little loopy and vulnerable. Holden is as safe as it gets." I patted her arm, hoping my words were enough to assure her that all was well in my world. It was. Dan's remains were probably still at the bottom of the hill unless the coyotes had finished what Killer had started.

"You're in a safe situation now?" She knelt beside me, searching for signs that I wasn't being honest.

"Yeah. Holden hasn't hurt me. He's really good to me actually."

The nurse stood and removed a business card from her pocket. "If you ever find yourself in trouble, call this number. They'll help with a good place to stay or a hotel."

I took the information from her and folded it in my hand. "Thank you."

The doors opened again, and the nurse wheeled me out of the elevator and down a long hall. She pushed the handicap button, then we exited the hospital. Several cars were lined up in the pick-up lane, and I shivered from the sudden cold and rubbed my arms.

"I'm here," Holden said as he jumped out of a sleek black Audi and opened the passenger door for me. He lifted me from the chair and placed me in the car. I winced as he pushed the button, and my seat moved back, allowing more legroom. Holden buckled me in, then thanked the nurse.

"Are you cold? I turned the heat on high." He held his fingers in front of the vent, testing the warmth of the blasting air stream. "I'll put a chair in the shower for you. We'll have to cover your leg, too. You can't get it wet." He glanced at me, his expression not revealing his feelings. "Let's go home."

"Home. The word sounds so *safe*." I rolled my head against the headrest of the car. "I've never had that before." I touched my fingertips to the leather dashboard, ignoring the concern etched into Holden's face.

"No one should have to live like that, River. No one."

"If you only knew. If you knew, Holden... you would leave me outside next to your garbage to be collected on pick up day."

For the first time in my life, I witnessed someone's heart crack open and bleed.

Chapter Eight

Despite my protests, Holden carried me into the house and downstairs. He deposited me on the leather couch, disappeared, then returned a few minutes later with several pillows to prop my leg up, along with a fresh ice pack. He placed a bottle of water and my meds on the end table and looked at his phone.

"You can have another pain pill in a few hours."

"Yes, sir." I gave him a half-hearted salute and snickered.

Holden sat near my feet and grabbed the remote control. "We have satellite, Netflix, Prime, and more channels to choose from than you'll ever have time for while you're healing."

"We're going to watch TV?" I attempted to remember what I wanted to ask a while ago, but it was just out of my reach.

"We can. I mean, you're pretty out of it and you need to rest."

I frowned at him. "You're kinda bossy. And I wanted to ask you something from earlier, but I can't remember. I'm not sure I'll even remember what I just said if you count to five. These pills are really fucking me up." I flashed him a smile, then it faltered when my brain registered his expression.

He twisted on the couch and looked at me. "River...."

His voice was a gentle touch to my battered soul.

"Yeah?" I wiggled my butt on the smooth leather in order to prop myself up better, so I could see him over my leg.

"Who hurt you? The bruises." He pinned me with his gaze, and I struggled not to squirm like I had when I was a young girl in the school counselor's office. My teacher had turned Dan in for abusing me, but they never did anything. Maybe the Child Protective Services thought I would be better off in the house with that bastard than in a foster home. How fucked up was that?

I searched the room, the sudden urge to flee consuming me.

"I'm not going to hurt you. I swear. Please try to believe me."

I chewed the inside of my cheek, wondering what I should tell him. I massaged my forehead, buying myself an extra moment or two. Thanks to the pain pill, my face no longer ached like a motherfucker.

"My legal guardian." There, I'd done it. I'd answered him, and we could move on now.

"What? River, he needs to be reported. You don't have to live like that anymore."

Anger surged through me. "And what? I've known you for all of five seconds and suddenly you're my knight in shining armor? You want to save poor little River from getting beaten and raped?" My tone dripped with sarcasm and venom.

Holden's shoulders visibly tightened, but he didn't apologize for his comment. In fact, he looked even more determined to learn more. What was with this guy?

"No thanks. I already took care of him." I sucked in a breath and wished like hell I could reel those words right back into my piehole.

"What do you mean?" Confusion washed over Holden's expression.

I rolled my eyes, which almost made me laugh. I wasn't the teen that tossed an eye roll whenever a person annoyed me. I valued my teeth in my head and not on the floor.

"What do *you* mean?" I asked, throwing his question back at him.

Maybe he would remember I was on pain meds and wasn't tracking the conversation well.

Confusion washed over his face. "What do you mean that you took care of Dan?"

"He's dead." The words flew out of my mouth without permission.

Surprise flickered across Holden's features, then he recovered. He leaned toward me, his eyes leveling mine. "Good. I hope it was slow and painful."

Tears blurred my vision. No one had ever been on my side before.

"I won't turn you in, River. You did what you had to do."

"I didn't kill him. I hid in a tree while it happened. The drug dealer's dog tore his throat out. It was pretty gross." *River, shut up already.* "Some men are looking for me, though. Dan owed them a lot of money. I overheard them talking about what they planned to do to me if they couldn't find him." I gulped, my stomach rolling at the thought of them getting their disgusting hands on me.

His brows furrowed as he pieced it all together. "So, you couldn't go home...."

I nodded. "They were watching our trailer, which was a total shithole. A week ago, I was accepted to a college in Oregon. I was on my way out, but ..." My long hair cloaked the tears that were now streaming down my cheeks. "I fought him as hard as I could." I sniffled and wiped my nose with my fingers. "He was too strong." A sob shook my shoulders, the images of that night replaying on a loop in my brain.

"River, it's not supposed to be like that. No one has a right to hit or force themselves on you."

I snapped my head up, the genuine tone of his words piercing my soul. "Maybe that's how you live. Maybe your world is full of kind people, but mine isn't."

I used the dirty sleeve of my sweatshirt and wiped the moisture from my face. "Is it possible that I can take you up on a shower and some of your sister's clothes?" I needed a break from this conversation. Over the last few days, my heart had gone through more than it could take. It was easier to protect it when you were in the middle of being abused. Hate had been my armor, but Holden was already putting chinks in it, and I couldn't let that happen.

"Of course. Let me grab you something to wear and put the chair in the shower for you."

"Thanks." My throat was tight and scratchy from my tears.

The second he was out of the room, I sagged against the arm of the couch and closed my eyes. I was going to have to fight harder against the pain meds. I'd revealed way too much to Holden. By the time six weeks passed, he would know me better than anyone else on the planet. I had to figure out how to leave before it was too late, and I'd allowed him to get too close to me.

"I found the crutches, too. You're all set up, but I'm going to carry you to the bathroom. After your shower and before your next pain pill, I'll make sure you know how to use them." Once again, he lifted me into his strong arms.

I chanced a peek at Holden. "I think you like carrying me around because it boosts your ego."

A low chuckle rumbled through his chest as he walked down the hall. He set me on the toilet seat, then turned on the water for me. "Don't laugh, but I don't know what to use to cover your leg, so...." He reached over on the white-and-tan granite counter and shook out a plastic trash bag.

I covered my mouth with my arm, trying not to giggle while he knelt and slipped the plastic over my cast. He gently smoothed it and released the trapped air. He smirked as he used the drawstring to tighten it above my knee and seal my lower leg from the water. "Perfect. You're good to go." He dusted his hands off as if his job was done.

Although Holden had thought a lot of things through, I'm not sure he'd figured out how I was going to get naked and in the shower on my own.

"Well, those jeans you have on are toast." He nodded at my cut pant leg. "You should be able to slip it over your cast pretty easily. Just don't lose your balance and fall off the toilet."

"Huh?" I wasn't tracking what he was saying.

"River, I'm really trying to figure out how to get you out of your clothes."

I gaped at him, and my cheeks flamed red.

Holden groaned. "I didn't mean it like that. I know you're loopy from the medication and I don't want you to hurt yourself again, but I can't undress you either."

"That makes more sense," I muttered. I looked at the shower. It was large enough for five people with a see-through door. Holden had placed a chair under the multiple showerheads and near the shelf that was full of shampoo, conditioner, and at least three kinds of body wash. "If I'm in the shower I can use a hand to stand and take my pants off. Like you said, they're trash anyway. I'll finish undressing in there." I grinned at him, rather proud of my plan.

"And when you're done?" He folded his arms across his broad chest.

I narrowed my eyes at the floor. Marble again. Shit, I'd bust my ass as soon as my wet foot hit the smooth stone. "Hang the towel on the shower handle. I'll hop over, open the door, then grab it from there."

Holden remained quiet. "As soon as you're wrapped up, yell for me."

I quirked an eyebrow at him. "You're bound and determined to see me naked, aren't you?"

This time Holden's cheeks turned red. He cleared his throat. "No, I'm trying to avoid another injury. I think one trip to the hospital was enough for the day." He strolled to the door. "Yell for me. I'll come in and carry you to Mallory's room. You can sit on her bed and get dressed again. Her clothes might be a little bit big on you, but not for long. I plan to feed you well while you're recovering."

What the fuck was with this guy? "I'm not some pet project for you to fix," I snapped.

Holden approached me with a steely, calm expression. "Let's get something straight. Unlike you, I come from a decent home. When I was younger, my parents taught me to be kind and to care about others that are less fortunate than we are."

My eyes flared in warning as the ugly truth filled the air, and a humorless laugh escaped me. I shot up on my good leg and punched him in the chest. His face registered shock as he staggered backward.

"Fuck you. I'm well-aware I'm trailer trash in the king's castle, but don't you ever speak to me like that again. I don't fucking need your pity. Now get out so I can get undressed and shower. The water has been running for a while, which is a goddamned waste if you weren't aware of it." My nostrils flared as I willed myself not to hit him again.

Holden hung the towel on the handle of the shower door, then quietly left the room. I hoped he felt like shit.

I sank onto the toilet again. At least I was alone. My anger had cleared my head a little, and I stood on my good leg, held onto the wall with one hand, and hopped over to other side of the room, where I discarded all my clothes other than my jeans in the trash. Even if I wanted to, I wouldn't be able to wear them again. Too bad my life wasn't as easily disposed of.

One thing was for sure, if the asshole continued to treat me like that, it would be pretty easy not to get attached to him.

Chapter Nine

True to his word, Holden had shown up when I'd called him from the bathroom. He was silent as he carried me to a large bedroom and carefully set me on the bed.

"I'm making dinner, so yell when you're dressed."

The second he was out of earshot, I groaned and fell back on the plush mattress. Guilt gnawed at me, and I closed my eyes. I'd been a bitch, but he'd clearly categorized me as belonging in the less fortunate pile of shit, and it pissed me off. Even if he ended up apologizing for being rude, he'd still verbalized it.

The little voice inside my head reminded me he'd been nothing but good and kind to me, and he was allowed to have a stupid moment.

I laid still, reveling in the soft comforter I was lying on. The tray ceiling and large windows made the huge room feel even more spacious. Finally, curiosity won, and I sat up, taking in all of the beautiful details. A white dresser matched the four-poster king-sized bed frame, and two bookshelves were filled with books. When I had the crutches, I'd have to take a look and see if there was anything good to read. Books had become my best friends over the years. They'd provided a safe place where I could mentally and emotionally hide. The characters had invited me into their homes, and I rarely wanted to leave to face the real world.

I ran my hand over the black-and-blue comforter, the soft, plush fibers brushing against my palm. A pair of gray Victoria's Secret sweat shorts and a matching sweatshirt laid on the bed next to me. A red bra and panty set with the tags still on them were near the shirt. I held the panties up with one finger. There wasn't much to them. The small triangle of fabric covered the front, then a string went up the ass. Well, they had a better chance of fitting me than the bra did. I fiddled with the tag and laughed. Mallory was smaller in the chest than I was, but not by much. Maybe it would fit okay.

Finally, my attention landed on my backpack, then my mouth gaped open in shock. Holden had found my knife and laid it next to the bag for me. He could have kept it, but he hadn't. I wasn't sure why, unless he wanted to help me feel safe. Unfortunately, it would take a hell of a lot more than a few kind gestures.

A half hour later, I was dressed and exhausted. I wasn't sure where I was going to sleep, but the bed was super comfy. I sighed as I adjusted my boobs in my new bra. It fit better than I thought it would, which meant I was covered and wouldn't have to try to hide my nipples from Holden.

Another minute passed, and I finally swallowed my pride. It was time to apologize for my outburst. I stood and held onto the wall as I hopped to the door, then opened it. Thank God I was in good shape, or my leg would have given out soon.

I hobbled down the hall, then to the edge of the living room. My mouth watered as the delicious smell of dinner wafted toward me.

"Hey," I said. Nervous energy tap danced over my ribcage as I waited.

Holden spun around, nearly dropping his beer on the floor. "Shit, you startled me."

Shame flooded me, and I had to tear my gaze away from his face. "I didn't mean to. I just thought I would save you from carrying me."

"Let me help you to the couch. Dinner will be ready in half an hour. Do you want a soda or anything?"

With long strides, Holden joined me. I wrapped my arm around his waist and leaned into him slightly as he protectively placed his hand on my back, steadying me. My stomach somersaulted, then flip-flopped again. Instead of wanting to flee, I found the warmth of his body calming. An air of protectiveness embraced me, and the voices in my head tapped me on my skull, reminding me that no one was safe and not to let my guard down. I ignored them and allowed myself to give in briefly.

After I was propped up on the sofa, Holden hurried over to the fireplace and flipped a switch. The fire immediately roared to life. He disappeared down the hall, then returned with a thick navy blanket and covered me.

"Do you happen to have any Dr Pepper?" I asked, a hint of hope in my tone. I'd rarely ever had one, but it was my first choice.

"Yup. It's my favorite soda so there's always some here." Holden took a few steps, then turned around slowly. "I'm sorry, River. I never meant to make you feel less than. You're not, and no one should ever treat you like that. I just opened my mouth and shit came out." He kneaded the back of his neck, apologizing with his dark brown eyes and lulling me into a false sense of security.

The ice walls I'd erected around my heart melted a little. "I'm sorry I hit you. I'm so used to having to defend myself, I ... It wasn't okay for me to do that."

"So we're good?"

"Yeah. We are." I flashed him a little smile, trying to feel safe enough with him to show another emotion other than anger or fear. "But, Holden?"

He leaned over the back of the couch, the soft leather dipping with the weight of his elbows. "Yeah?"

"You know part of my story. What's yours? What drives you to want to help me? I might have grown up in a bad situation, but it's taught me to read people, and I'm getting the feeling that somewhere along the way, someone you loved broke you. You were just lucky enough to be put back together."

Holden's mouth opened and closed like a fish out of water. I'd clearly caught him off guard. Although I hadn't meant to, I'd backed him into an awkward corner like he'd done to me earlier. Conflicted, he placed his hand on my forearm. This time I didn't flinch or pull away.

Before he could respond, the sliding glass door moved, and the platinum blonde I'd seen last night waltzed into the house. Two guys and one girl followed her in.

"Oh my God, Becky. Why did you stop like that?" one of the guys asked as he nearly knocked her over.

"Because of me," I answered for Becky, waving at them.

"Whoa, dude, who's the gorgeous chick that looks like she got hit by a fucking car?" A tall, tanned, hot as hell guy strode forward, his blue-gray eyes smiling. His broad shoulders were larger than Holden's, and he was in amazing shape. I wondered if he played football.

Holden cringed and swore under his breath. "Jace, she did get hit by a car, actually. In front of my house. Everyone, this is River, my cousin from Michigan."

This was the second time that story had saved us both from a ton of explaining that wasn't people's business. I appreciated Holden for not blabbing my situation to anyone who was interested.

"Oh, shit. I'm sorry. You just looked banged up, so I was being a smart-ass. I'm Jace, it's nice to meet you, River, cousin of Holden." He bowed, then plunked down on the couch, jostling the pillows beneath me, and I winced as a sharp pain stabbed my leg.

Holden slapped him on the side of the arm. "Careful, man! She's hurting pretty bad."

Becky continued to glare at me as she walked toward Holden, carrying a few bags. Instead of the see-through pajama shorts she had on last night, she wore a bright red, low-cut blouse tucked into light wash jeans. Her lipstick matched her top, and her foundation was a shade darker than the skin on her neck. I wasn't sure why she thought

63

it looked good, but I mentally raised my hand to tell her she needed a more natural look. Her black heels scraped the marble floor as she walked, and her hips swayed, calling attention to her too-tight pants. I wondered if anyone had told this girl that camel toe wasn't sexy.

"Hi." She batted her long eyelashes at Holden, and I nearly gagged. Thank fuck I wasn't eating yet because I would've tossed up my dinner in a heartbeat. Who *was* this girl?

The timer on the oven dinged a few times, breaking through the awkwardness everyone was feeling.

"We were about to eat. There's plenty if you guys are hungry," Holden announced.

"Starving" The tall blonde-haired guy I hadn't met yet graced me with a huge grin as he closed the sliding glass door. His blue eyes sparkled with a hint of mischievousness.

"Chance, you're a bottomless pit, dude." Holden laughed while he set the bags on the counter and unloaded a few six-packs of beer.

"Hi, I'm Brynn. It's nice to meet you." I glanced up at a gorgeous redhead with a slightly upturned nose and a dusting of freckles across her cheeks. Her brilliant green eyes sparkled as she spoke. She was stunning in dark wash jeans that showed off every single curve of her slender waist and hips. Her black sweater accentuated her boobs and flat stomach. I could only hope to look as beautiful as her.

"Hi, and you, too." I folded my hands in my lap and pretended I was more relaxed than I was. I was suddenly in a crowd of people I didn't know, and not one single thing felt good about it. The anxiety infiltrated my veins and slithered into every part of me.

"You'll get used to everyone." Brynn sat on the edge of the coffee table. "So, Michigan, huh? I've never been."

"You're not missing much." I attempted a smile, extremely self-conscious of my bruised face and wet hair. "It's cold in the winter with mosquitoes large enough to carry off a small dog in the summer. I'm glad I'm here for a while. The change of scenery ... Well, I was looking forward to it until I had my accident." There were times I scared myself, especially when it was that easy to lie. The only reason

I knew about Michigan was because Addison had lived there before Montana. Otherwise, I wouldn't have had a damned clue.

"Looks like the car won." Brynn wrinkled her freckle-covered nose at me. "I'm sorry. I hope you feel better soon."

"Oh, she will. I'm going to take good care of her," Holden said, giving me a Dr Pepper and my dinner. "There's plenty of food, so if you're still hungry let me know."

My mouth watered so bad I was afraid I would start drooling. Meatloaf, scalloped potatoes, and green beans. I frowned, then peered up at him. "Who *are* you?"

Brynn giggled and squeezed his arm. "He's the black sheep of the family because he's not a fucking douchebag. Well, his mom still loves him."

Holden visibly tensed. His mask of coolness was gone as a flicker of anger appeared in his expression. Just as quickly as it showed up, it disappeared, and he smiled while he patted Brynn's knuckles and said, "Thanks, Brynn. I appreciate that."

It was at that moment I realized that Holden had as many dark layers as I did. Although I wanted to know his secrets, I was afraid to crack that shell open. "Should I roll my eyes for you?" I offered.

"Please." Holden squeezed Brynn's hand before he returned to the kitchen.

"Black sheep?" I squeaked.

"You have no idea." Brynn giggled. "I'm teasing you. Holden is a great guy, but his family … Well, I'll save that conversation for another day. But welcome to Spokane, and to the wealthiest family in the Pacific Northwest. I promise you it will never be boring." Brynn winked, then hopped up and hurried over to the group and the food.

My fork bounced off the edge of my plate and clattered against the floor. Black sheep *and* wealthiest? What the hell had I just landed in the middle of?

Chapter Ten

The alcohol flowed, and each person sat down and talked to me ... except Becky, who kept herself busy by shooting me dirty looks from across the room while she practically humped Holden's leg. Such a multitasker, that one. If she was trying to mark her territory, then point taken. I was out of here as soon as I could walk.

Brynn hung out with me most of the evening, and it was difficult not to like her immediately. She was funny and kind. We had the same sarcastic sense of humor and a similar taste in music.

I'd popped another pain pill, and between the conversation and the exhaustion from the day, I struggled to keep my eyes open.

"Hey, princess. Let's get you to bed so you can get some sleep. It's after midnight." Holden looked down at me and grinned. "I can't have any of these assholes trying to pull your deep, dark secrets out of you while you're on meds, either."

"I didn't know she had secrets, but now that I do ..." Chance released a maniacal laugh and smirked.

"Fuck you, man. My cousin is off-limits ... period." Holden's expression tightened with his words. "In fact—" Holden cupped his hands around his mouth, using them to amplify his voice over the loud chatter and laughter. "—my cousin is off-limits while she's healing, and afterward too. That goes for men and women." Holden's gaze dropped to me. "Sorry to cock or pussy block you, but you're my responsibility, right?"

I stifled my giggle. "No shit. Getting knocked up while I'm here wouldn't settle well with the fam." I offered a lopsided and loopy grin.

"Definitely time to get you to bed." Holden bent down and picked me up.

Without thinking, I squeezed his rock-hard bicep. Even stoned on my meds, I didn't miss the scathing look Becky gave me.

"Night," everyone chimed in as Holden headed toward the stairs.

"Night." I waved, then rested my head against Holden's shoulder. "Becky must think we're into incest," I whispered against Holden's ear, causing him to stumble.

"Shit." He caught us right before we landed on the floor. "Are you all right?"

"Yup. Are you?" I couldn't control my snicker. "Was it the incest part that tripped you up? Like, literally?"

"Let's go upstairs, then we can talk. I'm not sure what's going to fly out of your mouth next and I would prefer not to have to take you back to the hospital."

"Yeah, that sucked. The leg sucks. I should be out of your hair already, but now you're stuck with me."

Holden didn't respond as he carried me up another flight of stairs from the main floor and down a hallway. "My room is next to yours if you need anything." He nodded to it as we passed by, then strolled through an open door.

"Crutches? Are you withholding them, so I don't try to run again?" I raised an eyebrow at him. "Are you keeping me a prisoner?" I gasped, and my hand flew to my mouth in mock surprise.

Holden laughed and set me down on a queen-sized bed. Instead of white furniture like in his sister's room, it was all a dark, rich brown wood. The bed had a million baby-blue-and-cream throw pillows and a matching comforter.

"No, it's just that everyone showed up and I forgot. Where's your phone?"

"In my bag." I sat up, realizing it wasn't here and neither was my weapon. "Shit, it's in the downstairs bedroom along with my knife."

"I'll get it for you. I'll program my number into your cell so you can text or call if you need anything. I'm hoping you'll sleep through the night, though."

I tried to suppress my yawn but didn't win the fight. "Who's the lesbian in the group?"

Holden's head tilted in question. "Are you? A lesbian I mean?"

"Nope, but I'm not opposed to experimenting."

Holden's brows shot to his hairline and the corner of his lips pulled up into a smile. "You're wasted. I doubt you'll even remember you said that by tomorrow."

"Maybe, but I really don't have an issue with it. I think gay people are human beings just like the rest of us and I don't give a flying fuck who they love or sleep with." I shrugged a shoulder.

Holden's dark eyes searched me. "Are you bi?"

"No. I've had sex twice with a guy ... willingly. It wasn't great sex. I was sixteen and it was mostly fumbling around until he found the hole."

Holden's chuckle filled the room. "It takes a little bit of practice for a guy to learn their way around."

I blew out a sigh. "To be fair, I haven't ever been with a girl, so I don't know if I would like it or not. Based on my two measly experiences, I definitely like dick."

Holden laughed so hard his chest shook, his eyes dancing with amusement. "I'm glad to hear it." He reached up and brushed the tips of his fingers against my cheek. "Is your face feeling better?"

I froze but didn't pull away, then he lowered his hand to his leg. If he wanted to rape me, he had the perfect opportunity. I kicked the fear in the ass and redirected my thoughts.

"Dude, everything feels good right now." I huffed out a laugh and smiled. "But who's ... wait." I smacked my palm against my forehead. "This doesn't make sense. There are two women downstairs, and Becky has basically pissed all over you marking her territory. I mean we're *cousins*." I used air quotes to emphasize cousin. "I have no clue why she perceives me as a threat unless you're into incest and I just don't know that about you yet."

Holden's nostrils flared. "Gross. No."

"I didn't get the vibe that Brynn was bi, but I'm not myself right now. Maybe I missed it."

"Those things are easy to miss. Becky is bi."

"Ahh. Well, you didn't need to warn her away from me. She already hates me."

He scratched his head, and an uncomfortable smile fluttered on his lips. "Please ignore her. Her bark is worse than her bite."

I leaned against the pillows, my brain hopping topics like a train running off the tracks. "Why?" My fingertips traced his angular jaw. "Why are you the black sheep? You've been nothing but kind to me ever since ... this morning. What makes you so bad, Holden Alastair?"

Holden wrapped his large hand around mine. "One day I'll tell you, but only if you share as well. Your secrets run dark and deep, and hopefully you'll trust me with them." He leaned over and placed a gentle kiss on my forehead, then stood. "I'll get your bag and grab a bottled water, along with your meds."

I didn't miss the sadness in Holden's eyes. The regret.

"Thanks," I said softly, my heart thumping erratically against my rib cage. Apparently, the pain meds not only made me feel vulnerable but bold. No way would I have allowed Holden to touch me without them.

I wiggled down into the bed, wondering whose bedroom this was. Images raced through my mind, recapping the last twenty-four hours as I stared at the white tray ceiling. This time last night, I'd been freezing my ass off in Holden's recycling bin after running for my life.

I shook my head at how everything had changed so damned fast. Even though I had a broken leg, I was in a beautiful home filled with luxuries. It would be hard to leave, but this wasn't where I belonged, and I knew it.

* * *

A sharp pain shot through my body, waking me from a sound sleep.

"Wake up, *Cousin River.*" Becky glared at me, then kicked my broken leg again.

"What the fuck is wrong with you?" I clenched my fists, ready to deck her if she got close enough.

"Here's your bag." Becky tossed it on the bed. "But this is interesting." She held up my knife, the blade reflecting the soft light of the lamp Holden must have turned on.

"Give it to me. You have no right to go through my things." I sat up, my mind automatically calculating how to defend myself. I hated to deflate Becky's ego, but I'd faced a lot worse than her.

"I have a right to do anything I want." Becky scrambled up the bed and over me, pinning me down when she straddled my waist. She leaned over me, her sneer full of anger. "I know you're not his cousin. I'm not sure what you're trying to hide, but I'm not buying any of it. I've known Holden since grade school and not once has he ever mentioned you."

"Our mothers have been estranged for years." I remained still, waiting for the right time to buck her off me. Since I couldn't run, I had to make sure I was close enough to the lamp so I could smash it over her head.

Becky leaned forward and pressed the blade of the knife against my throat, then licked my cheek. "You taste like white trash."

"I am white trash, bitch. Tell me something I don't know," I snarled. She was really pissing me off. "What the hell do you want?"

"Leave. I don't care if you can walk or not. Leave by tomorrow and don't ever contact Holden again. If you do ..." With a lethal glint in her eyes, she applied pressure to the knife, and I yelped as it pierced my skin.

"Why? Why am I such a threat to you?" I realized I should shut up, but apparently, the pain meds had me chattering away even when my life depended on me not saying another goddamned word.

"Because he cares about you, and I'm not going to lose my chance at marrying the wealthiest bachelor in the Pacific Northwest. He's mine, so take your sob story somewhere else." She leaned down, her breath tickling my ear as she spoke. "Don't ever repeat what I'm about to tell you. The Alastair family ... Holden's family isn't who they say they are. You need to leave. I'm sorry I hurt you, but this has to look legit."

Alarmed by her words, I froze. "What do you mean?" My body betrayed me and trembled beneath her.

Before Becky could continue, a movement caught the corner of my eye, and I tensed, preparing to punch her as soon as her attention left me.

"Becky, get the fuck off her right *now*." Holden's deep voice roared through the room.

Becky gasped and looked at Holden, the knife slipping from my neck. In one quick move, I hit her in the jaw, and she reeled backward, then onto the floor.

Holden took two long strides and stepped on her wrist with his bare foot. "Drop the knife."

Becky whimpered as she released it. "You're sick, Holden. You need therapy. She's trash and everyone knows she's not your cousin. For God's sake, you only met her today. Why are you protecting her?"

Those were excellent questions that I would love the answers to as well.

"Because she has something that you never will." He ground out the response, his jaw tightening.

71

I peered at Becky, who had tears streaming down her cheeks. If she wasn't careful, she would cry those fake eyelashes off.

"What's that?" she asked, hiccupping through her sobs.

"A heart." Holden knelt and collected my knife. "Get out. You're not welcome here anymore. No one threatens River's life and gets away with it. If I ever find out that you've talked to her again, you'll regret it." Holden lifted his foot and moved next to the bed, shielding me from her.

Becky scrambled off the floor and glowered at us. "This isn't over." With that, she stomped out of the room and down the hall.

Unanswered questions spun around in my head like leaves on a blustery day. Dammit. I didn't understand what Becky had tried to tell me.

"Are you okay?" Holden asked. "Dammit! Your neck is bleeding."

What the fuck? I swiped at my nicked skin, my fingers shining with a sticky crimson. "That bitch is crazy." Whatever she'd tried to tell me hadn't justified her actions. As far as I was concerned, Holden had been nothing but kind to me, and Becky was trying to mess with my head. At first, I was willing to give her the benefit of the doubt, that her attacking me was an act, but you don't cut someone for no reason unless you're fucked up.

"I'm really sorry, River. I had no idea she would come unhinged and threaten you. I need to make sure she leaves the house and property, though. I'll be right back."

Holden hurried out of the bedroom, and I sat up on the edge of the bed, wide awake. The last thing I wanted to do was bleed on the beautiful bedding. I used the nightstand to balance on and slid off the mattress, my good foot landing on the plushest carpet my little piggies had ever felt in their nineteen years.

Becky's screech echoed through the house along with a loud crash, confirming my earlier thoughts that she wasn't stable. Dammit, if I'd had crutches, I could see what was going on. Hell, I could have beaten her ass with one if they'd been next to me.

"Hey, are you all right?" Brynn said from the doorway. Jace's head popped up over hers.

"I hate to ask, but I need to get to the bathroom." I despised depending on people, and it was even harder to plead for help.

"This is silly. I'll find the crutches. I think they're in the kitchen. I realize Holden loves carrying you around, but you need to be able to get around without him." Brynn shook her head. "And cousin, my ass. Tell Holden no one believed him after the way he looked at you all night."

I could literally feel the color drain from my cheeks. "What do you mean?"

"Uh-oh." She peered up at Jace. "Would you get the crutches for River? I think I just said the wrong thing, and I should stay with her. She's pretty pale."

I sank onto the mattress again, my head woozy.

"All I meant was that he really cares about you already. And the guys will take care of Becky. I knew she had a screw or two loose when it came to Holden, but this was over the top even for her."

"Why? I'm broken and my face is more colorful than my language. Why would she ever feel threatened by me?"

Brynn's expressive eyes filled with compassion. "You don't know, do you?"

Chapter Eleven

My heart plummeted to my toes, a sinking feeling twisting my stomach into knots. "I guess not." I chewed on my already too short thumbnail.

"I'm sorry. The way Holden was acting, I thought maybe he'd told you. Holden and I have been friends for a long time, and I can't share his past with you. It's not my place. All I can say is that you resemble someone that was close to him, and Becky realized it." She offered me a sad smile.

"Even if that's true, it didn't give Becky a reason to attack me." I absentmindedly tucked my hair behind my ear as Becky's warning rang through my mind.

"I completely agree with you. But, I can promise you this, Holden is a wonderful guy. Smart, kind, and a hell of a football player. He'll give someone the shirt off his back. I'm not sure how his parents produced such an amazing kid when they're ..." Brynn stared at the floor, then at me. "It's not important. You're in good hands. Get to know him and understand that you're safe. I saw how on edge you were tonight, but after he told Becky to leave, I hope it put your fears to rest. You really can trust him."

Jace burst into the room and held out the crutches to me. "I tried to adjust them for your height." The sounds of sirens reached my ears, and I turned to the windows. He frowned. "What the hell?" He hurried to the window and raised the blind. "Holy shit. The cops and an ambulance." He spun on his heel and made a mad dash for the door. "I'm not sure if it's for Holden or Becky!" he yelled as he ran out.

"Can you make it down the stairs?" Brynn asked. "We have to see what's happening."

I hopped off the bed, gathered the crutches, and hauled ass out of the room and down the hall as quickly as my brain and body would allow me. When I reached the steps, I gave the crutches over to Brynn, sat down on the top step, and bounced down on my butt while I held my broken leg up with a free hand. Once I was at the bottom, I pulled myself up with the assistance of the banister.

"I can see you're quite resourceful." Brynn flashed me a wide smile as she helped me get situated again.

I glanced at the rooms on either side of me as we rushed to the ornate double wood doors of the main entrance.

I reached for the handle, but Brynn stopped me.

"Hang on. Let me look first. We have no idea what's going on." I moved to the side and allowed Brynn to peek through the peephole. "Oh for fuck's sake. Jace, move. I can't see anything."

The door swung open, and Brynn motioned me forward. I joined them on the front porch, gawking at what I saw.

Panic ripped the air from my lungs. "Holy shit," I whispered, trying to duck behind Jace. My fear was so strong I could taste it, sour and acidic.

"River, what's wrong?" Brynn asked, concern written all over her pretty features.

"There's a man holding a gun to Becky's head in the middle of the road, but ... he's hunting *me*." A whimper slipped through my parted lips, and I slapped my palm over my mouth. "I don't know how he found me, but he's dangerous. Please ... help."

Time stopped as I waited to see if Brynn and Jace would keep me safe. I looked into the street again where Billy, Logan's right-hand man, held Becky hostage. Three cop cars surrounded them, and multiple guns were trained on Billy. But where was Holden?

"Jace, stay in front of us and block anyone's view of River," Brynn ordered.

"Got it." Jace straightened his shoulders and stood at his full height to cover us.

Brynn slipped into the house, and I hobbled after her. Jace walked backward until he was inside again and quietly closed the door.

"Girl, you've got some serious explaining to do," Jace said, a combination of worry and irritation flickering across his face.

I shook my head adamantly, my attention bouncing between Brynn and Jace. "I don't ... How did he find me?" A prickle of anxiety rippled over my body, sending a shiver down my spine.

"He's a meth dealer in my old neighborhood." I licked my dry lips, attempting to form the rest of my words. "Becky doesn't deserve that. Oh, God." I crutched over to the stairs that led to the basement, suddenly feeling overwhelmed and fighting the urge to run. "There are rumors that they're involved with sex trafficking. My guardian ... he was mixed up with them." I sat on the top stair and bounced down on my ass.

"Jesus, this guy sounds like a real winner. I still don't understand why he's here," Brynn said, hot on my heels as I hurried to the extra bedroom.

"I don't know. I don't understand how he found me. I'm from a little town in Montana. I realize it's not that far, but I left in the middle of the night. No one knew except for the two people that helped me." I flipped on the light switch to Mallory's room. "Dammit. I forgot Becky brought my backpack upstairs." Tears welled in my eyes. "She has to be okay."

"There's not a damned thing we can do to help her," Holden said from behind us.

An unexpected calm washed over me. Holden was all right. "Where were you?" I asked, my voice shaking with the combination of relief and anxiety.

"Becky broke a lamp in the formal living room, and I was cleaning it up. After she screamed at me, she ran outside. I wanted to give her some time to cool off before I spoke to her, so I cleaned up the mess. Instead of dumping the broken pieces into the trash, I thought it would be safer to take them straight to the can in the alley. When I reached the container, I saw some guy had her at gunpoint. I called the cops and stayed on the phone with 911 until help arrived."

"You saw the whole thing?" Jace asked, running a hand over his short hair.

"Yeah, and this has definitely been a fucked-up evening. We're probably safest down here until the cops take care of the situation. He's completely surrounded, I just don't want Becky ..." His sad eyes connected with mine.

"It's all my fault." If Becky died, I would feel like shit, and Holden would never forgive me. I wasn't even sure if he'd forgive me for leading Billy, and ultimately Logan, to his house, either.

"Why is this your fault?" Holden looked at me quizzically.

"I need my backpack, then I can explain everything to you all at once." I sank onto Mallory's bed, my body trembling.

"I'll get it," Brynn offered and squeezed my shoulder.

"Thanks." I hated being helpless. It fucking sucked. If I hadn't been a dumbass and ran out in front of a car, I would have been able to catch a bus and head back to Coeur d'Alene and the homeless shelter.

"I wonder what's happening." Jace shoved his hands into his jean pockets, and fear etched into his expression.

"Nothing as of thirty seconds ago," Brynn said, entering the room again with my bag.

"Thanks." I unzipped it and dumped the items on my bed.

"What are you looking for?" Holden asked while he narrowed the gap between us and eyed my belongings.

"They had to have tracked me. Nothing else makes sense." I squeezed my eyes shut as I mentally reviewed everything Shirley and Ed had given to me. "Dammit." I grabbed the cell phone. I powered it on and waited until I saw Shirley's number. "Do you have a pen and paper?"

Holden opened a drawer in the nightstand and produced what I'd asked for. I jotted Shirley's contact information down, then went to work. "How do I get this damned thing open?" I searched for a way to pop open the back, but I was too rattled.

"Let me." Holden held his hand out while Brynn and Jace watched quietly.

Holden popped the back off, and a small circular device fell to the floor. He collected it, then held it up to the light. "Son of a bitch. It's a tracker." He lowered his arm slowly, his icy gaze landing on me. "What the fuck? Did you know someone was looking for you?"

Jace gently squeezed Holden's shoulder, attempting to calm him.

"Yes, but I had no idea about the tracker. I swear," I whispered. "I'll leave." I stood and moved to the door, but Brynn blocked my path.

"No, River. You won't. Holden needs to know the truth, and so do we. You need to tell us who you really are and what the hell is going on."

Chapter Twelve

I'd spent all of my nineteen years walking on eggshells in an attempt to stay alive. Dan had beaten me within an inch of my life more times than I could count, but this ... The tease of a different life and actual friends was at my fingertips, but still just out of my reach. I should have known my past would catch up with me. Even I had to admit I didn't belong here, in this house, or with these people who had been kind to me.

Three pairs of eyes stared in my direction, burning a hole right through me. The pain seared my soul, leaving me breathless as I scrambled to explain to them.

"A little over forty-eight hours ago, my guardian of sixteen years raped me ... and not for the first time." The tension in the air was heavy, but I owed them the truth before I left.

"Dan," Holden whispered, putting all of the bits and pieces of information together while Brynn's hand flew to her mouth.

"The bruises on your face were from him?" Jace asked.

I nodded.

"Where was your mom?" Brynn frowned.

"She disappeared when I was three." My chest ached as the few memories that I had of my mom consumed me, twisting my emotions, then blowing them apart.

"He was an alcoholic and addict, and he beat me on a regular basis." I glanced up at the ceiling for a moment, collecting more courage. "After he'd passed out on the couch, I packed what I could fit into my backpack. I was literally at the front door when he woke up and caught me. I hightailed it out of the trailer we lived in and ran, but he kept up pretty well. I hurried down a hill and to my favorite oak tree, then climbed it to hide."

My blood thundered through my head as I continued. "Billy, the man who has a gun to Becky's temple, is Logan's right-hand guy." I attempted to regulate my racing heartbeat. "Logan has a Doberman named Killer—"

"Who's Logan?" Brynn asked.

I studied the floor, mentally reliving the story as I explained it. "Logan lives in our trailer park. He's a meth dealer and is mixed up in dealing weapons, from the rumors I've heard." I paused to see if there were any additional questions, but they seemed as though they were waiting on me.

"I guess Killer heard all of the commotion because it wasn't long before he found Dan, who was standing under the tree that I was hiding in. Killer attacked him and ripped his throat out." Images of Dan's bloodied body slammed into my mind and my stomach flip-flopped. "There's no way he survived."

I glanced around at Holden, Brynn, and Jace, who were now pale and wide-eyed.

"After Killer started back up the hill, I headed toward the trailer. Once I reached my road again, I overheard Logan, Billy, and a few of their friends. They were looking for Dan. Apparently, he owed them a lot of money. One of the men said that if Dan had left town, they would take me as their payment." My pulse kicked into overdrive and my head buzzed. I stood and wished I could pace while I talked. It always cleared my brain when I was overwhelmed. "They began to talk about sharing me. That's when I realized that even though Dan was dead, I still wasn't safe. Not to mention I no longer had a home to return to."

Over the next few minutes, I shared with them how Shirley and Ed had helped me leave. "But the phone had a tracker in it. Shirley had to have put it there." Tears welled in my eyes. "I guess that's what I get for trusting them."

A pained expression twisted Holden's features.

With the mention of Shirley's name, the mixture of pain pills, adrenaline, and anger threatened to crash my system. Black spots danced before my eyes, and I clung to the side of the nightstand.

"River! I've got you." Strong arms lifted me and placed me on the bed.

I gasped for air and clawed at the comforter, then an uncontrollable sob erupted from me. "They betrayed me."

No longer able to hear what everyone was saying, the fear, anger, and heartache from the past several days surrounded me like a toxic fog, killing me slowly in the process. Curling up the best I could, I succumbed to the unfeeling blackness that called my name and slipped into a peaceful oblivion.

* * *

My head throbbed as I attempted to peel open my swollen eyes. The bright rays of sunshine instantly made me regret my decision. I struggled to move my arm, but my body was pinned to the bed. *Shit. Why can't I move?* Had Holden decided to turn me over to the authorities, or worse, the men that were looking for me? My pulse raced, my breathing rapid as I teetered on the edge of a full-on panic attack.

"River?" a seductive scratchy voice asked gently. "It's Holden. You're safe." He moved his arm, freeing me. "Sorry, I fell asleep, and I must have ..." He sat up and cleared his throat. "Uh, tossed my arm over you." He offered me a sheepish grin.

I pulled myself up into a sitting position as I tried to remember what had happened last night.

"How are you feeling?" Holden stood and stretched, his shirt hiking up and revealing a peek of his rippled abs.

"I don't know. What happened?" I smoothed the stray hairs from my face and tucked my long dark hair behind my ear.

"I think the events from the last few days, along with your pain meds, affected you. You had a mini meltdown."

My cheeks flamed red. "Oh, God. I'm sorry."

"Honestly, I'm not sure how you held on for so long." He walked around the bed, then sat next to me, the mattress dipping beneath his weight.

"Becky?" I grabbed his arm, my eyes widening. "Is she okay?" My hand trembled as I asked. I didn't like her, but she sure as hell didn't deserve to get caught up in my shit.

Holden gave me a gentle smile. "She is. Billy was arrested, too. For now, I think you're safe."

I flinched at his words. "I wish, but one of his men will eventually come looking for me. These assholes have a hierarchy. I can't stay, Holden. I've put you all in danger already." I tugged at the cover he was sitting on, but he refused to move.

"Now that I know who you're hiding from, I can protect you. You don't have to run anymore." Holden reached toward me and hesitated. "Don't be afraid of me," he whispered, a pleading look on his face. "Let me help." His dark brown eyes searched mine. "You're special. Different." His voice was deep and husky. It did strange things to my insides and turned them upside down.

I sucked in a breath as his fingers trailed down my cheek, and currents of electricity surged through me. What in God's name was happening?

"What about your parents? School? I can't stay here." I was rooted in a haze of uncertainty. My life was teetering on the edge of the unknown, and I hated it.

Deep concern was embedded in his features, and Holden took my hand in his. "My parents won't care. They won't be home for another month, then they'll be out the door again. As far as school, I have classes online and a few in person. Once classes start back up after winter break, I'll have football training, but our games are finished for the season. Seriously, if you don't stay, the house will just be empty."

Determination settled into my bones. "If I agree, then what can I do to pay my way?"

A gorgeous grin split Holden's face. "You'll stay, then?"

"I didn't say that." Although my words were firm, I couldn't hide my smile. "I'm used to working and paying my own way."

"How old were you when you started taking care of the bills for you and Dan?"

His question caught me off guard, and I frowned. "I didn't say that I did."

"You didn't have to. Dan was an addict and alcoholic, which meant his money went to his addiction."

I sunk my teeth into my lower lip, unhappy that I was so transparent. "I started working under the table when I was ten."

Anger flashed across Holden's expression, and he ran his fingers along his stubbled chin. "Sounds like you're way overdue for a sabbatical."

"What?"

"Take the time to heal, River. I have more than enough money to feed, clothe, and entertain you."

"Nope. That won't work. You'll grow to resent me if I'm a bump on your furniture. Besides, I need a project to focus on or something to study. I'll go nuts staring at the walls all day."

A mischievous spark flickered to life in his eyes. "Are you in college? I remember you mentioning you were accepted to one in Oregon, but were you at a community college in Montana? Do you even like school?"

"I was accepted to PSU in Oregon on a full scholarship. I was working and trying to lay low until I left in the fall. We both know how that turned out."

"What do you think about taking a few online classes while you heal?" He arched his eyebrow at me.

"I would love to, but I can't pay for them. I'll wait until the fall." Holden had no idea how much I wanted to attend, but it wasn't in the cards at the moment.

"What if I pay for it?" Holden's eyes flared with sincerity.

I pressed my lips into a thin line, wondering why Holden was so insistent on spending money on me. Did he think he could buy me, then I would be his slave? No thanks.

"River, I have a black American Express card. I could pay for the next four years of your college, and still have plenty of funds available."

My mouth dropped open. Becky wasn't kidding about Holden being rich. More than rich. Finally, I managed to form a question. "Won't your parents be pissed if you charge that much on your card?"

Holden gave a half shrug. "They don't pay the bill. I do."

I massaged my forehead and made the sound of my head exploding. "You? You're rich, not just your parents? I mean, because there's a difference."

"There is. And yes, I am independently wealthy, as well as my mom and dad."

"What do they do? What do *you* do?" I asked, suddenly wanting every detail about this guy sitting in front of me who was willing to take me in and help me heal not only my leg, but my mind and heart.

Holden took my hand in his, sadness and unease flashing in his chocolate brown eyes. "I'll tell you another time. I don't want you to think that you're a burden in any way. It would make me very happy if you stayed. We'll come up with some things to keep you occupied while I'm in classes."

"Do you know what they say about the nice ones?" I raised my eyebrow at him.

Holden shook his head.

"That they will win you over with their kindness, then they'll break your spirit."

Holden stared at me, disbelief clouding his expression. "I can't speak for anyone else, but I would never do that to you. Never."

"Maybe, but sometimes it happens unintentionally."

It was clear that I wouldn't receive any more answers from him at the moment, but I would eventually find out why he had taken such an interest the first time he laid eyes on me. Little did I know that when I learned his secrets, I would have regrets for the rest of my life.

Chapter Thirteen

Holden had continued to randomly ask my thoughts about college. He had a subtle way of convincing someone he was right. After a week of negotiations, I agreed to take a few online classes, but only under the condition that it was a loan, and as soon as I found a job, I would pay him back in monthly install- ments. I even insisted on a contract. Once we both signed it, Holden handed me a brand-new laptop and iPhone for school and to be able to reach him if I needed anything. He hadn't voiced his concerns, but we were both worried that Logan's men would show up again. At least I could call or text Holden if I had to.

I glared at him. "This will be added to what I owe you. I don't do charity."

"Charity is for people who don't have much. You have a lot." He waved his hand, indicating his house was also mine.

A waterfall of emotions washed over me—gratitude, excitement, guilt. I was secretly giddy to have a computer and phone. I'd only used the ones at the library, and I'd missed having communication with Addison and Mrs. Donaldson.

I didn't waste any more time as I typed out an email to Addison and included my new cell number. I wouldn't divulge details over the internet, but I let her know that I wasn't in Montana anymore. I realized she would have questions, but if her parents had heard that Dan was dead, she'd be freaking out by now. Unfortunately, that was out of my control.

As I flipped through the contacts, I realized Holden had already programmed his, Jace's, and Brynn's contact information in as well.

I also needed to call Shirley and confront her about the tracker, but every time I thought about it, my stomach lurched, and my body shook uncontrollably. If she and Ed had helped Logan and his men track me, it seemed like the best way to handle the situation was to stay off the radar. My instincts agreed with me, so for now, I wasn't going to reach out. However, I gave myself permission to change my mind if I needed to.

I spent the next few hours searching through the college catalog, overjoyed and overwhelmed with the choices. I hadn't decided on a major yet because deep down inside, I never thought I would really make it to school.

"What's up?" Brynn asked, strolling through the basement sliding glass door. Even though the house was over ten thousand square feet, we practically lived down here. What I appreciated most was the heat. I'd finally begun to warm up after years of freezing my ass off in the trailer.

"Hey," I said, smiling at her. She looked gorgeous in a soft pink sweater that hugged her curves. Her dark wash jeans were tucked into mid-calf black boots. Her makeup was flawless, and her green eyes twinkled as she sat down next to me.

"Are you bored?" she asked.

"I'm going to college!" I squealed. "And before you say anything, I signed a contract that I would pay Holden back for the classes and computer."

Brynn laughed. "He won't miss the money, River. He would,

however, miss you horribly if you left. I think it's his way of keeping you close. He's like that. He wants to take care of the people that are really important to him." She winked at me. "Well, I brought over one of my favorite movies of all time. I say we pop open a bottle of wine ... Oh, wait. Are you finished with your pain pills? You can't mix those."

"I'm all done, but better yet, I don't hurt much. Advil seems to do the trick."

"Excellent. What do you like? Wine? Beer?" Brynn's face scrunched up. "Beer is nasty, but if you like it ..." She lifted her hands in front of her, palms facing me in a sign that she wasn't judging me if my tastes were different than hers. I suspected everything about us was different.

I wrinkled my nose. "I don't like beer. I've only had a few wine coolers. Since Dan was an alcoholic, I stayed away from it."

"Shit. That's right. I'm sorry," Brynn said.

"No, I'm fine. I would love to try something new." I beamed at her. As much as I tried to fight it, I really liked Brynn.

Brynn stood and tapped her finger against her lower lip. "Let's start off with ... What's your preference? Sweet or salty?"

"Sweet. Just not overly sweet," I explained.

"Two White Russians coming right up!" Jace yelled as he waltzed into Holden's house, the freezing air rushing into the room with him.

I shivered, then waved at him. Jace was as gorgeous as Holden and Chance, but he was the clown out of the group, which I loved.

"Where's Holden?" he asked, searching for him.

"Upstairs. He should be down soon," I replied.

"Awesome. I'll make the drinks. I think we're going to play video games while you girls watch a chick flick." He wiggled his brows at us, then headed to the kitchen.

"What movie?" I asked, excited to have a girl's night.

"Two actually." Brynn held the DVDs up and grinned. "*Magic Mike* and *Magic Mike XXL*. Have you seen them?" She gave them to me.

I flipped the case over and read the back, a furious flush traveling up my neck. "Strippers?" My voice cracked, and Jace howled with laughter.

"Oh man, are you a virg—" Jace froze, then swallowed visibly. "Um, sorry." He turned away from us, busying himself.

I realized Jace didn't mean anything by it, and he stopped as soon as his brain connected with his mouth, but I think I was just as mortified as he was. I'd shared about the rape, which meant I wasn't a virgin, but I wasn't used to casual conversation about sex either.

Brynn sat down on the edge of the coffee table. "River, have you been with anyone willingly?" Tears welled in her eyes. "Every girl deserves to be loved and worshipped. I hope—"

I held up my hand, halting her before she said anything else. "Twice willingly when I was sixteen. But no, I haven't had the experience you're referring to."

"It's amazing when you're with someone you love, or if you're having fun. There are times that the no-strings-attached romps are just as important." Brynn twirled a strand of her red hair around her finger.

I returned the movies to her. "They look fun." I chewed on my bottom lip and peeked over my shoulder at Jace. "The guys won't be in here with us though, right?" I whispered.

"Nope, we're banning them from being down here with us. They'll play games in the game room upstairs."

"Okay," I said, trying to suppress the giggle that was bubbling up.

Holden's sweet and spicy scent tickled my nose before he even reached downstairs. He descended the steps, and I glanced over my shoulder. He was freshly showered, his hair still slightly damp. His navy long-sleeved T-shirt clung to his broad chest, and my fingertips itched to touch him. After a sneak peek of his abs, I was curious to see him without a shirt. I had a feeling I wouldn't be disappointed. His jeans hung low on his hips, hugging his butt and thighs perfectly.

Holden Alastair was pure, mouthwatering perfection.

"Are you ready for me to kick your ass?" Holden asked Jace. He walked over to me, chuckling. "Our boy Jace whines like a little bitch when he loses." Holden winked at me, then strolled around the couch and hugged Brynn.

"We'll see who's crying like a little girl in a while. Until then, I made cocktails for everyone." Jace approached us with four glasses on a tray.

"Madam," he bowed to me, his grin infectious.

"Why thank you, good sir." I hesitated, unsure of which one was for me.

"The white one," Brynn said.

"Got it." I selected mine and eyed the others. "What are those?" I pointed to the light tan-colored drinks.

"Long Islands," Holden said, taking his. "Thanks, man."

"Thank you, dude. It's *your* liquor." Jace clicked his tongue and winked at Holden.

I laughed, then took a sip. "Oh, this is tasty."

"Brynn would agree with you, River. A word of advice, though, take it slow. Those can sneak up on you. Right, Brynn?" Holden snickered.

"Hey, just because I can drink you all under the table doesn't mean you can tease me about how many times I puked the next day." Brynn crossed her arms over her chest and shot the guys a playful glare.

"Damn, I bet that tastes awful coming back up." I curled my upper lip in disgust before I took another sip.

After the laughter died down, Jace and Holden told us goodbye, then hurried up the stairs while talking shit to each other. I didn't miss Brynn's attention following them, or the longing evident in her wistful expression. I wasn't sure who she was secretly in love with, though. Holden or Jace? A stab of jealousy pricked my chest, and I mentally scolded myself. This wasn't my world, no matter how much Holden wanted me to think it was. I still planned on moving on when I was healed, which meant emotional attachments were firmly off the table.

"Let's get the entertainment started." Brynn loaded the DVD player, then settled in next to me and dimmed the lights. The huge television flickered to life, then the music blared through the speakers. Since I had to wear shorts most of the time due to my leg, I was constantly snuggled under a blanket.

"Where's Chance?" I asked.

Brynn's fingers tightened around her glass. "He's at work."

My eyebrows knitted together. "He works? I thought you all were like ... super rich."

Brynn smiled. "We are. He likes to work for his own money separate from his parents."

"Gotcha, just like Holden." I paused momentarily, waiting to see if Brynn was going to tell me what the guys did for work, but she didn't. As much as I wanted to ask, Holden had said he'd tell me later, and I wanted to respect his wishes. I understood not wanting your secrets exposed.

"You're going to love the eye candy," Brynn said, changing the topic. We grew silent, our attention glued to the drool-worthy men on the screen.

* * *

Voices roused me from a deep sleep. "Shit, I fell asleep during the last movie." I wiped my mouth with the back of my hand as Holden chuckled.

"You know how they say that when people are asleep, they look angelic?" I quirked an eyebrow at him, not sure where this conversation was heading.

"Yeah?" I glanced at Brynn, who was still sitting at the other end of the couch, but now Jace was with her, too. *Great. I had a fucking audience while I was drooling.*

A playful grin pulled at the corner of his mouth. "You looked like one too, but I think your halo is held up by horns."

91

I laughed at him. "If that's all you've got, it was completely lame." I shook my head, smiling.

"I don't know you well enough to insult you and get away with it. I mean ... I insulted you on accident that one time." Holden stopped short, his eyes cutting over to Brynn and Jace.

"I'm not going to ask what came out of your mouth, but River, did you at least hit him really hard when he was being an ass?" Jace asked.

Holden rubbed his chest, then answered for me. "She's got a hell of a punch."

"Yes!" Jace hurried over with his hand in the air, ready to high-five me.

I slapped his palm and smiled. It was obvious that Brynn and Jace were good for Holden.

"What time is it?" I asked.

"Midnight," Brynn replied. "I need to head out. I'll see you tomorrow." She stood and stretched, yawning.

"Yup, me too." Jace draped his arm around Brynn's shoulder. "I'll walk you to your car."

She beamed up at him. "Thanks."

We all said goodbye, then Holden locked the sliding glass door behind them.

"I'm still learning your facial expressions, but I think I see some wheels turning." He approached and sat on the edge of the coffee table.

"How does the phone work that you gave me? I mean, how many minutes do I have available?"

"It's unlimited, River. You can call ten people a day and talk for hours. It still won't run out."

"Really?" A sudden excitement blossomed inside me, and I sat up straighter. I could call Addison.

"Really. You also have unlimited texting and data." He propped his elbows on his knees and grinned. "You can use the internet as much as you want as long as you have a cell signal."

My brain started calculating dollars like an obsessed accountant. I would be in debt to him for years.

"From the look on your face, I'm guessing you're trying to figure out how to pay me back. The phone and laptop are a gift, River. You don't need to pay me back. If those assholes come after you, I need to know you can call 911, then me. So, in a way it's a selfish present. I need to be able to text and talk to you when I'm at school instead of stressing that something bad might have happened to you again. Brynn, Chance, and Jace aren't any closer in an emergency, either. They're on campus with me. I did program their numbers in your cell, though. Just in case you can't reach me. Plus, you and Brynn are becoming friends."

I leaned forward as much as I possibly could with my broken leg. "I want to know why, Holden. Why me? Why are you helping and not asking anything in return?"

Holden swallowed, his Adam's apple bobbing up and down. "I ..." He massaged the back of his neck, fear and anxiety flickering to life in his features.

"Holden, you don't need to explain it to me right this minute, but I want to know. I'm spinning inside and trying my damnedest to understand and not second guess your every move, but until you tell me what's driving you, I can't."

Pain slashed across his face, and a muscle clenched in his jaw as he visibly struggled to hold it together. Seconds felt like hours as I watched him attempt to rein in his feelings.

I took his hand in mine, my heart already breaking for him. "What's happening right now? I don't understand, Holden." His eyes misted over, and tears welled in mine.

"Promise me you won't leave." His voice barely hovered above a whisper.

The hair on the back of my neck bristled. *How bad was it?* "I can't promise you that. I have no idea what you're about to say."

Holden sank to his knees, his head hanging down. I mentally prepared myself for the worst and tried to figure out how to leave with only one good leg. I wouldn't take the laptop with me, but I needed the phone. Maybe he wouldn't turn it off right away.

"Her name was Hannah," he started.

Chapter Fourteen

The word *was* echoed in my mind.

"She was my older sister by three years. The color of your hair and eyes are very similar to hers."

My pulse stuttered against my wrist. "I look like her?"

"No, just those two features. I swear." His face clouded with emotions I didn't understand. "When I was fifteen ..." He wiped the moisture away from his eyes and inhaled deeply. "I won't go into all of the details, but she'd gotten into trouble—drugs, alcohol, and she was involved with some bad people. I was able to talk her into going to rehab, but as soon as she got out, she went right back to partying. My parents kicked her out the day she turned eighteen. They washed their hands of her."

"I can't imagine how hard that was on everyone," I said softly.

"It was difficult for them, but not for the reasons most people would think. My parents have a certain standard and reputation they work hard to manage. Hannah didn't fit that image."

I pursed my lips together, the voice inside my head whispering that I sure as hell didn't fit into their perfect world, either.

"When Brynn said I was the black sheep it was because I was the only one in the family that refused to give up on Hannah and it caused problems. I would buy her clothes and pay her rent, but it didn't seem to make any difference ..." He trailed off, his features darkening.

"Over the next two years, Hannah couch-hopped, but she was so deep into the drugs, she stole from her friends to support her habit. Anything that she could find of value, she took."

Holden's gaze connected with mine and my pulse pounded in my head. The pain in his expression gutted me, and I wanted to reach inside of him, hold his heart in my palm, and breathe hope and life into it again. This wasn't the same Holden that had made me break-fast a week and a half ago. This Holden was broken and dark. I understood this man more than he would ever realize.

"Eventually, she burned bridges with everyone who loved her. She ended up on the streets and was homeless for about a year." A storm brewed in his eyes, and he studied the floor for a moment.

Realizing I still had his hand in mine, I rubbed my thumb over his fingers in an attempt to help him get through the hell he was reliving.

"I searched for her for weeks, but she moved around a lot. The last time I'd spoken to her, she'd tried to convince me she was in danger, and someone was following her, but she couldn't give me any details, so I assumed it was the drugs talking ... until."

I wasn't sure I could hear anymore. The grief in his expression was ripping my soul in two. "Holden, you don't need to say anything else. I have enough information to put the pieces together."

His demeanor softened. "I need to tell you. It's important that you feel safe and can trust me."

"Okay." The heat from his skin soothed my anxiety as I waited for him to continue.

"One afternoon Hannah called me. She was crying so hard I couldn't understand what she was trying to tell me. Again, she mentioned that she was in danger and asked if I could meet her. Of course I agreed. She was my sister, and I would do anything for her.

"I was supposed to meet her under the Maple Street Bridge, but I couldn't find her. I'd almost given up, thinking the drugs were messing with her head, when I spotted someone laying on their back. I hurried over to see if the person needed help ... She did." Holden rubbed his face with his hand, his eyes glistening with moisture. "She'd been beaten, and I was pretty sure raped as well. Her clothes were filthy and torn, her shirt was open, and the buttons had landed on the ground next to her. I covered her with my coat while I removed my phone from my back pocket and called 911. It was then that I noticed the needle sticking out of her arm." Pain slashed across his expression, and a muscle clenched in his jaw as he visibly struggled to hold it together. Holden stood quickly and paced the room with his back to me. "She died in my arms," Holden whispered, his shoulders shaking.

"Holden." I hurried to him. When I stood in front of him, I dropped one of my crutches and slipped my arm around his waist, hugging him hard. "I'm so sorry. And I hate when someone says that shit to me, but it's true."

Holden wrapped me in his warm embrace as he sniffled. He rested his chin on the top of my head. "I thought I'd worked through it, but I think I just shoved all the pain down. After that I was numb. Over the last few years, I pretended. Pretended that I was happy, pretended that my heart hadn't shattered, pretended to give a fuck about my life." He lifted his chin, and I gazed up at him.

"I know all about pretending." I bit my lower lip, and Holden's gaze briefly landed on my mouth.

"The day I found you in the recycling bin ... it was the first time I've felt something real in a long time."

I leaned into him, feeling the warmth of his body against mine. He was safe and comforting.

In slow motion, my brain pieced everything together. Hannah and I had similar hair and eyes. We were both homeless. Holden tried to save her and failed. Intense pressure settled on my chest as the truth fell into place. *Son of a fucking bitch.*

The similarities doused me like a large bucket of ice-cold water, intertwining with my past and ripping through me at Mach speed. I clenched my jaw and pain shot through me. This couldn't be happening. "I remind you of Hannah, and I'm your key to redemption, aren't I?" I jerked my arms away from him, nearly knocking myself off balance. "All I am to you is salvation. You don't give a crap about me as a person. You're using me to feel better about yourself. I'm just a pawn in your rich life. You'll use and discard me as soon as you're done." He watched me as I processed the stages of my emotions. The anger, the desperate need to react, and the way I was barely keeping my shit together. I was more than a charity case. I was his second chance at life, but he hadn't bothered to clue me in. This wasn't what I'd signed up for, and I could make it without him.

"River, please." Holden bent down and handed me the crutch from the floor. "I swear it's not like that."

"Really?" I steadied myself, then hobbled away from him. "Did you pay for your sister's college too?"

He met my question with deafening silence, and I headed to the stairs. "I'm out of here. I'll pack and be on my way. I'm not Hannah. I'm River Collins, in case you forgot that we're two different people."

"River, stop."

His stern tone halted my next step. My breathing became shallow as his footfalls grew closer. He stood in front of me, a determined expression on his face. "You're quick to run, and I understand that, but you need to hear me out."

I jutted my chin up. I didn't have to do shit. "Move."

"No." He held firm, refusing to let me through.

My nostrils flared. "So now you're resorting to holding me hostage?"

The muscle in his jaw twitched. I'd hit a nerve, but I wasn't sure why my question had affected him.

"You're free to go *after* you listen to what I have to say." His chest heaved, and a crackle of electricity connected the small space between us.

"Fine. Go ahead and I'll *pretend* I give a fuck. I mean, after all, we're really good at pretending aren't we?" I gripped my crutches so hard my knuckles turned white.

His gaze narrowed briefly. I was definitely dancing on his last nerve. Good. At least he was feeling something now.

"You're infuriating. Why don't you try to let someone in for a change? You're just giving the entire world a big fuck you because you've had a shit life. A lot of people have shit lives, so stop hiding behind it." He rubbed his forehead. "This conversation wasn't supposed to go down like this. Eventually I would have told you about Hannah, but I didn't want to scare you." His shoulders sagged, and he stared at the ceiling briefly before looking at me again. "I don't know what the hell you're doing to me, but in the last week and a half —" He shook his head. "Never mind." He pursed his lips. "River, this isn't just my chance to live again, it's yours too. Hopefully you're not too prideful to take the opportunity that's landed in your lap."

I gasped. *Who the hell does he think he is?*

"If you're bound and determined to leave, I'll drive you to the bus station and pay for a ticket anywhere you want to go." With that, he walked away from me, leaving me in a swell of unwanted feelings that I had no fucking clue how to handle. I'd used my anger as a shield my entire life, and he was asking me to put it down and let him in. Tears spilled down my cheeks. I didn't want to be his redemption project. I wanted to be someone he genuinely cared about, without an agenda. But maybe that wasn't possible. Maybe he was as broken as I was. We just hid behind different walls, making sure we weren't vulnerable to the outside world.

I crutched over to the couch and sank onto the edge of it. The harsh truth seeped into the cracks of my heart that I'd been stupid enough to allow Holden into. Exhaustion tugged at me, and I picked up my phone from the coffee table. It was almost two in the morning. It was a perfect time to slip out of the house and be on my way, but was it what I really wanted?

Chapter Fifteen

The bright sunshine streamed through the partly closed window shade of the downstairs living room. I groaned as a sharp pain stabbed my neck. After debating with myself for a few hours on whether to stay or leave, I'd finally fallen asleep.

I sat up, stretched, and attempted to clear my muddled head.

"Hey," Holden said, descending the stairs. His hair was still damp, and he was dressed in a black, long-sleeved polo shirt and jeans. My nose twitched as the clean citrus scent of his cologne reached me.

"Hey," I said, embarrassed that I'd overreacted last night.

"I'm sorry," we said in unison.

"I shouldn't have behaved the way I did. I can't imagine how hard that was for you with Hannah." I self-consciously tucked a strand of hair behind my ear.

Holden approached the couch and sat on the opposite end. "I don't talk about it to anyone. It was all brushed under the rug. The cops never looked into the case to see if she was murdered." Holden leaned forward and propped his elbows on his knees. "I know it was a lot of information, but Hannah has nothing to do with how I feel about you."

My brows shot up to my hairline. "What?" I squeaked.

"I can't seem to keep my mouth shut around you." He sank back into the couch. "I laid in bed all night trying to figure out how to explain that not only are you making me feel again ... I'm feeling things for you, too."

My cheeks flamed red. "I think you're just confused. It's a difficult line to balance. I have similarities to your sister that are triggering a lot of memories and pain. But Holden, I really think the feelings you have for me are deeply intertwined with losing your sister. Give it some time and you'll be able to separate them."

He glanced down at the floor, then back to me. "Are you leaving?" His voice caught in his throat, sadness dancing across his gorgeous features.

With tears in my eyes, I exhaled, ridding my body of the anger and frustration from last night. "I don't want to, but you have to promise to be up front with me. No more secrets."

Holden grinned at me. "Deal." He stood, serious again. "I'll send Brynn over after her classes today. She'll take you shopping and out for a spa day. Expect her around eleven."

I narrowed my eyes at him, not following why a spa day was necessary.

"You said no more secrets, right?" he asked.

I nodded slowly, still skeptical.

"You asked me where my money came from. Tonight, I'll show you. It requires a gorgeous dress, heels ... in your case one high heel, your hair and makeup done. You'll have a day of being pampered, which you deserve. I want you to feel good." His eyes sparkled with mischievousness. "After tonight, I'll ask you again if you want to stay. My business has the potential to—" He rubbed his jawline with his hand. "—to set you on edge. I don't want that to happen. If you want to be here, then you need to know exactly who I am."

Chills shot down my spine as Becky's words bounced around in my head. *Holden's family isn't who they say they are.* "Oh, shit. We didn't already get through the part that would send me out the door?"

"No." Holden walked over to me. "I have classes, but I'll see you tonight." He leaned over and pressed a gentle kiss to my forehead.

I propped myself up, allowing myself a better view. My heart was in my throat, and my eyes were glued to him as he walked toward the slider. His jeans hugged the curve of his ass and his thick thighs. As he reached for the door, the muscles in his back flexed through his T-shirt. A tingling sensation spread through me and into my neck, releasing warmth throughout my entire body. I'd had a little preview of his abs that one time, but I suddenly wanted more. I wasn't okay with that. My goal had been to not grow attached to him or his friends, but apparently my attempt had turned into an epic failure.

I kerplunked back onto the couch and rubbed my temples. I'd had crushes before, but after the years of Dan hurting me, it was a part of myself that I'd shut off. I didn't want anyone to notice my body or how big my breasts were. All I wanted was to stay safe. An idea nudged me. "No," I said aloud to an empty house. "I'm not crushing on Holden." Dammit. This wasn't happening. He would just break my heart. We were from two opposite worlds, and we both knew I would never blend into his.

In an attempt to stop my mind from spinning out, I turned on the TV and selected HBO Max. After scrolling for a bit, I chose *Gossip Girl*. I'd never had cable, and the antenna on our TV at the trailer wasn't worth shit, so I never saw the show. Until Brynn arrived, I was limited on my choices of things to do other than keep my leg up.

Two hours later, Brynn opened and strolled through the door.

"Ooh, *Gossip Girl*. It's still one of my favorite shows."

"Oh wow. I got sucked in, and fast. I had no idea what time it was." I propped up into a sitting position and smiled at her. For the first time since I'd met her, Brynn's face was free of makeup, and I inwardly groaned. She was gorgeous without it too. Instead of jeans and a sweater, she'd opted for sweats and a matching sweatshirt.

"Are you ready to be spoiled and pampered?" she asked as she strolled into the kitchen for a glass of water.

"Well, I'm struggling a little. I don't understand why it's necessary. Holden didn't tell me where we were going tonight, just that I needed to ..." I frowned, unable to articulate my feelings well. "I know he has money, Brynn, but I'm having a hell of a time dealing with him paying for a spa day. All he's done is take care of me." My throat grew tight, and my words trailed off. "I know about his sister, and we had words last night. Big ones."

Her head snapped my way, eyes open wide and filled with curiosity. Brynn flew out of the kitchen and sat on the edge of the coffee table before I even had time to take a breath.

"Oh fuck. What did he tell you?" She clasped her hands together and placed them in her lap.

Brynn was smart as hell, and it was one reason that I liked her so much. She knew not to dive in and talk to me about Holden's sister. She was testing the waters to see exactly what he'd said to me. It also told me she was loyal to her friends and their trust in her was important. I hoped I would earn the same loyalty from her someday. Just because I had to leave when my leg was better didn't mean I couldn't find a studio apartment nearby and still see her.

"He told me about the drugs and her living on the street. Holden also mentioned that she was afraid someone was following her, but he couldn't find any proof. After she died in his arms ..." I massaged my forehead, grief for him clogging my throat. "He said he went to the cops, but they didn't take his concern seriously."

"It was awful. He was so broken, River." She placed her palm over her heart. "Even though he acts like everything is fine, we know he isn't okay. That was until you busted into his life a few weeks ago." She grinned. "Sorry for the pun." She gently tapped my cast.

"Really?" Holden had said the same thing to me, but for some reason, it made a difference coming out of Brynn's mouth.

"Really. It's like you turned the light on inside him again." She crossed her legs at the ankles.

Heat traveled up my neck and cheeks. "It's because my circumstances are so similar to Hannah's, which I have a hard time with. I think it's a chance for redemption, and when he feels better, he won't have a need for me anymore." Tears clouded my vision and I quickly looked down at my lap, hiding them from Brynn.

"I'm going to be blatantly honest with you. Yes, Holden sees a chance to do for you what he couldn't do for Hannah. However, he's very clear on the fact that you and Hannah are two different people. First of all, Hannah didn't have your fight. She wasn't feisty. Hannah kept everything bottled up inside until she wasn't able to control her feelings anymore. They controlled her. I guess the best way to describe her personality was mousy. And you, River, are anything but. Holden loves that about you. We all do."

Unable to hide my surprise, I grinned at her like an idiot. "I like you guys too," I admitted.

"Good, because even after your leg is all better, you're stuck with us." Brynn stood and placed her hand on my knee. "Our group is very loyal to each other. Jace, Chance, Holden, and I have practically grown up together. We're incredibly picky who we let into our circle, and you're in it. We have so much respect for you, and I adore you. With those feelings comes some spoiling. We all have more money than sense, and it makes us feel good to take care of each other." She held her palm out to me. "So, let's go, babe. We have manicures, massages and facials scheduled in two hours, which gives us enough time to shop for a dress and heels for you. I'll let you borrow some of my diamond earrings and a necklace."

My mouth hung open. "Real diamonds?" My breath stuttered in my throat. She was trusting me with something valuable, which said a lot about how she saw me, which was as a worthy friend.

"Yep. Even if you leave us, we're still going to be your family. You're one of us now. Get used to it, River."

My heart overflowed with more emotions than I could name. I'd always wanted a real family. A sister. I was so overwhelmed that they'd accepted me this fast that I missed the nagging feeling inside my gut.

Chapter Sixteen

Brynn held a dress up against me while I balanced on the crutches. "I think you'd look dick-hardening hot in this."

I choked on my spit. "Not sure I want that kind of reaction from anyone, Brynn."

She quirked an eyebrow at me. "Not even Holden?"

I glanced around the store. Brynn had seriously caught me off guard.

She put the dress back on the rack. "Listen, I know you've had some shitty experiences, but it doesn't have to stay that way. Holden isn't Dan."

"I didn't say he was," I said defensively. "Sorry. That came out wrong. It's just difficult to talk about."

"I get it. I really do." She paused, then beamed at me. "You and Holden are seriously cute with the little looks you give each other, though. Jace and I notice these things." Brynn grinned at me, then selected an emerald-green cocktail dress and a navy one. "Let's have you try these on."

Grateful for the change in conversation, I crutched along behind her, my wheels spinning about Holden. I still thought he had feelings for me because of his sister, and they would fade quickly. If I were honest with myself, I wasn't sure I wanted them to. I did want to be liked for me, though, and not because of my similarities to Hannah.

"All right, hot stuff. Let's see what you've got." Brynn grinned and stepped into the largest dressing room available.

I waited for her to come back out, but she didn't. "Umm, are you coming out here?"

Brynn poked her head out. "Nope. We'll be changing around each other a lot, so no embarrassment is allowed." She waved me in. "Besides, I don't want you to lose your balance and fall over trying to take your shirt off. Holden would ground me like a teenager if I let anything happen to you." She laughed and ushered me in with a wave of her hand. "Come on, babe. We don't have all day."

The dressing room was large enough for both of us, and I sat down on the little seat that was anchored to the wall. I slipped off my worn tennis shoe, then shimmied out of my shorts. "I'm glad it's warm in the store. Plus, I'm getting a helluva workout today." I flexed my muscle, my small bicep bump showing. I threw my head back and laughed.

After another few minutes, I stood in front of the mirror in the navy dress.

"Damn, girl. You've got to stop hiding behind baggy clothes. You're fucking hot as hell. I'd be happy to trade boobs with you." Brynn gently patted my butt like we were on a football team together.

My brows shot up to my hairline and I wondered if Brynn smacked all her female friends on the ass.

"You're having a sister experience." She giggled, then opened the door. "Let's get you in front of multiple mirrors so we can really see the dress. Sometimes it's harder in the little rooms. Not to mention the lighting sucks."

"It does, plus the space is tiny." Although I'd been able to see the front of the dress, I couldn't see the side or back. My stupid cast was also distracting me. I entered the hall and walked to the mirrors. I gasped. The lights were a lot better. "The dress is see-through!"

"It's supposed to be. We're going to buy you a sweet bra and panty set to wear beneath it. You'll be fully covered."

I struggled internally with the concept while my cheeks blazed with embarrassment.

"Or not. It's okay, River. I'm used to dressing like this, but there's no pressure. We can find you something you're more comfortable in." She walked toward me. "You'll be with Holden, Jace, and me all night. No one will ever hurt you again."

I hiccupped, unable to hide the fear that had blossomed inside my chest. "I don't want to be afraid anymore, Brynn. I want to be ... normal. Hell, I don't even know what sex with someone I'm in love with is like. I've never orgasmed or had the chance to experiment and learn what I might enjoy. Every time I think I would like to, that fucking son of a bitch's face is leering at me again."

Brynn wrapped me in a hug. "I'm sorry. I never meant to upset or trigger you." She pulled back and wiped away the tears that had escaped.

"I have no idea how to begin to heal." I sniffled and attempted to pull myself back together.

Brynn cocked her head and closed one eye. "What about simply getting familiar with your body and what feels good?"

Puzzled, I frowned. "I don't understand."

Brynn leaned into me, then whispered in my ear. "A vibrator."

My eyes popped open wide. "Never had the money for one, so I never considered it. I have no idea how to answer that question."

"It might be a safe way for you to be in total control and see what you like and don't."

I chewed on my bottom lip, pondering the idea. "You think it might work?"

"It's worth a try. If you don't like it, no harm done. But if you're open to it, we'll go by Adam & Eve and I'll help you pick something out."

My brows shot up to my hairline. Shopping at a sex store seemed like it should be done in private. "Girls do that together?"

"Girls do shit like that together all the time," she assured me.

I barked out a laugh. "I can't believe I'm saying this, but if we have enough time, I'm in."

"Awesome. I need to pick up a few things as well."

After another half an hour and four more dresses, I found the one I loved.

"It's perfect," Brynn gushed.

The dark green dress dipped low, revealing my back, but the front covered me fully. I'd never paid attention to the curves of my body before, but now I couldn't ignore them. It accentuated my breasts, hips, and ass perfectly. Since I would be with Holden, Jace, and Brynn all night, I felt safe enough to wear it. I wondered if Holden would like it, too.

"Hang on. I'll be right back." Brynn hightailed it out of the dressing room, and in a few minutes, she returned with a pair of black heels with a peek-a-boo toe and ankle strap. "I checked the size of your Converse." She beamed at me, then set the right shoe on the floor. "They're not so high you'll break your neck."

"Ugh, the last thing I want is to hurt myself again." I balanced on the crutches, then slipped my foot in it. Surprisingly, it was more comfortable than I'd anticipated.

"Well?"

"They feel pretty good. How do they look?"

Brynn blew me a kiss. "By the time we're done getting pampered, you're going to take Holden's breath away." Brynn laughed and hurried to the dressing room. "I'll take these back while you change clothes." She reached into her bra and produced a black Amex. "Holden gave it to me for today." She wiggled her brows at me.

"Shit!" I fumbled around for the price tag. "Jesus! Fifteen hundred dollars?" I slapped my palm against the wall for support, so I wouldn't fall over. "At this rate I'll be his indentured servant for the rest of my life."

Brynn's face fell and all of the excitement drained from her expression. "I can't express this enough, River. There are no strings attached. Ever. You could walk away tomorrow with the phone, laptop, and clothes, and the only thing Holden would miss is you."

I blinked rapidly, trying to comprehend what she'd just said.

Saving me from saying anything, Brynn piped up. "Our massage and facial appointments are next. We'll get a manicure and pedicure after that, then we're off to the salon."

"Good grief, I'll need a nap before we go out tonight!"

Brynn waved her first finger at me. "Can't. You would mess up your hair and makeup. You'll have to sleep sitting up on the couch."

We laughed, but I knew she was right. "What time will we see the guys? Holden made it sound like he wouldn't see me until tonight."

"We'll meet them at nine."

My pulse kicked up a notch at the thought of seeing Holden. If I had to dress nice, I wondered what he would be wearing. A tux? A suit? My heart hammered against my ribcage in anticipation.

* * *

We'd swung by Brynn's house, and she hurried in to grab her new dress she'd bought the other day, along with her heels and a duffle bag. From the street view, her home was almost as large and gorgeous as Holden's. I hadn't seen a brick home in Spokane until we pulled up to Brynn's. I loved the whitewashed effect instead of the more common red. Well-trimmed shrubs lined the walkway to the black double doors. The windows in the front allowed a peek inside the living room, where Victorian furniture filled the space. Brynn and Holden definitely ran in the same financial circles.

It was seven-thirty by the time we arrived back at Holden's. Brynn offered to take my new purchase from Adam & Eve to my bedroom and tuck it in the nightstand. I admitted that I'd be horrified if Holden found it.

Five minutes after we were at Holden's, the doorbell rang, and I froze. What if Logan was at the door? I'm sure he knew where I was and had just sent Billy to Holden's house instead.

"It's probably the pizza. Hang tight." Brynn's long legs took her up the stairs and to the front door.

Shortly after, she returned with two large pizza boxes, and the tension in my neck and shoulders eased.

"We have to eat up. We're going to burn some major calories tonight."

"Dancing?" I wasn't sure if she'd meant to let the hint slip or not. She'd been very tight-lipped about the upcoming evening.

"Eat." She flipped open the box and grabbed a huge slice of cheese pizza. "What do you want to drink?"

"Is there a Dr Pepper?" I asked around my first bite. I hadn't realized how hungry I was. Apparently, being pampered all day worked up an appetite.

"It's Holden's favorite, so he never runs out. It's like he has it on tap or something." She grinned, gathered a few cans, and gave me one.

We ate in silence, then we brushed our teeth and slipped into our evening dresses.

"I've never worn anything like this before." I stared at myself in the mirror, dumbfounded by the transformation. My long dark hair had been washed, conditioned, trimmed, and straightened. My makeup was a perfect blend of smoky eyeshadow, eyeliner, and a dab of mascara on my dark lashes. The foundation had concealed the rest of my bruises, and unless someone had seen me a few days ago, they would never know they were there.

"You're stunning, girl. Walk like you know it." Brynn applied a light gloss to her lips, then set the tube down.

"Oh shit, I almost forgot." Brynn rummaged around in her duffle bag, then produced a black box. She flipped the lid open, and my mouth hit the floor.

"Let me put it on you." Brynn slipped the choker necklace around my neck and fastened it. "There. Take a look."

I peered at my reflection in the mirror, skimming my fingers over the fancy diamond H embedded in the gold. My stomach flip-flopped. I'd never worn something this valuable before, and I was nervous as hell that I'd lose or break it.

"What's the H stand for? Hannah?"

"No, Holden would never give you her jewelry to wear. This is for you, and he'll explain later."

I was more curious now than ever, but I decided to see what he had to say when I met him at the club. "Thank you. I promise I'll take care of it tonight."

"Girl, I'm not even worried about it. I know you will." She returned to the black box and produced teardrop diamond earrings.

I put them in and tilted my chin up, catching the reflection of the diamonds. Dan had refused to pay for my ears to be pierced, so Addison and I took it into our own hands. My ears had hurt for days after Addison had done it the old-fashioned way with ice, a potato, and a needle. But it had worked. I only owned a few pairs of earrings, but occasionally I'd worked a few double shifts, so I'd splurge a few dollars on another set. I smiled at the memory, my heart aching for the one friend that had been consistent in my life. I had to figure out why Addison hadn't responded.

"Here." Brynn picked up the lip gloss from the counter, then dabbed some on my lips. She stepped away, and her approving gaze skimmed over me. "Even with the cast, you're fucking gorgeous. No wonder Becky was so jealous. She saw your potential."

I flinched at her name. "How is she?"

Brynn sighed. "She's fine. I suspect she's still a bit shaken about having a gun to her head, but maybe she'll keep her drama down to a dull roar. If she hadn't thrown a fit, she wouldn't have barged out of the house and right into that guy's arms."

"What? That shit show wasn't Becky's fault. It was mine." I placed my palm against my chest. Her words sank deep into the pit of my stomach, weighing me down with guilt. "If I hadn't been hit by a car, none of this would have taken place."

Brynn shoved her makeup in her bag, then picked it up. "River, what happened to Becky wasn't on you. Becky has been teetering for a while, and she's pulled some real crap with girls that showed an interest in Holden. All I'm saying is that if she'd behaved better, she wouldn't have found herself in a shitty situation. That's all."

"Why do I get the feeling there's a lot you're not telling me?" I resisted chewing on my bottom lip since I had gloss on. Even though I'd decided that Becky was nuts, her words continued to haunt me on occasion.

"Because you're right, there is, but she's in the past now, and you have a great future in front of you. Let's get through tonight, and if you decide to stick around, maybe I'll fill you in."

"Holden said the same thing. I mean the 'if I stay' part." My voice cracked with anxiety as I recalled why we were dressed up. "He said I might have a difficult time with how he makes his money."

Brynn looked at me, her gaze full of compassion. "I think you'll be okay, but yeah, it might trigger you. None of us want that, and I told Holden it was too soon, but he said he promised you that there wouldn't be any more secrets."

"When did he tell you that?"

"He called me after your argument. Holden didn't tell me what you two argued about, so I was genuinely shocked when you said he'd told you about Hannah."

An alarm on Brynn's phone filled the bathroom. "That's us. It's time to go. Are you ready to learn more about Holden?"

Yes and no. I was terrified the truth might send me packing and out of his life. At the same time, I needed to know who I was falling for.

Chapter Seventeen

The restless wind grazed the tops of the trees as we left the house through the front door. Brynn walked next to me as I slowly crutched along. My arms were sore as fuck after shopping all day, but I was too nervous about Holden's secret to mention it.

"Ooh, someone is having a special night." I nodded to the black limousine parked at the corner of the street.

"That's ours. I'm going to have him bring the car closer, so you don't have as far to go." She removed her phone from her clutch, and seconds later, the vehicle backed up.

"Holy shit, I've never seen a limo other than on television!" I wasn't able to hide the excitement in my voice.

"She's beautiful. I've been in several, but this one is my fave," Brynn said.

"Who rented it?" I asked as we approached the man in a black suit and white shirt that held the door open for us.

"It's Holden's. He uses it for business." She flashed me a warm smile.

I should have known, but it hadn't occurred to me. Reaching the vehicle, I turned around and placed my butt on the soft black leather of the seat, then held my casted leg while I spun around and brought my feet in. "That was sexy, huh?" I giggled, slightly embarrassed. Brynn laughed and climbed in as well. It was then that I paid attention to the driver. His light brown hair and emerald-green eyes were mesmerizing, and I found myself lost in his gaze. He was at least six-three, and his stoic expression was a little disarming, but my hormones and body were completely fine with it.

My core pulsed and heat pumped through every willing part of me. Holy shit, what in the hell was happening? "Thank you. What's your name?" I asked, a bit breathless.

"Zayne. I'm your driver and bodyguard."

I gulped. Bodyguard? I nearly gave myself whiplash looking at Brynn.

"Wait until you see the rest of them. They're hot as hell." Brynn fanned herself. "Group sex has never looked so good," she whispered.

"Are you safely in the vehicle?" Zayne asked, his gaze landing on Brynn briefly, then me.

"Yes, thank you." A blush crept across my cheeks.

He closed the door, then my focus landed on the bar that was loaded with alcohol. I ran my fingertips over the soft, buttery leather and relaxed into the luxury of the vehicle. Music played through the sound system as the car started to move.

"Do you want a drink?" Brynn pulled out a bottle of vodka along with some orange juice.

I nodded. "I have a feeling I might need one or two."

"If you drink too much, Holden will have to carry you around for the evening." Brynn giggled softly. "You'll see Chance tonight, too."

Hell, I'd almost forgotten about Chance since I rarely saw him. "I haven't spent much time with him yet, so it will be nice to get to know him better."

"He's a good guy." Brynn's tone carried a hint of something for her friend that I couldn't identify.

Brynn made small talk as we drank our screwdrivers. Half an hour later, the limo stopped. I gathered my crutches as the back door of the car opened.

"Where are we?" I asked, staring into the night at a dark building.

"It's safe. I promise." Brynn hopped out of the vehicle and joined me.

"Ladies, after you." Zayne motioned for us to proceed, and he fell into step behind us.

When we reached a brick wall, Brynn stopped and stood still. A little red light scanned her iris, then the wall opened.

"What the fuck?" I whispered.

Brynn didn't answer as we walked down a dimly lit hall and stopped at a steel door. The scanner activated and Brynn stood still while it swept over her eye again.

The lock clicked, and she pushed it open. Blue, green, and purple strobe lights cut through the poorly lit room.

"Follow me!" she roared over the deafening noise of the music and people.

The floor vibrated beneath my foot and crutches, and a gentle hand landed on my left shoulder, steadying me.

"Are you all right?" Zayne asked near my ear.

I nodded, grateful he was there to catch me if I lost my balance.

Zayne was glued to my side as I followed Brynn. A techno version of "My Own Monster" by the X Ambassadors thumped through the club's speakers. Brynn led us around one of the dance floors and to an elevator. Once inside, I leaned against the wall as the doors slid closed. "He owns a club?" I asked her, still confused about why he thought I would have an issue with it. I'd love to dance as soon as my cast was off. Not only did I have friends, but a safe place to go now.

"Yes," Brynn said as we arrived at the next floor. "This time, we used the back entrance, so you didn't see the sign out front. It's called 4 Play. This is the VIP section."

I gawked at the club that seemed completely separate from the one we'd walked through minutes ago. "Futureproof" by Nothing But Thieves played, but instead of a packed dance floor, men and women were sitting on couches along the wall. Each of the six sections had their own gorgeous and scantily clad waitress in a white halter top and short black skirt that barely covered their ass cheeks. I had no clue how they worked all night in stilettos, but they seemed to be doing fine.

Brynn led us to the back corner, where I spotted Holden chatting with a shorter dark-haired guy. Holden threw his head back and laughed, then his eyes softened as his attention landed on me. He patted his friend on the shoulder and approached, his heated gaze assessing me. He swallowed hard, then placed his hands on his hips, his black suit jacket flapping behind him.

Suddenly my palms grew sweaty, and a strong desire I'd never felt before swirled in my lower belly. My head swam with the scent of his cologne, and my lips parted slightly. He ran his fingers through his short hair, and I imagined them roaming over me. I cleared my throat, attempting to rein in my sudden hormonal overdrive. I gripped my crutches tighter, mentally reminding myself that we were from different worlds, and he would break my heart if I allowed myself to feel anything for him. I'd had enough heartache in the last nineteen years. Sweeping my gaze over him, I settled on his focused eyes.

"You look stunning," he said.

"Thank you." My cheeks flushed, and a newfound heat coursed through my body. No guy had ever called me stunning. Bitch, slut, or loser, sure, but never stunning. In some ways, it was easier to deal with the harsh words than the nice ones. I knew how to fuel my anger to protect myself when someone was being an asshole, but not when they were kind. "It was all Brynn's doing."

"No, you can't make someone this beautiful." He cleared his throat and nodded to Zayne. They obviously knew each other.

"Let's get you off the crutches." Holden stepped to my side and placed his warm palm against the bare skin of my lower back. His gentle touch sent currents of electricity pulsating through me.

As we made our way to our section, my attention landed on a man with a blonde and brunette on either side of him. One lady was rubbing his crotch while he kissed the other. I quickly looked away, feeling strange that I was witnessing what should be a private moment.

"Here we are." Holden indicated the curved, dark brown leather couches with three small round tables in front of them. Bottles of champagne were chilling in silver buckets and glass flutes were waiting for us. I sat down and nearly slid off the seat and onto the floor.

Holden laughed and caught me. "Sorry about that. They were cleaned before we opened."

I eased my way to the center while Brynn joined me on one side and Holden on the other. Zayne stood silently, his arms at his sides and gaze attentive. I had to admit, I felt safer with him around.

Holden signaled to our waitress, and she popped the top on a bottle of bubbly and filled the glasses for us. I took a sip and nearly moaned. It was light and smooth.

"Drink up, girl." Brynn laughed and clinked her flute against mine, then Holden's.

The lighting was better here than downstairs, and I could see the other VIP sections. Men and women were laughing and drinking, and some were grinding on each other.

"Did you have a good day?" Holden asked, focusing on my neck.

"I did. Thank you." I touched the necklace. "Brynn was sweet enough to loan me some jewelry for the evening."

Holden glanced at Brynn, a look of understanding passing between them. Brynn nodded.

I took another sip of my drink, trying to relax. I was as uptight and nervous as a working girl in the back of a Southern church.

"It's actually mine. I asked Brynn to give it to you. The diamond H lets others know you're under my protection."

Mortified, I was suddenly grateful I didn't have any champagne in my mouth. I would have spewed it all over Holden on accident. "Protect me from what?"

Chapter Eighteen

Dark thoughts rolled into my mind, clouding my vision for a moment. What was Holden into?

"This business has some interesting characters, but when they see the necklace, they'll understand that you're off-limits. Men come here to hook up. I needed them to know that you aren't a possibility."

"We've got you taken care of." Brynn reached over and squeezed my hand. I returned the gesture thankful she was with me. I released a slow breath. The necklace was a sign of protection. I was all right with that, especially while my leg was healing.

"We should dance." A smile graced his mouth and my tummy flip-flopped. A part of me wanted to peel all of Holden's layers away and see who he truly was. He'd offered me glimpses, but this man had as much darkness as light in him. The more time we spent together, the more intrigued I became.

"I can't. I have my cast." I pressed my lips together in frustration.

"Nonsense." Holden stood and held his palm out to me. I slid my butt along the seat, then took his hand. He grabbed my crutches and helped me up, patiently waiting while I found my balance before he started walking. Completely confused about how this was going to work, I followed him.

"Watch your step," he said, pointing at the two stairs.

"I don't think sliding down them on my ass would exactly be appropriate in this dress." I gave him a shy grin.

Holden hopped down the stairs, then faced me. He picked me up, then gently set my good foot on the dance floor. A squeal escaped me, but the music was too loud for anyone other than Holden to notice.

He guided me over to the side of the room, where he moved one of my hands to his shoulder. "Use me for balance."

I leaned on him while he took my crutches and propped them against the wall.

"Take off your shoe."

"What?" I laughed.

"Take off your shoe," he repeated.

I gave him a quizzical look but removed it and scooted it over near the wall.

"Now, stand on my foot," he ordered.

"Bossy much?" Apprehension tugged at my insides. "Holden, I'm going to hurt you."

"You won't, but please don't stand on my other foot with your cast. That *will* hurt." A wide grin played across his lips before he slid his arms around my waist and held me tightly. Once I was situated, he walked us backward into the center of the floor. I was sure the people on our side of the club could hear me giggling my ass off. I'd never danced with anyone before, and I was happy that my first time would be with Holden.

"Sex and Candy" by Alexander Jean started to play, and Holden gently swayed with me.

"I don't think this is a slow song." I glanced up at him beneath my eyelashes, suddenly incredibly self-conscious of how close we were and where his hands were ... on my hips.

"With the right person, any song is a slow song." He winked at me.

I looked around the club, realizing that several people were staring at us. Only five or six other couples were dancing, so we were easy to spot.

"We're the center of attention." I placed my palm against his muscular chest and inwardly sighed. I gently rubbed the soft material of his white shirt, and I wondered what he would look like without it.

"You're new, and the new women are always intriguing. Plus, you have a cast on your leg."

I nodded. It made sense. "Brynn said Chance will be here?"

"He's downstairs. There are three floors to the club and five in the building. I'll take you to the lower level later. For now, let's just have some fun."

He smoothed a stray hair from my face and tucked it behind my ear, his fingertips grazing my cheek. "I love seeing you like this. You're breathtaking, River." His heated gaze landed on my slightly parted mouth.

I stifled a moan, my hormones suddenly kicking my brain out of the driver's seat and taking over. The heady and breathless feeling left me dizzy. The heat of Holden's touch had me wondering if I could have sex and leave my past behind.

"Save Your Soul" by Damned Anthem played next, and Holden and I continued to exist inside our little bubble. The sway of his movements and our bodies pressed together was almost more than I could handle. Butterflies broke out and ran crazy in my tummy as his hand trailed up my bare back and I arched into him. Electricity swirled around us, igniting the air and causing all my senses to heighten.

His attention remained on my mouth, and I stifled the urge to stand on my tiptoes and suck on his lower lip. My God, what was this man doing to me?

After the song ended, we made our way to the wall, and with shaky legs, I collected my crutches and hobbled back to our table.

Holden gathered my shoe, then slipped an arm around me until I sat down safely.

"Where's Brynn?" I frowned, feeling her absence. Holden and I had spent plenty of time alone, talking, laughing, and watching television, but tonight was different.

"She probably went downstairs to let Chance know we're here."

Still reeling from Holden's close proximity while we danced, I mentally swore as I reached for my champagne with a shaky hand. Dammit. I couldn't look at Holden right now. I was too embarrassed that he'd most likely witnessed the effect he was having on me.

I gripped my glass tighter, taking a drink and allowing the golden liquid to travel down my throat and calm my overactive nerves. Without a word, Holden reached for the bottle and topped off our drinks. I tipped it back and guzzled half of its contents.

"Holy shit. That was seriously unladylike." I grimaced and peeked at him, but he just laughed.

Our gazes connected again, goosebumps peppering my skin under his heated stare.

"I really want to kiss you, but I have to make sure it's what you want too, River." He reached up and ran his thumb over my bottom lip. "You were wrong before. I don't have feelings for you because of Hannah. I have feelings for you because you're smart, beautiful, and you're not afraid to fight for what you want."

I gulped, wishing he would show me what it would be like to be wanted by someone who cared about me. Closing my eyes, I attempted to rid myself of the longing for him. It would only lead to trouble, but no matter how hard I tried to fight it, nothing and no one else existed that night except for him.

He leaned into me, his mouth next to my ear. "Can I touch you?"

I nodded. Oh God, I wanted him to. I wanted his caress to erase all of the horrible memories from my mind and replace them with something good.

He trailed his fingertips slowly up my arm, and my flesh

responded with a delightful chill. He skimmed over my collarbone, up my neck, then under my hair, and across my upper back.

I grabbed the edge of the seat as he continued.

"You're so soft, River." His warm breath caressed my cheek and I shuddered.

"It was the massage today, which felt amazing by the way, but this ... this is ..." I captured my bottom lip with my teeth while his fingers traveled down my spine.

"I'm glad you're enjoying it." He nipped at my earlobe, and I moaned.

I was shameless putty in his hands.

"Jesus, River. You don't understand what you're doing to me."

I was pretty sure I had a good idea, because my body was on fire, begging for a release, but I'd never had one, so I wasn't sure what it felt like. If this was anything close, I would happily cooperate.

My core throbbed while Holden continued to lightly stroke my skin. Not once did he move lower, and although my hormones were encouraging him, I was grateful he was taking it slow. I needed time.

"Hey, man," a deep voice from behind me said.

My head jerked up, spotting Chance in a stunning, dark silver suit, matching tie, and white shirt. Holden flattened his palm against my back and focused on his friend.

"You remember River?"

Chance's brown eyes widened. "I do, but wow, you clean up nice." He released a low whistle.

I was unsure of how to handle the new attention, and I hadn't realized I'd scooted closer to Holden. "Thanks. It's a new look for me, too." I offered him a smile, pretending that I wasn't feeling incredibly awkward.

"Are you ready?" Holden asked me.

I looked at him, locking in my mind's eye the beauty of his face and the adoring gleam in his eye. Regardless of what happened between us in the future, I wanted to recall him like this forever. "For?"

His expression faltered, the tic in his jaw revealing how nervous he was. "To learn my secret."

Chapter Nineteen

My hormones screeched to a halt as I remembered the real reason I was here. Holden was afraid his secret would send me running. My heart hammered against my chest, and my hands grew moist. One thing I'd never done was back down from a challenge, though. I'd excelled in school because of it. Maybe I needed to prove myself since I came from a shithole home, or perhaps it was a massive fuck you to my absent mom who left me with a sorry son of a bitch that thought my body was his property.

I drew in a deep breath, tipped my chin up, and squared my shoulders. "After you, Holden."

His eyes flashed darkly, and I held his intense gaze with mine. He said it was my choice to stay or leave after tonight, so I was ready to find out what he was so afraid of me learning.

Holden stood and smoothed his white dress shirt. I gathered my crutches, my mind spinning scenarios from drug dealing to him housing the homeless. *Fuck.* I had no idea, but whatever it was, he was nervous as hell.

He shoved his hands in his pockets, then we followed Chance to the elevator. Zayne trailed a few steps behind us.

Sometimes my imagination was worse than the actual reality. At least that's what I was trying to convince myself of as the elevator slowly lowered, then stopped. The doors whooshed open, and we exited. The stark white hallway nearly blinded me after the dark room upstairs.

Chance strolled down the corridor, then paused in front of a door.

"Zayne, please stay here." Holden's attention landed on me. "Remember, River. It's your choice to accept my life or not. There's absolutely no pressure." He paused and massaged the back of his neck. "But I hope you can. I hope you stay." His eyes pleaded with me, and my heart plummeted to my toes. Holden had accepted me as I was, and I hoped I could do the same for him, but I'd learned long ago never to make promises. Promises had been easily forgotten, broken, and had left my soul scattered across the floor in a million pieces. I never wanted to do that to someone I cared about.

"I appreciate the reminder." I wanted to reassure him it would be all right, but I couldn't say anything until I understood what was on the other side of the wall.

Chance moved out of the way and Holden approached the black box. A green light scanned his eye, then the lock clicked.

Little sweat beads formed on the nape of my neck, and my pulse throbbed wildly as we all entered a dimly lit hall. Doors lined each side as far down as I could see. Holden stopped at the second one on the right and grabbed the handle. He glanced at me, fear evident in his face.

"I'll meet up with you in a few, Holden. And River, it's always a pleasure. I hope to see you in a few minutes with Holden, but if not, I wish you all the best. You deserve it." Chance leaned down and pressed a sweet kiss to my cheek.

My throat clogged up. No one had ever said that to me before. I hoped like hell I would be okay with whatever was on the opposite side, because I really loved my group of new friends.

I'd heard that we control our destiny, but I wasn't buying it. My fate was in the hands of the unknown. My stomach churned and butterflies ran amok in my chest.

"Let's do this," I said.

Panic flashed across Holden's expression, then it dropped away. "When we're inside, I have to close the door, but it won't be locked. You can leave at any time. I don't want you to feel trapped." Holden entered, and I followed. The small area glowed with soft blue light, and I immediately noticed how sparsely furnished the space was, with only a couch and lounger.

"This room is for observation." Holden flipped a switch, and a hidden screen slowly slid up and into the ceiling, revealing a glass wall.

I gasped, my mind struggling to comprehend what I was seeing. "What the hell?" Although I was stunned, I couldn't pull my attention away. The man who had been with the two girls upstairs was now in a room with a California king bed and both women. Naked. The platinum blonde backed up against the other, and the guy sat in a chair, watching and stroking his long cock. The dark-haired girl wrapped her fingers around the blonde's throat, and the blonde moaned as the other chick pinched her nipple, then slipped her hand between her legs. The guy stood and joined them on the bed, sucking the blonde's tits.

I tore my gaze away, horrified that I was witnessing people having sex. My brows knitted together. "Holden, what is this?"

He visibly swallowed and his forehead creased before he spoke. "River, I own the club upstairs, but I also own a membership-only sex club."

My mouth opened and closed as I attempted to speak while I focused on the threesome. Hands groped and mouths licked and sucked while they continued like this was a normal thing for them.

I turned around. "So, you have a bunch of rooms for people to fuck and be watched in?"

He massaged the back of his neck, obviously nervous about my reaction. "This room is for voyeurism. Each room has a different purpose."

Turning my back to him, I started toward the door.

Holden moved in front of me. "River, you have my word that everyone is here with full consent. They are required to sign a form before they're allowed in. We also run a deep background check on everyone that applies for membership. I've never had any trouble. No one has ever been hurt or raped. It's a clean operation and everyone has fun."

As appalled as I should have been that this was Holden's life, my G-string was soaked. Holden's secret was my greatest fear ... sex.

The man's grunts from behind the glass pulled my attention back to the group. The dark-haired girl was riding him hard while the blonde sat on his face.

I ground my molars together. "I want to leave."

Pain was etched into Holden's features as he opened the door for me again.

I sucked in a huge breath and continued down the hall. Then I stopped and looked at him over my shoulder. "Show me more rooms."

"River ..." Holden closed the gap between us. "Are you sure? If you have questions, I'll answer anything you want to know. I'm an open book."

"I want to see more, but how did this start?" I stared at my cast, angry with myself for being curious and feeling dirty for wanting to know. My heart and head were in a full-on tug-of-war between right and what I perceived as wrong. What I struggled to understand was that, if everyone consented, was it really bad? I also wondered how it would feel to be free of the fear and guilt associated with my past. To have safe and fun experiences.

"I don't want to sound like a rich prick, but a group of us got really bored during high school. We'd tried it all: drugs, sex, dating, racing cars—you name it, we did it. We wanted a high without the drugs. One night, I talked to Jace, Chance, Brynn, Payton, and Sariah. There were a few others we were close to, but this is the group I started the sex club with. We agreed to screen applicants, but it had to remain secret and underground."

"High school?" Disbelief clung to my words.

"Yeah, our freshman year, actually. I think when you have a shit ton of money, it's all about the next thrill. Over time you can't find it anymore. At least this way we were having sex with people we trusted with our health and life. That certainly wasn't the case before I formed the group."

Holden shoved his hand into his pocket, an apology flashing in his gaze. "I can't let you into the other rooms while they're occupied, but I can show you one more."

A giggle floated down the hall, and a couple entered the room we'd just left. A pang of jealousy stabbed my chest. They seemed so comfortable with the idea of watching the threesome. They appeared free in their desire, and that wasn't an opportunity I'd ever had.

"I want to see it." A sharp prickle of anxiety rolled over me and I willed myself not to chicken out. Hell, I'd never even seen porn, and here I was watching people fuck right in front of me.

I counted ten more doors before we reached the one at the end of the hall.

Holden paused, his forehead creasing with worry lines. "Are you sure? You can't go back from it, River. Once you see it, you can't unsee it."

Holy shit. It must be bad. "Are people being beaten in there or something?" I resisted the urge to shoulder check him and barge in, rescuing anyone that was being hurt.

"No. As I said, everything that happens here is consensual."

A beat of silence hung in the air.

"Then let's do this." My tone didn't hold as much conviction as I'd intended, but Holden opened the door anyway.

It took my eyes a minute to adjust to the low light, but it was stronger than in the hallway.

"What the fuck?"

Chapter Twenty

"This is *our* room. We call it the Master's Playroom," Holden explained quietly.

I lost my words as I noticed a naked woman strapped to a wheel. A blindfold covered her eyes, and she was smiling. She was spread eagle, and her wrists and ankles were tied to the platform.

Several couches and a few chairs took up half the space in the large area, and a full bar was in the back of the room. Shelves and hooks lined a wall, and rows of sex toys and other options I'd never seen before were also available.

Six people stood around her, all naked and with their backs to me. One of the guys approached the wheel and spun it slowly.

A deep chuckle permeated the place. "Nipple clamps, darlin'."

Oh. My. God. I recognized Jace's voice. I'd just seen his ass. The moment I realized it, he turned around, and I slapped a hand over my mouth as his long dick saluted me. I stood there, my cheeks blazing, eyes burning, and every muscle in my body taut as a bowstring. Shit, I'd seen my new friend naked.

Jace returned to his place, then a petite black-haired girl stepped forward and spun the wheel.

She giggled when it stopped. "Hold on, Red. I need to get situated."

Red bit her lip and grinned. "I hope it's what I think it is."

"Jesus, that's Brynn?" I whisper-yelled at Holden.

"Yeah. We're all in the club, River."

Reality slapped me in the face, nearly knocking me off balance. Holden, Jace, Chance, Brynn, and a few others had all been having sex and playing sex games for years. They were way more than just friends. They'd licked, fucked, and sucked each other.

The petite girl knelt, then ran her tongue along the inside of Brynn's leg.

"Holy shit." My body responded without my permission as I watched this girl perform oral sex on Brynn. From the sound of Brynn's moans, she clearly enjoyed the hell out of it.

"Anything goes?" I squeaked.

"As long as no one gets hurt, then yes. Spanking, BDSM, girls with girls. I do have a boundary. I won't cross swords. Another guy is off-limits for me, but some are okay with it."

I stole one last glance at the group, my chest rising and falling as the light bulb went off in my head. The next person approached, and I looked away. Guilt gnawed at me for feeling aroused, and for witnessing my friends in a private moment. I wasn't sure this was what I wanted, but I wasn't opposed to it either. What did that say about me? Maybe I was more like my mother than I realized. A whore.

"I'm done." My heart sank as Holden stared at me, disappointment and sadness springing to life in his gorgeous features.

"I understand, River."

* * *

My thoughts spun out of control on the way back to Holden's. He'd opted for his navy BMW i8 and left the limo for Brynn, Jace, and Chance. I'd never asked him how many cars he owned, and honestly,

I didn't care. I was too angry even to admire the beauty of the one that I was sitting in.

Once we were safely in the foyer of Holden's house, I spun around and glared at him.

"You said that Brynn wasn't bisexual. You lied to me." Anger flared from deep inside. I was suddenly being forced to choose between my old life and this new one.

"I didn't lie. You mentioned that your pain meds might be messing with you, and I agreed. I never answered if Brynn was bi. I mentioned that Becky was."

"Was Becky a member, too? Did you two use a room?"

"River, I can't give out any information. It's all confidential. I can tell you that we dated for a few months, but I just wasn't into her. Then after she pulled that shit with you, I was done."

I smashed my lips together, growing angrier by the second. "So why did you take me to the club, Holden? Do you need redemption about this, too?"

"I promised no more secrets ..." His voice trailed off. "Hannah was introduced to drugs at 4 Play."

Holden's shoulders slumped and he hung his head. "When I found out, I took over and cleared out the drug dealers and pimps. Less than a year later, I was running a drug-free, high-end club. I felt a sense of accomplishment and I had my own money. 4 Play has a reputation for being safe. It was only last year that I moved *our* sex club to one of the rooms, so we could use it whenever we wanted to. Before that, we used each other's houses when the parents were gone."

"I don't even know what to do with this information, Holden." I shook my head and stared at the white-and-black marble floors. "I need some time to think. Tonight has been a lot."

Without looking at him, I crutched my way up the wide stairs and into the bedroom. I quietly closed the door behind me, then flopped down on the bed. I heaved a sigh while I watched the blades of the ceiling fan spin, the string pinging rhythmically against the light. Massaging my temples, I tried to separate out the hurricane of feelings that were crashing down on me. It was Holden's secret, but it was also Brynn's, Jace's, and Chance's. These people were so rich they got bored and had started a sex club.

I fisted my hands and pounded the bed, frustration seeping out of my pores. I sat up and looked around. I was too tired and overwhelmed to make any decisions tonight except for one. I traced the diamond H of the choker I was still wearing, and I felt around for the clasp. The necklace fell forward, the weight of the diamonds and gold hit my palm, then I placed it carefully on the nightstand.

I stood and leaned against the mattress for balance as I slipped out of my dress. My nipples hardened against the cool air, and I shivered slightly. It took me a minute to wiggle out of my G-string, and I swore at the blasted cast on my leg. Sprawling out on the bed, I propped up on one elbow, then tugged on the drawer of my nightstand. When Brynn and I had arrived earlier that day, she'd brought the Adam & Eve bag to my room, opened the package, and wrapped the vibrator in a soft purple pillowcase. Even though I was shocked about the club, it also left me wanting more. Maybe Brynn's idea would work.

I loaded the magic wand with batteries, then flipped on the switch. Staring at the long, dick-shaped toy, I thought about earlier in the evening when Holden and I danced. His citrusy clean scent and touch had been intoxicating. The way his fingertips had glided over my skin had left me spinning.

Chewing on my bottom lip, I placed the vibrator between my legs as it hummed. Heat rushed to my core, and I lifted my hips and angled the toy against my clit. A soft moan escaped me. It felt good. Really good.

I spread myself apart, my fingers becoming slick with my own juices. I'd been so turned on at the club, not only with Holden but while watching the sex game and the threesome.

Easing the tip into my slit, I forced myself to relax. It wasn't Dan slamming his disgusting dick inside me. I had complete control. I eased it in deeper and slowly pulled it out, then pumped my wet pussy as soft moans of pleasure escaped me.

"Oh, God," I whispered and arched off the bed. I never knew I could feel like this. My nipples ached to be sucked as I continued to experiment with what felt good.

I closed my eyes, thinking about what it would feel like to have Holden kiss me. The vibrator slid in a little deeper, my core clenching it.

The door creaked open, and I paused. Goddammit, I'd forgotten to lock it. I looked over to see Holden, shirtless and in gray sweats, staring at me.

Horrified, I froze.

Chapter Twenty-One

A deafening silence filled the room, then Holden gulped. "I knocked and when you didn't answer ..." His heated gaze swept over me, his eyes darkening with desire. "Don't stop, River. Please ... don't stop." My name rolled off his tongue in a sweet whisper with a hint of promise and spice, and I wondered what his mouth would feel like all over my body.

He closed the door behind him and approached the bed. "Jesus. You're so beautiful." He ran his hand through his hair, and I gawked at him, speechless. "Can I show you? Can I show you how good it can feel, River? I'll use the vibrator, and you're in full control."

I stared at him like an idiot but finally managed to speak. "Yeah."

Holden walked over to the other side of the bed and laid down next to me. "You have the most perfect tits I've ever seen."

I looked at him as though he were crazy. He'd been with tons of women, and I couldn't imagine there was anything special about mine. But even crazier was me lying here naked beside him with a vibrator still buzzing inside me.

"Can I taste your nipple? Suck on it?"

"Please," I said breathlessly.

His warm mouth closed over my breast and his tongue toyed with my taut bud.

"Oh God. That feels so good." I moved the vibrator again, catching a new rhythm as his other hand caressed my left tit.

"I'm so turned on right now. You're so sexy in a sweet, naive way. I want to taste every inch of you. I want you to come over and over. Show you what it's all about."

"I've never had one," I admitted, my cheeks flaming red with my confession.

Confusion filled Holden's expression.

"An orgasm. I've never had an orgasm before."

"That's about to change." His fingers snaked down my stomach, then he paused. "Can I use the vibrator on you?" His eyes darkened with need, and I glanced down at the huge bulge in his sweatpants. I wanted to touch and feel him too, but I didn't have any experience, so I kept my mouth closed.

I nodded, giving him permission to continue.

"River, I need you to say yes or no. I have to be a thousand percent clear that you're okay with this. Consent is everything."

"I understand. Yes."

My body tensed as he trailed his fingertips down my flat stomach, then between my thighs.

"You're so fucking wet." He placed a kiss on my cheek, then took the vibrator and pulled it out of me. "Can I lick your pussy while I use the toy on you?" His tone was pure silk, gliding over me and massaging my sensitive skin.

I was pretty sure that I nearly came with the mere thought of it.

"Yeah." Apparently, that was the only word I could speak, but it was all he needed.

Holden stood and walked to the foot of the bed, then crawled between my legs and carefully parted them. Holden didn't even seem to care about the cast.

He dipped his head and gently licked my clit. My hands

wandered over his well-defined shoulders, then I dug my fingernails into his skin and arched my hips up.

As he continued, he slipped the vibrator inside me. Desire burned every inch of me, and I panted as he pumped me with the toy and worshipped my pussy. I didn't want him to ever stop.

"Oh shit!" I threaded my fingers through his hair as every nerve in my body sprung to life.

"That's it, baby. Just relax into it."

My eyes slammed closed. "Holden, what are you doing to me?" I moaned, then shattered with the intense pleasure.

"You're so beautiful when you come. I love seeing you like this." Holden ran his tongue over my bundle of nerves again, and I trembled against him. He removed the vibrator and sat up.

"Oh my God. Oh. My. God." I giggled and covered my mouth, completely embarrassed yet comfortable with him at the same time. I bit my lip and peered up at him, tears forming in my eyes. My emotions overflowed, rippling through me like a storm over the sea. The push and pull was chaotic and uncontrollable. My shoulders shook and I turned away from him.

"Hey, what's the matter?" He scrambled up the side of the bed, smoothed my hair, and held me while I snotted all over the gorgeous comforter.

"That meant nothing to you. It was just another sex game, but it was everything to me," I admitted. I peered at him through my wet eyelashes, feeling vulnerable and exposed. I should have never let him close to me, but after everything tonight, I needed to know if I was capable of having a normal sexual experience. Now that I had my answer, I wasn't sure it was what I wanted. I'd never anticipated the feelings that might accompany it.

"River, look at me." He gently tilted my chin up, then he kissed my forehead. "I stopped being a member of the club months ago. It wasn't fulfilling anymore. Sure, it felt good, but even that became boring. Tonight, with you, it was different. Special. I haven't experienced anything like it before. You're working your way into my heart, and I don't know how to handle it. All I know is that I want to make you laugh and feel good."

I looked up at him as he gently cupped my cheek.

Fear flickered through his expression. "Does our time together tonight mean you're going to stay, or is this it for us?"

Chapter Twenty-Two

I turned my head away from him. My mind was clouded with what had just happened between us, and I hadn't had time to think about what I wanted. If I were brutally honest with myself, I knew I was full of shit. It had only been a week and a half, but Holden and I had spent almost every minute together. His kindness had cracked the ice around my heart, thawing it a little each day. I wanted to be with him, even if it didn't include an intimate relationship.

With every stolen glance and beautiful smile, Holden made me feel as though no one else existed in his world except me. I had no idea how to manage my feelings for him, though. Then, there was Hannah and how similar we were. My biggest concern was that he was blinded by his past and couldn't see the truth. If I fell for him, then he dumped me when he realized he was just trying to save Hannah again ... I wasn't sure I would recover. What if I made a mistake? Inwardly I scrambled backward from the idea of allowing him any closer.

"What are you thinking?" He took my hand, his soft lips brushing across my knuckles.

I turned my head again, and our gazes connected. "I don't want to ever return to the life I had before, Holden. You've given me a glimpse into an entire world of possibilities, but ..." I peered down at his strong hand over mine. "But I can't use you. I have to be sure that I'm staying for the right reasons."

Hope flickered to life in his brown eyes.

"Do you ..." He paused. "Do you have feelings for me, River?"

My pulse fluttered with every blink of his dark lashes.

"I think so, but what if it's for the wrong reasons? You've been so good to me. It would really fuck me up if I hurt you." I chewed on my lower lip, and his gaze latched onto my mouth.

He shifted on the bed, and I peeked down at his sweats. He was still fully erect, and I was lying in front of him naked, yet he hadn't forced himself on me or touched me without permission. He hadn't called me a whore or a slut for what we'd done. "Also, I'm not sure what to do about the club. You make your money from sex, the one thing that nearly destroyed my life." I rubbed my forehead with my palm. "At the same time, I hate that I'm not free enough inside myself to ask for a membership." I barked out a laugh. "And yet I'm naked in front of you right now, trying to have a really important conversation."

"I have no problem with that." A playful smile tugged at the corner of his mouth.

"Yeah, but all I want is your mouth all over me. I want you to kiss me. I want to stroke you and ... I'm scared. All of these feelings bubbled up inside me just from you using the vibrator ... what happens if we have sex?" I whispered, afraid to acknowledge the possibility that my emotions would be heightened if we were together.

Holden's eyes darkened. "We can take it slow. You're in the driver's seat. We don't ever have to play around again, but I can't handle it if you walk out of the door and my life."

"What if I don't want to take it slow?" My voice cracked with my boldness. "What if I want you inside of me right now?"

A low growl rumbled through Holden's chest. "Your honesty is a breath of fresh air. The games women have played with me weren't the ones that I was interested in. It was a turn off, but you ..." He stroked my cheek with the pad of his thumb. "You're stealing my heart, River."

Terror spiked inside me, sending my pulse racing. Shit. Holden had just shown his vulnerability. "Holden ... I'm not sure I can give what you need."

Disappointment and pain clouded Holden's features and he looked away briefly.

"I'm not sure I'm capable of being more than friends with benefits. But I feel safe enough to see if you can set me free from the cage that's confined me most of my life. Sex has been my enemy, and I want that to change."

"Are you asking me personally or are you wanting to join the club?" Holden ran a hand over his short hair.

A flutter of nerves and excitement shot through me. "Can we start with just us, then let me see how I do?"

He pierced me with his intense gaze. "Will you trust and allow me to open this new world for you? It can be more than sex. Let me take you out, buy you clothes, and be on my arm at events. I can give you anything you want. Sex, money, and connections to make all your dreams come true. All I'm asking for is a chance. Let me prove to you that my feelings are for you and have nothing to do with Hannah."

My eyes widened.

"There's one additional condition if you accept, River."

"What is it?" I whispered, afraid to wake myself up from the dream I was obviously having.

"No sex with anyone else unless we agree on who we're inviting into our bed. That goes for me too. If you want to experiment with a threesome, I'm fine with it, but not with someone that's close to me."

"That's fair." I reached up and touched his cheek. "Will you teach me what you like? Help me find out what I like?"

Holden kissed my palm. "Yeah."

Anxiety pulled and twisted my insides. "This sounds like a relationship."

"It is. I'll give you everything you want—"

"In hopes that someday I'll love you," I finished for him, realizing that his need to be loved and accepted was as deep as mine. The only difference was that he was willing to give me his heart, but I wasn't willing to give him mine yet.

"Let's not complicate it." Holden kissed me on the forehead.

I needed to see if he would honor his word and if my feelings ran deeper than I'd admitted. I did care about him, and the connection was there, but I wasn't clear about the reason behind it. Until we had more time together, I was okay with him on these terms.

"All right. I'm in."

"One more thing," Holden said. "When you're at any club, whether it's with me or other people, you need to wear the collar."

My brow shot up. "Collar?" I was completely confused.

"The necklace Brynn gave you with the diamond H on it. It's a collar for branding you as mine."

I sucked in a breath. Something was definitely wrong with me. His comment should have pissed me off, but instead, I felt safe and protected for the first time in my life. "Is that what you want?"

His deep brown eyes searched my face. "Yes. I want you for myself."

"Since you explained that it protects me from others, and you've been up front about your feelings and intentions, I'll wear it."

"Say it, River. Say you'll be mine."

My core pulsated at his words. Holy shit, this was hot.

I propped up on my elbow and leaned into him, our lips nearly brushing. "I'm yours."

Holden groaned, then pressed his mouth to mine in a tender kiss. "You taste so sweet." He pulled away and leaned his forehead against mine.

"Please be patient with me, Holden. I have a lot of flashbacks.

Sometimes I can still feel Dan's grubby hands on me, pinning me down."

Holden's nostrils flared. "He's gone. He can't ever hurt you again. Now you're under my protection, babe. If anyone wants you, they'll have to go through me."

A flutter of nerves and excitement filled my stomach. I hadn't ever had the opportunity to feel safe. It was funny how safety seemed like an opportunity to me rather than a right.

"Do I have your permission to kiss and touch you without asking every time?"

I nodded. "Yes. Do I need to ask you?"

"No, I'm all yours."

"Then take off your sweats," I demanded.

Holden stood, then tugged his pants down, his long, thick cock bobbing free. My eyes roamed the dips and valleys of his abs, the broad corded muscles in his chest and arms. A bead of precum glistened on the tip of his dick, and I had a sudden urge to lick it off. His gaze traveled over my body, and his lips softly parted, as if he couldn't wait.

"Can you roll over and prop up on your hands and knees okay with your cast?"

My mouth opened and closed before I was able to form my question. "What? Why?"

"I'll have better access to your pussy, babe. I won't hurt you. I promise."

My heart warmed a little with his sudden use of the word babe. I rolled over on my stomach, then pushed up on all fours.

"Are you comfortable?" he asked, moving behind me.

I peered over my shoulder. "Yeah, I'm fine."

He knelt on the floor and nipped at my ass cheek. "I'm going to make you come so hard." His breath tickled my inner thigh as he spoke. He gently spread my sensitive, wet flesh apart. Holden gripped my hip, then he ran a finger up and down my slit.

He pulled me closer to the edge of the bed and groaned. "Goddamn. I'm going to come while eating you out." He shoved his tongue inside me, then lapped at my pussy like it was the last thing he'd ever do in his young life. My body burned with desire as he once again made me feel things I'd never known were possible before. I closed my eyes and dragged in gulps of air, heat curling deep in my belly. As I teetered on the edge of a mind-blowing orgasm, Holden stopped.

"Roll over, River." His voice was husky and thick with need.

I rolled over and laid back against the pillow, my hand gliding over the dips and valleys of his muscular body.

"Can we ..."

"What do you want?" he asked.

"I want you inside of me, Holden." There, I'd said it.

"I'll be right back. I need a condom from my room."

He must have run because he was back in seconds, ripping open the foil package. Holden stilled and lowered his arms. "River, I want you so bad I can't stand it. But you had a big night. Hormones and emotions are flying high. I have to do this right. Don't misunderstand me, I want you ..." He sat on the edge of the bed, the mattress dipping beneath his weight. "River, you've never had a man treat you the way you deserve. All they did was take and take and left you to fend for yourself. I love your courage and fight, but I want to be the one that shows you how special you are. I want to give you everything that was stolen from you ..."

With a shake of his head, sadness clouded his handsome features. "But I can't have sex with you. River, you deserve a better man, and I want to be that for you. We need to wait."

Confused and feeling rejected, I pulled the comforter over my body, shielding it from his gaze.

"Don't, River. I love seeing you like this." Holden tossed the package onto the nightstand beside the necklace and crawled into bed next to me. "Look at me."

I didn't want to. I'd just shared a moment with him that I'd never experienced before, then he turned me down. My inner voice reminded me that I was only good for one thing. To be used and discarded like a used diaper.

Holden placed his fingers below my chin and gently tipped it up, forcing me to look at him. "All your life you've been used and hurt, River. Let's take this slow so you're a hundred percent sure that my intentions are good. I want you ... bad. But I also want you to have a positive experience because I care so much about you."

Tears welled in my eyes, and I blinked furiously, willing them to go away.

Holden rolled over on his side and placed his hand over my heart. "I want to give you the world, but I also want to make sure we cherish this."

Unable to speak, I nodded. Maybe I was more than a game to him. Maybe he wasn't lying, and he really cared about me after all. Only time would tell.

Holden pressed his mouth against mine. "Let's get some sleep, babe."

"Okay," I whispered, doubting I would be able to drift off after everything that had happened tonight. Since I had to lay on my back, Holden stayed on his side with his palm against my chest.

Minutes later, his soft snore filled the room. My attention landed on him, my walls softening now that he wasn't awake. I didn't have to mask my emotions. He couldn't see the fear and confusion in my eyes as Becky's words came back to haunt me again. With a heavy sigh, I decided to do some digging and find out exactly who the Alastairs really were. I just wasn't sure where to start.

Chapter Twenty-Three

Over the next four weeks Holden kept his word and refused to rush sex between us, even though I continued to reassure him that I was ready. Instead, we made out like horny teenagers, and although my heart was still torn, he was winning me over with his continual efforts. Each time he said he would do something, he followed through. He was always punctual, answered my calls, and reassured me that we could make this work.

Holden was also full of surprises and showered me with flowers, chocolates, diamond earrings, or his black American Express card to shop with Brynn. The gestures were fun, but his actions were all the proof that I needed.

The evenings were my favorite time with him, though. Most nights we snuggled up and watched movies, talked, and laughed. At times, we would share about what we wanted in the future. His future included me. The fact that he saw me in it was shocking, but those moments had worked their way into my heart. I hadn't really talked about my dreams with anyone before him because I'd never had any goals other than college. Dan had snuffed out any hope that I'd ever escape that life and could make my dreams a reality. But not Holden; he was helping me rebuild them. Although I'd fought it, my feelings for him had turned into something so deep I didn't have a name for them. Maybe it was love.

Even though I was getting to know Holden better, there were moments that I was still skittish, and I struggled not to relive the awful years with Dan. My brain knew Holden wasn't Dan, but some days I couldn't separate my feelings. When I talked to Brynn about it, she explained to me that I most likely had PTSD. She and I were also growing closer. For the first time in a long time, I felt as though I had a chance to live and not just survive and tread water. But I was constantly waiting for the other shoe to drop.

Weekends were filled with Brynn, Jace, and Chance. Although it was super awkward after I saw them at the club, I finally adjusted to the idea that I knew what they looked like underneath their clothes. I'd never admitted it to anyone, but I was attracted to Jace and Chance as well as Holden. I brushed it off as exploring my options, but in the back of my mind, I understood that it was a safety net if Holden and I fell apart.

On the days Holden was at college and I was home alone, I began my research on Holden's family. Oddly enough, the Alastairs were difficult to find information on, but I wasn't the best at digging, either. There wasn't any news on Hannah, which bothered me. I found articles on Mallory and Holden for sports, college acceptances, and other minor things. I was only searching for them because I was curious. When Becky had attacked me, she said *the Alastairs*, which led me to believe there was something off about Mr. and Mrs., not the kids. When I asked Holden more about their careers, he explained they had started their financial company years ago and were now working with businesses around the world. He finally admitted that he didn't know much, either. I thought it was strange, but it didn't seem as unusual if you rarely saw them.

"Are you ready for tomorrow?" Holden asked as he played with my hair.

I rested my head in his lap while my cast was propped up on the arm of the couch.

"So ready. I wonder if it will feel strange. I mean I haven't walked on this leg for six weeks." I glanced at it and laughed. One evening, after several drinks, Holden, Jace, Chance, and Brynn had made the cast a work of art. Before Holden finished his awful sketch of a bridge, he licked and nipped the inside of my thigh. My neck and face flamed red in front of everyone. When I asked him about it later, he chuckled and said he was just reminding his friends who I belonged to. I wondered if it came from a place of pride or jealousy. I might have been okay with both.

"We should celebrate." Holden slid my finger into his mouth, his skilled tongue driving me insane as he licked and sucked on it.

"I can't think straight when you do that," I groaned. "Did you say something about celebrating?"

A low chuckle rumbled through his chest. He laid a hand on my stomach, then his fingers slipped beneath his football jersey I'd thrown on earlier.

"What would you like to do?" His eyes darkened with need as he traced small circles on the swell of my right breast. I had to admit my boobs looked phenomenal in the new bras Brynn had helped me pick out.

Holden moved the lace material to the side and pinched my nipple. "What are my choices?" I arched into his touch, my greedy body wanting more.

"You haven't mentioned going back to the club, so I haven't brought it up again. But if you just want to dance and drink, we can go anytime, River. I would love to show you off." A playful smile eased across his face, his brown eyes flickering with mischievousness. "It would be good for you to get out of the house. Doctor's appointments don't count."

Holden located my other breast and he cupped it, then raised my shirt.

"How long are we going to mess around without having sex?" A little whimper escaped me as he massaged my boob more firmly.

"I'm waiting for the right time."

"Yeah? I think we have a difference of opinion on what the right time is." I smirked, then pulled his sweater up and dotted kisses over his lower abs and to the waist of his jeans.

I continued to tease him as his head fell back on the couch and a soft moan escaped him. Fumbling with his button and zipper, I finally freed his thick erection from its prison.

I peeked up at him as I ran my tongue along the tip of his cock. "Does that feel good?"

"Shit," he hissed. His hand traveled down to the inside of my thigh while I slicked him up with my mouth, then hollowed out my cheeks.

"Fuck!" His head shot off the couch and he thrust into my mouth. "When did you learn that?"

I giggled but continued. It wasn't polite to talk with my mouth full. Rolling over, I gave him my undivided attention and worshipped every inch of his dick. I wasn't sure if I was in love with Holden, but I was definitely addicted to this part of him.

"Sit up, babe." Holden gently nudged me away.

I did as he asked.

"Take off your shorts," he growled.

While I shimmied out of the rest of my clothes, Holden stepped out of his jeans, then tossed his sweater on the floor.

"Scoot up," he ordered.

After I was situated, Holden crawled on top of me and placed his dick between my lips. I moaned as he fucked my mouth, and I dug my manicured, hot pink nails into his ass cheeks. Holden moved my good leg off the couch, then spread my folds.

"My favorite meal of the day," he said before lowering his head and kissing my pussy.

I bucked against him and dragged my fingernails down his thighs. His tongue lapped at my swollen clit while his fingers pumped into me. I cupped his balls and sucked them gently. He raised his head, a moan of pleasure escaping him as I continued.

"River, babe. You need to stop."

I gave him one more firm stroke, then he hopped off the couch.

"What is it?" I asked, fearful I'd done something wrong.

"Oh, God. Nothing. I was about to lose my shit, and I don't want it to be over yet." He scrubbed his face with his hands and blew out a sigh. My attention traveled over his muscular body to the dusting of hair and the V of his lower abdomen.

"Take me to your room," I whispered.

Without any effort at all, he swept me up, his strong arms slipping under my knees and around my back as he scooped me off the couch. I placed my head against his shoulder.

"This is where you belong, River. Next to me." He placed a kiss on my hair, then hurried up both sets of stairs.

He gently lowered me onto his bed, and I sank into the plush navy comforter. "Are you comfortable?" He eyed my cast.

I reached up and traced his strong jawline. "Holden ..." A lump formed in my throat. "I—"

Holden's cell phone interrupted what I was about to tell him, and I inwardly sighed. If it was Holden's dad, his timing sucked.

"Sorry, babe. I need to take it. It's Dad."

I gulped. What would his dad think if he knew we were naked in his son's room?

I watched Holden leave, appreciating the mouthwatering view of his muscular ass and legs.

Earlier, my insides quaked when Holden had looked at me with so much love in his eyes. It was as if Holden had reached inside of me and held my heart, massaging it back to life.

"Sounds good, Dad. Tell Mom hi." Holden waltzed back into the room, then placed his phone on the nightstand.

"How are they?" I asked as he crawled into bed next to me.

"Fine. Dad just needs me to run some errands for him tomorrow. I'll do it after you get your cast off." He rolled over on his side and propped his head up on his fist. "What were you going to say before Dad called?"

I chewed on my bottom lip. "I don't remember." I offered him a smile in an attempt to hide my lie.

"Will this help you to remember?" He lowered his mouth to my breast and tugged my nipple between his teeth.

"Maybe?" I slid my fingers into the back of his dark hair. "Have you ever used the Voyeur Room?" I mentally scolded myself for blurting out my question.

"Yeah."

Curiosity stirred inside me. "Which side of the wall were you on? The one with the bed, or the one with the couch where you could watch?"

Holden cleared his throat. "Both." He paused. "River, I'll answer any questions you have, but where is this coming from?" He took my hand in his, softly kissing my knuckles.

"I just wondered what it was like." I looked away from him, embarrassed that I'd asked.

"Do you want to try it? Is that why you're asking?"

I gave him a half shrug. "Maybe. I'm not sure."

"What if we made sure you could leave, and let you set the rules?" Kindness filled his expression.

I pondered his suggestion for a moment. "I don't know what guidelines to try."

"I would recommend that we start as observers. At any time, we can leave the room. If you're not comfortable after a few minutes, then that's it. No pressure, babe. I realize this is all a new experience for you."

I wondered how I'd managed to fall for someone that was so patient with me. "What about tomorrow night?" My voice hovered above a whisper as my pulse skyrocketed.

Holden pinned me with his stare, and I assumed he was searching for any signs that I wasn't ready to try it. "I'll reserve the room for us. If you change your mind, then we'll find another way to celebrate."

"Okay." Overwhelmed with gratitude that he continued to allow me to explore without any judgment, I leaned up and kissed him. His mouth parted, and he gently sucked on my tongue, my scent still on his lips from earlier.

"Holden?"

"Yeah, babe." He nuzzled my neck and nipped at my ear.

"It's working." I tilted my head, allowing him better access to the sensitive skin.

"What is?" Holden's kisses dotted my collarbone and I shuddered.

I leaned in close to his ear. "I'm falling for you."

Chapter Twenty-Four

Holden looked up, our gaze connecting. I placed his hand on my chest.

"You're falling for me like ... as in the boy next door who is hot?" He lifted a brow at me, a playful grin spreading across his handsome face.

I laughed softly, appreciating that he was allowing me to ease into this conversation. "No."

He brushed his mouth against mine. "As in ... you think about me all the time, miss me when I'm not with you, and can't wait until you see me again?"

I nodded. "Like that."

"It's the same for me." He smoothed my hair, then placed his palm on my chest. "Your heart is racing, River."

"I know. That's what you do to me."

Holden rubbed my cheek with his thumb, his features growing serious. "That's good, River, because I'm already in love with you."

"What?" My brows knitted together. "You are?"

He peered right inside me, setting my world on fire. "Madly, insanely, and crazily in love with you."

Every steel wall I'd built around myself shattered at his words. My body trembled from the intensity of how much I cared about him. It scared the shit out of me, but he'd proven over and over that his feelings had nothing to do with Hannah. With him, I felt as though I came first with someone and that I was the center of his universe.

"Make love to me, Holden. Show me how much you love me." Tears blurred my vision as my emotions started to free fall through space and time.

"Are you sure?" His intense gaze probed mine for permission.

"Yes." Raw need surged through my body, but now my feelings were involved, which intensified my desire for him.

Holden rolled over, opened the nightstand drawer, and removed a condom. He ripped the foil packet open, then slid it over his erection. My eyes followed his every movement.

"I want to make sure you're ready." His hand danced between my thighs, his fingers slickening with my juices. Holden massaged my clit in gentle circles as I lifted my hips, needing more. Needing all of him.

I parted my legs, allowing him better access.

Holden hovered over me. The muscles in his biceps bulged as he stayed there, searching for any signs of fear or resistance. "You're sure?" he asked.

I leaned up and kissed him deeply, our tongues tangling as I was once again swept up in the moment with him. "Please don't make me wait any longer." I nipped his lower lip and he moaned softly.

Holden's eyes never left mine as he positioned himself at my entrance. "If at any time you need to stop, tell me."

"I promise."

Pressure filled my core as he slid into me. "I know my feelings are ahead of yours, but I love you, River. From the moment I saw you, I knew you owned my heart."

Tears streamed down my cheeks as he gently eased in and out of me, and he kissed them away. "River, you're the light in my world ..."

Holden's gentle words were a healing salve to my broken soul. No one had loved or cherished me as much as he had. He continued to move in a sweet, slow rhythm. I ran my hands over the dips and valleys of his muscular back and hiccupped through my tears.

He paused and shuddered. "I'm sorry. It's been a while, and it's more intense than I anticipated." He leaned his forehead against mine. "What they say is true, though. Sex is so much better when you love the person that you're with." With a strong thrust, he groaned. "Jesus. You feel so good."

I lifted my hips, encouraging him to continue as I dug my fingernails into his ass cheeks. Our bodies rocked in sync, my climax stirring deep inside me.

I nipped at his shoulder, then his ear. "I love you inside of me, Holden."

His lips claimed mine and my mouth melted into his, moaning as his hot tongue explored me.

Jolts of pleasure rippled over me, and I whimpered. I broke our kiss. "Baby, oh God." I rocked against him, picking up the pace. The world stopped as I shattered, drowning in waves of intense pleasure, coming apart and being made whole at the same time.

"You're so goddamn beautiful when you come." His thrusts quickened as he pushed into me two more times before he came, my name on his lips as he released.

Holden relaxed on top of me and kissed me as I wrapped my arms around him. "Thank you," I whispered.

He lifted his head. "For what?" Love and awe filled his expression.

"For replacing those awful memories with something I'll cherish for the rest of my life." Even as the words filled the air, I realized there wasn't anything I could say that could help him understand the gift he'd given me.

"You don't have to tell me until you're ready, but I love you so much. I haven't ever felt this way about anyone before." Holden kissed the tip of my nose, then pulled out of me. "I'll be right back."

I grinned like a fool as he strolled into the bathroom. The sound of water running filled the otherwise quiet room. He returned with a washcloth and carefully cleaned me up. As stupid as it sounded, that act felt more intimate than the sex we'd had.

The floor creaked as Holden headed toward the clothes hamper in the closet.

"Holy shit!" a male voice said from the doorway of the bedroom.

My scream split the air as I struggled to cover myself.

Before I realized what happened, Holden barreled across the room and shoved Jace backward. "Don't fucking look at her!" Then he slammed the door in Jace's face.

"Why is he here?" I scrambled to find my clothes, but then I remembered they were downstairs.

"God dammit. I never lock the doors, and they're used to walking into the house unannounced." Holden's head hung down. "Are you okay?"

"Just startled. Plus, he saw me naked." Heat dusted my cheeks as I tugged the comforter up to my neck.

Holden sat down on the bed next to me, the mattress dipping slightly beneath his weight. "You have my word that no one will ever touch you without your permission again. If Jace, Chance, or anyone else lays a hand on you, I'll destroy them." Fierce protectiveness rolled off him in waves.

"Do you think he would?" My forehead creased in confusion.

"No, but you need to understand that I'll never let anything happen to you."

Even though I knew that his words were too big of a promise for him to ever be able to keep, I lied to myself anyway and anchored his words in my heart.

Chapter Twenty-Five

"Oh my God. This feels so weird." I looked at Holden, then walked slowly with my new cane. I was surprised at how much lighter my leg was once the cast had been removed.

"It's only for a few weeks," Holden assured me, his hand on my lower back as we entered the house through the front door. He quickly locked it and set the alarm. "I let everyone know they have to text and use the doorbell from now on." A sheepish grin spread across his handsome face.

My stomach flip-flopped with the reminder of Jace walking in on me naked in Holden's bed after we'd made love for the first time. Horrified didn't even begin to explain how I felt. But the memory of Holden inside of me made my core throb with longing.

Grinning, I looked around the gorgeous foyer. "Now that I can walk without crutches, will you finally give me a tour of the rest of the house? We're always either in your room or downstairs, and I know there's more to see."

"Babe, it's a ten thousand square foot home. Are you sure? It's a lot of walking right out of the gate."

I looked around and pondered how this might go down. Sucking on my bottom lip, I approached him, then ran my fingernails over his chest and down his black fitted long-sleeved shirt. "If I get tired, will you give me a ride?" I peeked up at him through my eyelashes as I caressed his dick through his jeans.

Holden leaned down and brushed his lips against mine. "You can have as many rides as you need."

"Then let's do it." I grabbed his ass for good measure.

Holden slipped his arm around my waist and led me to the left of the foyer. "I'll show you the game room, formal dining room, and the guest bedrooms first."

"There's more bedrooms?" I couldn't hide the shock in my tone. There were already two downstairs and three upstairs.

"There's also a kitchen and a mudroom that leads to the four-car garage. My parents' room and office are on the other side of the house. They wanted to ensure they have privacy when they're home and working."

"Holy shit," I said as we entered a dining room with a large chandelier hanging over the center of a long cherrywood table that easily sat twelve. I wondered why they had so many chairs when Holden hadn't ever discussed relatives or holidays. A beautiful hutch matched the other furniture, and a full set of white china and wine glasses sparkled behind the glass doors.

"It's not been used since ... Hannah left."

I didn't miss the sadness in his words.

"I'm so sorry." If anything, I understood the loneliness that accompanied not having a family, but I suspected it was amplified when you did have one and weren't close.

Holden showed me the guest rooms next. By the time we arrived at the last one, my leg throbbed with each additional step, but I pushed through it.

"Growing up, I spent a lot of days here with Jace, Chance, Hannah, and Brynn. We still use it, but not as often."

"Holy crap." I gawked at the largest television I'd seen in my life.

A pool table sat to one side of the room and a foosball table next to it. Rows of shelves were lined with games and DVDs. A fully stocked bar and two black sectional couches filled the space. "You could add a weight set in here, too."

"We have a gym."

I rolled my eyes at him. "Of course, you do." I laughed. "Will you teach me to play pool some time?"

Holden's brows shot up. "You've never played?"

"Nope." I ran my fingertips along the back of the couches, the soft leather feeling cool against my skin. "What was it like?" I turned to him. "To grow up wealthy and not wondering where your next meal was coming from?"

Holden sat on the back of the sofa, his expression serious. "It never crossed my mind. I always had food, clothes, limos, and house-keepers." He folded his arms across his chest. "I'll never pretend to understand what it was like for you, but I'm guessing that we both had a lot of lonely years. The majority of my memories with my parents were when I was younger. Right after my tenth birthday, they started traveling all of the time. We had a nanny, but I think that Hannah's lack of supervision and an active parent in her life drove her to find that love and security elsewhere. Unfortunately, she looked for it in the wrong places and it cost Hannah her life." Guilt and pain clung to Holden's words, piercing my heart.

I leaned on my cane, shifting my weight from my healing leg to my good one. "I'm learning that loneliness doesn't have boundaries. Regardless, if someone is poor or rich, the feelings of abandonment can be the same."

Holden placed a sweet kiss on my palm. The warmth of his touch traveled up my arm. "I'm not lonely anymore." His words caressed my soul, whispering promises of safety and a new life with him.

"Me either." I closed the gap between us, then kissed him tenderly.

Holden's mouth opened, and his tongue swept across mine, tasting and taking what I was giving him. His hand slid up my bare thigh, and he palmed my ass through my shorts, pulling me between his legs.

The sound of the doorbell startled me, and I jumped.

Holden checked his watch. "It should be Brynn. I asked her to pick you up a few things for tonight."

"Oh?" I couldn't help but grin. Brynn had amazing taste in clothes, so I was always excited to see what she selected.

Holden pulled his phone from his back pocket, and his fingers danced across the screen. "I can unlock the front door with my cell now." He held it up.

"Really? I had no idea someone could do that." I peeked at the app he was referring to.

"After Jace showing up unannounced, I thought I'd better look into a solution that allowed them into the house without me having to run to answer it every time they showed up."

"And it works beautifully," Brynn said, smiling as she joined us in the game room, carrying a black garment bag. Her long red hair flowed down her back and her blue blouse accentuated her eyes. I made a mental note to ask Brynn what kind of jeans she wore. Her ass and long legs always looked amazing.

"Hey." I returned her smile and walked toward her for a hug.

"I'm so excited that you have your cast off." Brynn gave me a warm embrace with her free arm. "Are you ready to see what's in the bag?" She wiggled her eyebrows at me, then turned her attention to Holden. "We'll see you later. It's girl time."

Holden chuckled. "Be ready by eight."

"Why so early?" I asked.

"I need to be there before the clients arrive," he explained.

It finally dawned on me that he hadn't given Brynn details of our plans tonight, which I appreciated. She wouldn't think anything of Holden and me going to the club to celebrate that my cast had been removed. The fact that Holden and I were going to try out the Voyeur Room was too personal for me to share. Maybe that would change soon.

"Let's go." Brynn took my hand and led me upstairs to the bedroom I'd used before I moved into Holden's.

"I feel like it's been forever since I saw you, but it's only been a few days." It wasn't as though I had much to tell Brynn. I was sure she'd heard all about Jace walking in on us.

As if she were in my mind, she grinned as we reached the guest bedroom. "So, when did you move into Holden's bed?" She closed the door and hung the garment bag in the closet.

"Last night." I lowered my head, my cheeks flaming red.

"Oh. You two finally got past all the playing around and slept together." Brynn's eyes widened, then a huge grin eased across her face.

"Yeah. He kept making me wait." I giggled, suddenly shy.

"That's because he wanted to make sure that you were ready," Brynn assured me. "Well thank God I brought my dress over, too. I figured you had some deets to share." She rubbed her palms together, nearly giddy. "I'm so excited that you two are a couple. I mean, I knew that you were into each other, but when Jace walked in on you naked ..." She planted her hands on her slender hips. "Is it wrong to say that I'm jealous he saw you without any clothes?"

I made a choking sound. "He discussed what he saw with you?"

Brynn waved it off. "Babe, we all discuss everything."

She strolled across the room, then reached into the bathroom, flipping on the light. "Well, we did until you came along. Holden's been really discreet about what's going on with you. We see the looks and kisses, but he won't discuss anything." She approached me and placed her hands on my shoulders. "I've never seen him happier." Brynn wrapped me in a warm embrace. "He deserves something good in his life." She stepped back, assessing me. "Why don't you take a shower and wash the cast residue off your leg? I'll dry and fix your hair and makeup." She beamed at me.

"Okay." I glanced down, then grinned like a little kid. "I can wear jeans now!" I laughed.

"Do you own any? I've only ever seen you in shorts and the cast."

My forehead creased as I realized I had one pair left in my backpack. The ones I was wearing when I got hit by the car had been torn and ruined.

"One." Suddenly embarrassed by the fact that I didn't own many clothes, I sat on the edge of the bed. "Um, Brynn ... I'm just trailer trash." My voice cracked at the horrible reminder that I didn't fit into Holden's world. "Holden offered to let me borrow Mallory's shirts and shorts since we're the same size. I mean, you and I bought bras and underwear at the same time we purchased my dress for the club, but ..."

Brynn sat down on the bed and tucked her legs beneath her. "You're not trash, River. You're one of us. Trash is someone that's mean and vicious without a second thought about others. Trash is someone that refuses to see their value and lives the same life of crime and never makes changes. That's not you. Holden would never fall for trash." Brynn reached up and brushed a stray hair from my cheek. "If you don't believe me, then just keep spending time with us and I'll keep hammering it into that beautiful head of yours." She sighed, her shoulders slumping slightly. "River, we haven't talked about the club and what you saw the night Holden showed you the rooms."

"What's there to talk about?" I wasn't sure I wanted to have this conversation.

"The fact that Jace, Chance, Holden, and I are very close friends. The sex club," she said softly. "I know it had to have been a lot to digest. And you learned things about me that I hadn't told you because it was more than my secret to share. When Holden said he needed to be honest with you, he sat every member down and asked our permission."

"That was cool of him." My knee bounced up and down, my anxiety shooting through the roof.

"I also don't want you to be concerned that because I'm bisexual that it changes our friendship. It doesn't ... at least not on my side."

I finally realized where she was headed. "Brynn, I'm straight, but who you sleep with is no one's business, even mine, and I consider us friends. I was surprised, but I was also a little jealous."

Brynn frowned. "Jealous?"

"You all are so free, and sex almost destroyed my life ... until now. I wonder how different I would be if I had met you all sooner."

Brynn gave me an understanding smile. "I get it. You're with Holden now, too, so it's safe to explore. And if you have any questions about toys or BDSM or anything, I'm here for you. I want you to be happy. You deserve an amazing guy like Holden."

"I'm scared, Brynn. I'm afraid I'll lose him and if I do, then I lose you too. I'm not sure I could handle it."

Brynn waved me off as her eyes grew misty. "You know what? I've always wanted a sister. Now I have one."

"Yeah? Me too."

"Definitely. No matter what happens between you and Holden, you're stuck with me." Brynn laughed, then a peaceful silence filled the space between us. "For now, take a shower so we can get ready." Brynn hopped off the bed and took her phone from her purse. "Sail" by Awolnation played from her speakers. "Gotta have tunes." She winked at me. "I'm starving. Do you want anything from the kitchen?"

"Something to drink would be great."

Brynn left the room and I stood, the pain in my leg better now that I'd had a break. Shit, I still hadn't seen all the rooms in the house before the throbbing had started. I didn't mind, though. I could explore later.

* * *

The sight of Holden standing near the front door wearing a black suit and light blue dress shirt stole my breath as I descended the stairs. He adjusted his cufflinks, then glanced up at me. The adoration and love in his eyes sent my heart into overdrive. He melted me on the spot.

Approaching the bottom step, he held his hand out to me. "You're beautiful," he whispered.

"Thank you." I took the last stair gingerly with the cane and the black strappy heels I was wearing. "You look amazing yourself."

Holden leaned down and gently brushed his lips against mine. "I'm glad I chose the gold dress for you." His fingers glided down my sides and rested on my hip.

"What? You picked it out?" The material glittered as it caught the light from the chandelier in the foyer. I'd nearly had a shit fit when I tried it on. The length had barely covered my ass cheeks. Brynn had adjusted it, but it was still shorter than I would ever worn before.

Holden grinned. "And the shoes."

"He has better taste than I do," Brynn said from behind me, taking the stairs in her stilettos like it was nothing. Her black dress dipped into a deep V in the front, exposing most of her breasts and stomach, then ended right below her belly button. "I have dibs on taking her shopping for jeans and anything else she needs now that she has her cast off."

"We'll see," Holden chuckled. "I might need to help her in the dressing room."

My cheeks burned at his words. At times I forgot how close he was to Brynn, and a comment like that meant nothing to them. It was all just fun and games.

"I didn't mean to embarrass you." Holden took my free hand and led me to the closet. He pulled out a see-through black wrap and placed it around my shoulders. Brynn followed us as we exited the house.

I shivered as the chilly evening air brushed against my bare legs. The limo was waiting for us, and I immediately recognized Zayne, who stood next to the back door.

"Zayne," Holden said.

"Sir."

I glanced at Brynn, who was appreciating the fit of Zayne's black slacks and white shirt that accentuated his broad chest and muscular arms. I was pretty sure she would be happy to help him out of his clothes if he was willing.

Once we were settled in, Zayne closed the door. I snuggled up to Holden while Brynn sat across from us, her dress riding up her toned thigh. I peeked at Holden, wondering if he was thinking about sex he'd had with Brynn in the past. Inwardly I sighed with relief when I realized his eyes were on my legs, not hers. I loved Brynn, but she was gorgeous, and it was weird to know that Holden and Brynn had slept together ... a lot.

A combination of anxiety and eagerness flooded my senses as I pondered what our time in the Voyeur Room would be like. Regardless, if I bolted out of there or was able to relax and have an amazing experience, I promised I wouldn't judge myself. This was new, and as long as Holden was next to me, I felt safe enough to explore.

Half an hour later, the four of us entered 4 Play through another entrance that led us to the elevator. Instead of going down, Holden pushed the up button. "Drinks first." He winked at me. "Plus, the guys are here, and they want to say hi."

"At least I have my clothes on," I mumbled.

Brynn snickered. "I'm guessing not for long."

I glared at her, not wanting Zayne to overhear.

The doors slid open, allowing the music from the VIP level to reach my ears. "Break My Heart Myself" by Bebe Rexha blared through the speakers, the boom of the bass shaking the floor beneath me.

Holden held his arm out, and I slid mine through his. I self-consciously reached up and touched my necklace with the diamond H on it. Holden's brown eyes flashed with pride, then he lowered his mouth to my ear. "Everyone knows you're mine and it makes my cock so hard it hurts."

A gasp escaped me, and my core pulsed at his words. I was naïve in some areas, but I wasn't stupid. Holden had marked me, branded me, and for some reason, it turned me on. Images of being handcuffed and blindfolded with him sent ripples of heat through my body. I made a mental note to ask if he liked that scenario, but first I needed to make it through the evening.

"Let's grab a drink, then we need to head downstairs before my clients arrive."

I nodded, afraid my voice would betray my fear and excitement.

Over the next hour, I had a few White Russians and enjoyed the time spent with Jace, Chance, and Brynn. Zayne remained next to our corner table, his alert green eyes constantly surveying the area. Butterflies fluttered in the pit of my stomach with each minute that ticked by. I knew Holden wanted me as relaxed as possible before we visited the Voyeur Room, but wouldn't our friends know where we went?

As if on cue, Brynn stood and smoothed a hand over her fitted black dress. "Anyone want to join me?" Her attention bounced between Jace and Chance. Chance rose, the bulge in his gray slacks obvious. Jace slipped his arm around her petite waist, and they all exchanged looks.

"We'll see you guys later." Brynn gave us a little wave as she walked away with the guys.

"Master's Playroom?" I asked, my eyes glued to the three of them.

"Yes." Holden tilted his glass, swirling the brandy around before he finished his drink. He glanced at his watch, then stood. "Are you ready?"

Chapter Twenty-Six

My heart jackhammered in my chest, but I stood anyway. Without a word, Holden took my hand in his and led us back to the elevator. Every eye was on us as we walked past the other customers. I wasn't sure if it was because I was with Holden or because of the cane.

Minutes later, we arrived at the entrance of the Voyeur Room. "Just remember, we can leave at any time. You're in complete control, River." Holden leaned down and kissed me before he opened the door.

On shaky legs, I hurried to the couch and sat on the edge of it.

"I have an idea." He sat on the chaise lounge, then parted his legs and patted the space between them. I settled in, then rested my back against his chest.

"Are you comfortable?" He stroked my arm.

"Yeah." I relaxed into him, allowing my body to mold to his.

"My dick has been hard ever since I watched you walk down the stairs tonight." He tilted his hips up, his erection pressing into me.

Holden gathered my long hair, then placed it over one shoulder. I glanced up at him, and saw his eyes filled with raw desire. His fingers danced over the necklace, then trailed over my collarbone and to the edge of my strapless dress. Delightful shivers traveled up my spine as his hand disappeared into the bodice, and he gently pulled on my nipple.

"What do you think about when I'm not touching you, River?" His minty breath caressed my cheek as he spoke. Holden lowered the top, exposing my breasts. "What do you want to try?" His voice was low and gruff.

"Tonight?" I squeaked.

"Or any time that you're ready, babe."

I looked down as he continued to play with my tits.

"Spread your legs," he ordered.

I did as he asked.

"Earlier today, I thought about bending you over the pool table, tugging down your shorts, and giving that sweet ass a good spanking."

A gasp escaped me. "Spanking?" People did that?

"One of my favorite things, River." His confession stoked the fire that was already burning through me. "When I was done, I would fuck you hard. Your tight, hot pussy would clench around my cock as I plowed into you." He rubbed the inside of my thigh as he spoke, then slowly trailed up to my core. "Jesus, fuck, you're not wearing panties."

"Do you like it? It was my little secret, and I thought about your hand sliding up my dress all night." I sucked in a breath as he circled my clit and I panted. "What else do you think about?" Maybe I should have run after the spanking confession, but I found it insanely hot.

"You sucking my dick until I come all over your perfect tits. Then I'd fuck you with a dual vibrator."

I lifted my hips up, needing his fingers inside me.

"I've never tried one." I bit my lip as the curtain began to rise, revealing a couple that appeared to be in their twenties. The blonde-haired woman had a butterfly tattoo on her right ass cheek. The dark-haired guy was tall, muscular, and incredibly well-endowed.

168

Holden and I fell silent as we watched the duo. The girl was bent over the man's knee, and he smacked her butt. She cried out in pain as he spanked her again.

Oh my God. He had been testing me to see my reaction before he raised the curtain. "You knew. You knew we'd be seeing this."

Holden pinched my bundle of nerves, and I threw my head back, pleasure coursing through me.

"Open your eyes," he demanded.

I nodded and focused on the activity on the other side of the viewing glass. Another man entered the room, his thick erection resting in his palm. He stood there, stroking his hard dick in his hand while the other guy continued to spank the girl. Her cry filled the room, then the second man rubbed her red skin.

"Your pussy is dripping wet," the second guy said as he knelt, spread her apart, and started tongue fucking her.

"Oh shit." *My God, why is this turning me on so bad?*

"Do you like that?" Holden asked.

"Yeah," I confessed.

The girl moaned with pleasure as the guy lapped up her juices. Once he was finished, he stood and spanked her.

The man on the bed laid down, then she crawled on top of him, sliding down on his cock. He grabbed her hips and bucked into her. With her back to us, she leaned forward, allowing us a full view of the situation.

"I want you to ride me like that, babe." Holden eased two fingers inside me, pumping me while I nearly came. "That's it." Holden's breathing became jagged as I squirmed on the seat in front of him and he ground his hips against me.

My attention returned to the threesome. The man who had been eating her out straddled the other guy's legs. He ran his cock over her folds, then eased into her puckered hole.

She leaned forward, taking him in.

"I hear a girl comes twice as hard that way." Holden removed his slick fingers, then spread my ass cheeks. "I won't hurt you. I swear."

His finger massaged my asshole, then he slid it in just a little while his other played with my clit. "Are you okay?"

"Yes. Oh. God!" My body had a mind of its own as I bucked against him, wanting and needing more. Heat curled deep inside me as he continued. I slammed my eyes closed, black dots floating before my eyelids. I gripped his forearm and screamed his name as I came apart in an earth-shattering orgasm. Before I completely returned to my senses, he lifted his hips, and I tugged his pants down along with his boxer briefs. His cock sprung free, and my tongue darted across my lower lip. With a quick move, I shoved him into me, startling him. "By the way, I'm on the pill."

"You feel so good like this, I almost don't care if you're on birth control," he moaned, gripping my thighs. The heels of my palms pushed on the back of the sofa for additional leverage as I slid up and down his cock. My tits bounced as I rode him hard.

"That's it, River." He fisted my hair and pulled my head back as he sucked on my nipple.

Holden and I had made love last night, but this was pure, animalistic lust driving us this time. He bit my nipple just hard enough to cause pain and pleasure mixed into one.

I raised up, and he moved his hand to my butt, then fucked my ass with his finger. The sensation overwhelmed me, my pants and groans growing louder.

"Do you feel safe?" Holden asked me.

"Yes." My cheeks flushed and a newfound heat coursed through my body.

He quickly lifted me off him. "On your knees."

I whimpered as I dropped to the floor. Holden stroked his cock, and I licked my lips in anticipation. "If you're a good girl, I'll let you suck it. For now, bend over my lap."

I knew where this was going, and although I wasn't sure what to expect, I knew without a shadow of a doubt I was okay with Holden.

I positioned myself over his legs, and he spread my slick folds. He pinched my butt cheek, and I yelped in pain. Holden rubbed it out, then spanked me.

I moaned, liking it way too much.

"You're hot as hell bent over my lap like this." He spanked me again, and I bit my lip as the sting traveled through my legs. My body lurched forward as he smacked me harder. But instead of begging him to stop, I encouraged him.

"Is this what you like Holden? Control? Pain?"

He growled as he shoved two fingers inside me. "You're drenched." His cock lay against his stomach, precum on the tip. I grabbed him and angled my head so I could suck it off.

He raised his hand again. The harder he spanked me the harder I sucked. He seemed to forget that I was used to pain, and this kind was so much better.

Holden moved me away, and his dick popped out of my mouth. Without a word, he stood, then bent me over. He pushed at my entrance, only giving me a little at a time.

"Holden," I whimpered. "Fuck me, please."

He kneaded my ass cheeks as he continued to torture me. *"Please."*

He held me firm, then plunged into me. Holden slammed into me over and over until I was moaning his name again. My core clenched around him as sheer ecstasy claimed me.

"Fuck!" Holden yelled as he buried himself deep inside.

To my surprise, he pulled out. I peeked over my shoulder as he jacked off and came on me.

He sank to his knees and kissed my inner thigh, his hot breath grazing my sensitive skin.

"River?" He stood and tugged his pants up while I collapsed on the furniture, still attempting to recover.

"Yeah?" I looked up at him, expecting to see a hungry look in his expression, but there was nothing but gentleness.

"Are you okay?"

I sat up and adjusted my boobs back into the top of my dress. I smiled at him shyly. "I liked it." Guilt knotted my stomach into little balls. Maybe I shouldn't have liked my introduction to rough sex, but I did. At the same time, I felt dirty and wanted to find comfort in his arms.

He sat on the floor in front of me, his dark brown eyes searching me for any signs that I wasn't telling him everything. He rubbed his clean-shaven jaw. "I like sex. A lot. But crossing lines won't work."

I frowned. "Did I do something wrong?"

Holden shook his head. "No, but I'm afraid I pushed you tonight. It's easy to get caught up in the moment." His shoulders slumped. "If I went too far, I'd feel like shit."

I sat up and placed my hands on both sides of his face. "Do you love me?"

Holden's intense gaze connected with mine. "I love you more than life itself."

I leaned forward and kissed him gently. "That's why I'm okay trying out what I like. What works for us. I know you'd never hurt me, baby. You have my word that I'll tell you if we need to stop."

"Swear it to me." Holden's words hitched in his throat.

"I swear."

Although we were establishing clear lines in our relationship, I couldn't help but wonder what had happened in his past for him to be so worried. For now, I would revel in the bliss of the hottest night of sex I'd ever had in my life, not to mention with the man that I loved.

After we arrived home and crawled into our bed, Holden made slow, sweet love to me that night. My body was sore from our earlier sexcapade, but I longed for his healing touch. His eyes never left mine as he poured his heart into me. With every thrust, Holden claimed another piece of my soul, and I willingly gave it to him.

Chapter Twenty-Seven

The bright morning sunlight spilled through the parted curtains. I stretched, the ache in my body reminding me of the crazy time at the club the evening before. I grinned as I rolled over, the soft, dark blue sheets rubbing against my bare skin.

My lip jutted out when I saw that Holden had already left the bed. After we'd made love, he held me most of the night. Apparently, I'd gotten too hot and moved away from him. I sat up slowly and eyed the alarm clock on his nightstand. *Holy shit!* I'd slept until almost one in the afternoon.

I flung the covers off me and headed straight to Holden's shower. He wouldn't be home for a while since he had a late class, but I'd wanted to have time to clean up the house. Although a housekeeper came in a few times a week, I still wanted to contribute. It was the least I could do for Holden taking me in. Plus, I wanted to surprise him with lasagna tonight. Addison and I had made the recipe for her parents, and I loved it as much as they had.

An ache clutched my chest. I needed to call her. I'd been a shit friend by not reaching out more. After Holden had given me a phone,

I'd text her several times, but her responses were short, and she hadn't reached back out to me. I wanted to explain what had happened, but a part of me had slammed the door on Dan and his abuse. I didn't want to open that box of horror again. I was finally moving forward with Holden. Who I was a few months ago wasn't the same girl standing naked and happy in her boyfriend's bathroom. But maybe Addison had found someone too. It was painful to admit we were different people than we were five months ago when she left for college.

After I showered and dressed in a Victoria's Secret sweatshirt and shorts, I realized I had no idea where the washer and dryer were. Grabbing my cane, I wandered down the hall, then down the stairs to the main floor. Logically, it would make sense that there were a few in this large of a house. Although Holden had shown me the guest and game rooms, I still didn't know where his parents slept. I stood in the foyer, debating which direction to turn.

The cold marble floors chilled my bare feet as I turned left on the main floor. From what I recalled, Holden's parents' master bedroom and the office were on this side.

An eerie feeling settled on my shoulders as I called out, "Hello," just in case anyone was here. My voice echoed through the emptiness. I bit my lip and walked down the hall, noticing that there was a bathroom on the left. Pausing before a closed door on the right, I gently tried the doorknob, but it was locked. Once I reached the end, I located the utility room on the left and another closed door across from it. I glanced behind me, convinced I wasn't alone. I tried the handle in front of me, but it was locked, too. I blew out a sigh, realizing my nerves and overactive imagination were fucking with me. It was spooky walking around Holden's house without him here.

I hurried back down the hallway as fast as I could with my cane. I'd look for another laundry room. This part of the home was freaking me out. Before I searched downstairs, I realized it would be easier to gather our dirty clothes and bring them down with me. I laughed softly. Slide them down the stairs was more like it. I couldn't carry the basket with only one hand. With a plan in place, I made my way to Holden's room again. My heart hammered something fierce as I sat on the edge of our bed. Becky's words flashed across my mind again, and this time I couldn't shake the feeling that something was wrong.

I stood and chided myself for being silly. My old fears were screwing with me. I'd had to constantly look over my shoulder and wait for Dan's wrath. That was all—just lingering feelings. Holden had been nothing but amazing to me since he'd found me in his recycling bin.

* * *

After poking around on the lower level, I located a utility room, and for the remainder of the afternoon, I cleaned and vacuumed. I listened to Spotify while I busied myself with dinner. For some reason, I felt safer in the walk-out basement or in Holden's room than in the rest of the house.

A little after five in the evening, the sound of the slider opening caught my attention from the kitchen and my head popped up.

"Hey, babe." Holden closed the door behind him, and I sighed with relief.

"Hey." I gave him a warm smile, then laid the last lasagna noodle down.

"You're the best thing I've seen all day." Holden strolled over to me. He gathered me in his arms, then lifted me.

My giggle filled the room. "I missed you today."

Holden kissed me gently, then set my feet on the floor.

"It looks like you've been busy." He grinned as he eyed the pan of lasagna that was almost ready to pop in the oven.

I picked up the bag of shredded cheese and sprinkled it on extra thick. "It's been so good to have my cast off, I ended up cleaning and doing our laundry. I hope that was okay."

"I'm glad to see you up and moving. You don't need to clean the house, but I'm sure Tina will appreciate it."

I wiped my hands off on a towel, then opened the oven. Heat rushed out, and I took a step back. Once it had diminished, I slid the pan of goodness in and closed the door. My gaze roamed over the control panel again until I found the timer option and set it.

The buzzer on the dryer alerted me that it was finished, and I grabbed my cane and moved in that direction.

Holden chuckled and followed me. "I'll help."

We filed into the room, and I removed the clothes.

"I'm going to take you up on that since it will be harder for me to drag it up the stairs. It was a lot easier letting the basket slide down on its own."

"I've got it, babe." He leaned down and kissed me again, then he grasped the handles, and we headed to his room. I mentally debated asking him about the locked rooms down the hall, but I didn't want him to think I was snooping.

We folded our jeans and shorts and put them in his dresser. He'd given me a few drawers and half the closet, but I didn't have anything to hang up other than the dresses I'd worn to 4 Play. Now that my cast was off, I definitely needed more clothes.

Holden disappeared into the huge walk-in and gathered some hangers. It was strange to realize how domestic we were. How easily we had fallen into a routine, sharing a space and bed.

"Babe?" Holden asked as he hung up our shirts.

"Yeah?"

"You seem out of it. Are you sure you're okay? I mean with what happened at the club last night?" He leaned against the doorframe, worry lines creasing his forehead as he studied me.

"I'm fine. I promise. I was just thinking how easily we fell into a routine is all." My attention swept over the room before landing on his desk. I walked over and realized something had gotten caught beneath the glass top and the wood. Hoping that whatever it was hadn't been damaged, I gently tugged at it, recognizing it as a picture.

The faces came into view, and my mouth dropped open, horror coursing through my body.

"What the hell?" I spun around, my eyes widening.

My hand trembled as I held the image up for him to see.

"Babe, what's wrong?" Holden hurried toward me, and I flipped up my cane and jabbed the end of it into his chest.

"Don't. Touch. Me." My voice was laced with steel. I mentally calculated how I could move around him and out of the bedroom. Currently, I was cornered.

Holden stepped back and raised his palms in surrender. "River, I don't understand what's happening. Please talk to me." He backed away farther after realizing I was trapped.

My chest heaved as I held up the picture. "Do you know who this is?"

"Yeah. It's my dad and Hannah. Dad had a business partner over for dinner. Afterward he wanted a picture of everyone together. Mom is to the left."

I flipped the image around, identifying his parents, him, Hannah, and Mallory. "Who is this? Do you know his friend?" My arm trembled from holding my cane in the air.

"Babe, I was four then. Dad and Mom had people over all the time. I have no idea who he is, but it's one of the few pictures I have of my family together. Be upset with me but talk to me. Please." Pain and fear clung to his expression, and my heart broke.

"You don't know him?" My words stuck in my throat, and I swallowed over the dryness.

"I swear I don't."

I stared at him, unblinking. He seemed genuine and sincere. My mind sifted through my memories since I'd been here with Holden. As far as I knew, he'd never lied to me ... even about the club. I lowered the cane, my knees buckling beneath me as I sank to the floor and burst into tears.

"River." Holden's arms were around me in seconds, and he

pulled me into his lap. "It's okay, baby. I've got you." He kissed my hair and rocked me.

I clutched his shirt, my tears flowing faster as I gasped for air, shoving down the scream that threatened to tear through my throat.

"River?" Holden asked as I attempted to piece myself back together. "Do you know who the other man is?"

Chapter Twenty-Eight

"It's ... Logan." My voice cracked with the mention of his name and my anxiety skyrocketed. "Holden, your father knows Logan." The one person I'd finally allowed myself to feel safe with had just been ripped away from me. What if Holden's dad was still in touch with Logan, or worse, they worked together? I would become a target the second his father set eyes on me, and there would be nowhere to run. I inwardly cringed as a dark thought clouded my mind. Holden was young, but he was in the picture, too. What if he knew Logan and had reached out to let him know where I was? The room spun, and I willed myself not to hurl all over Holden.

"What the fuck?" Holden lifted me off his lap and stood. I'd dropped the photo, and it had fluttered to the carpet beside me. He picked it up and studied it for a long moment, the muscle in his jaw tensing. "This was years ago. Are you sure it's him?" He ran his fingers through his hair, a look of desperation flickering across his features.

I scrambled off the floor and peered at the man again as he held it for me. "Yes. He has a scar near his left eye." I pointed at the image. "His hair has receded, but I have no doubt in my mind he's the man between your dad and mom. Logan still has that evil glint in his eyes, too."

Nausea swam up to my throat and I swallowed my fear back.

"Dammit. River, did you think I was the one that told Logan where you were?" Disbelief clung to his words. He dropped the picture on the bed and wrapped me in a tight embrace. "You have my word that I don't know him. Hell, I don't even remember him or that day. I was just a little kid." He released me and placed his finger under my chin, tilting it up and forcing me to look at him. "I'll kill anyone that ever lays a hand on you again, River. I swear it."

My racing pulse slowed as I digested what he'd said. The shocked expression on his face and his words tugged at my insides. He was telling the truth. "I believe you." Another tear streamed down my cheek, and Holden kissed it away. I needed a plan before his father came home.

"River, I was waiting for a better time to tell you, but—"

"Well, who do we have here?" a deep voice said from Holden's doorway.

I screamed and jerked away from Holden, stumbling backward into the desk.

"Whoa, babe. Are you okay?" Holden reached for me and rubbed my back, soothing my frayed nerves.

Shaking like a leaf, I pressed my hand to my mouth and attempted to calm my galloping pulse. "I'm sorry. You scared me," I finally managed.

"I heard." With my heart in my throat, I came face-to-face with the older version of the man in the picture next to Logan. He and Holden shared the same dark hair and beautiful cheekbones, but that was all. Mr. Alastair was shorter and thicker than his son. He was barrel-chested and muscular, where Holden was leaner and cleared his father by several inches.

"Dad, this is River. River, this is Tim Alastair, my dad."

I gave him a wave and a sheepish smile. "Nice to meet you," I said, finally remembering my manners. If he already knew who I was, then I was in deep shit. Until I could gather my wits about me, being polite and not getting tossed out on my ass right into Logan's arms was imperative.

Tim's brown eyes darkened as his gaze lingered on my chest, then slowly traveled down my legs. Holden cleared his throat. "What are you doing home? I thought you wouldn't be here for another week."

"I have some business to attend to." Tim shoved his hands into the pockets of his black dress slacks. "I arrived around ten this morning."

I sucked in a breath. He'd been in the house, and I hadn't known. Holden gently squeezed my shoulder.

"River's staying with me," Holden announced, not even blinking an eye.

"Fine. If that's her food in the oven, the timer is going off."

"Thank you. I didn't hear it." *Over the pounding of my heart.* I picked my cane up from off the floor and made my way past Holden, but Tim was blocking the doorway.

"Excuse me," I said softly, unsure of who this man really was. I'd just found a picture of him and Logan together. Maybe I should give him the benefit of the doubt since it was years ago, but Becky's nagging words broke through my thoughts once again. His behavior wasn't helping the situation either. His tongue might as well have been hanging out of his mouth when he looked me up and down like I was a gourmet meal. Not to mention, he wasn't allowing me around him. I mentally swore.

"Dad." Holden's voice was firm, threatening.

Tim smirked, then moved out of my way. I shuffled by him as fast as I could. This wouldn't work. There was no way in hell Holden could leave me alone in the house with his father. Ever.

My overloaded brain tried to piece the new information together. *Logan. Tim.* Tim had been home earlier in the day, and I suspected his bedroom was one of the locked doors.

Peeking at the lasagna, I was grateful I'd cooked. Maybe it would be a way to break the ice with Holden's dad and move toward a better experience.

"My goodness that smells amazing." Heels clicked on the floor as someone descended the stairs. "And the downstairs is spotless. What a surprise!" A stunning woman patted her chest as she looked around, then her attention landed on me. "I should never be surprised to come home and find a gorgeous girl in my son's kitchen." She chuckled and tucked a dark lock of her shoulder-length hair behind her ear, her diamond rings catching the light.

Holden's mom. I wasn't sure if she was trying to make me feel crappy with her remark about the gorgeous girls in the house or if it was meant as a compliment. Either way, I was in uncharted territory, and I suspected there was at least one shark in the water.

"Hi, I'm River." I carefully placed the pan of food on the cooktop.

"Yes, the girl who my son found in our recycling bin. I'm Catherine, Holden's mother." She flashed a warm smile as she approached me. "How's your leg, dear?"

Unnerved, I removed the oven mitt from my hand and faced her, attempting to assess the situation. Friend or foe?

"Holden told you?" Funny, he hadn't mentioned anything to me.

"Holden tells me everything." She strolled across the kitchen, collected a glass from the cabinet, then made herself what appeared to be a strong alcoholic drink. I wasn't sure I didn't want to join her. I brushed off the thought. I needed to stay aware and keep my head clear.

"Everything?" My tone came across as challenging, and I internally cringed.

"Well, almost. He doesn't need to tell me you two are sleeping together. Do you need help with birth control? I don't see kids in my son's future."

Everything inside me bristled. "No, thank you." If this had been anyone else's mother, I would have already put her in check. My sexual relationship with Holden wasn't any of her goddamned business. I'd visited Planned Parenthood and started birth control after the first time Dan raped me and had stolen my virginity.

She took a sip of her drink, then frowned. "I'm sorry, River. From what Holden has told me, I already like you. I just arrived home from an eleven-hour flight and that doesn't count the layovers and driving. I tend to be direct and rude when I'm exhausted."

I blanched at her apology. She was continuing to catch me off guard, and I didn't like it.

"That's a long flight. I would be exhausted, too." What I really wanted to say was I'd be a cranky bitch, too, but that wouldn't help matters any.

"I'm going to go change, then I can give you a hand with the rest of dinner. I'm looking forward to getting to know you, hon." She gave me a little wave, then disappeared up the stairs.

I leaned against the counter, my heart jackhammering in my chest so hard it hurt. Sucking in a deep breath, I tried to reduce the panic that was blossoming inside of me. *Fuck, fuck, fuck!* And where was Holden? We definitely needed to discuss what had gone down with both of his parents.

"Hey, babe." Holden hurried down the stairs. "I just ran into Mom. She said you two met." He stopped short, his attention on me. "Oh Shit. What happened? You're really pale, River."

I picked up the oven glove, walked over to him, and smacked him on the chest. "You tell your mother everything?" I hissed. "She asked me if I needed birth control in the first five minutes we talked!" I hit him again for good measure, knowing full well I wasn't hurting him, but I was mortified and pissed. "And why the hell didn't you tell me your father was a creeper?"

Confusion furrowed his brows. "Umm, I don't tell Mom everything. She knows about 4 Play, but not about the lower level, or how close Brynn, Jace, Chance, and some other high school friends really are. She's only assuming you're in my bed, babe. I needed to tell her that you were living here, though. Naturally, she had questions."

Regret twisted Holden's features. "I've never seen my dad behave like that, though. I have no idea what's up his ass."

I blew out a big sigh and covered my face with my hands while I attempted to rein in my emotions—anger, fear, and major skepticism. I'd finally settled in with Holden and Brynn. Now I felt like I was backed into a corner again and questioning everyone.

Holden wrapped his arms around me, then whispered against my hair, "I know that picture has you on edge, and it does me too. We just need a few minutes to figure out what's going on."

I peeked up at him, and he stroked my cheek with the pad of his thumb. "Mom does know I'm in love with you. She really gets a bit ... obnoxious when she's exhausted. Given a few conversations, I think the two of you will hit it off. In fact, I know you will. Mom has mad respect for someone who survived what you have. You're strong, smart, and can fend for yourself. She came from a rough background, too. Give her a bit of time to adjust, okay?"

Holden's explanation and faith that Catherine and I could get along helped calm my nerves. "All right. If you and she are close, then I want to get to know her."

"I'll remind her not to be so forward." He flashed me a boyish grin, then it fell. "As far as my father is concerned, keep your distance until we figure out what the hell is going on."

I nodded against his chest as I bunched the material of his soft white shirt up in my fingers. "I don't think he knows who I am, but I can't tell for sure. What if he tells Logan that I'm here?"

Holden leaned his forehead against mine. "Dad wouldn't want that kind of attention. He would wait until you went somewhere, then Logan would show up."

"So, I'm trapped inside the house with the devil?" I cringed. "Sorry, I didn't mean to say that about your dad."

A soft chuckle rumbled through Holden's chest. "We'll discuss it after they've gone to their part of the house. Maybe we should go to 4 Play after dinner and grab a conference room and talk. We wouldn't have to worry about anyone else being around or overhearing us."

I swallowed hard, my hormones kicking my brain out of the driver's seat. "If we go to the club, then we should use it." I bit my lower lip as the bulge in his pants told me he was on board with the idea.

"Let's go casual when we leave the house. Jeans and a shirt. That way we won't tip them off. And babe, they know I own 4 Play, they just don't have any idea about the lower floor," he reminded me.

Footsteps grew closer, and we immediately stopped talking.

"I'm back, River. Why don't we whip up a salad and garlic bread to go with the lasagna?" Catherine squeezed Holden's shoulder as we dropped our embrace.

"How was the trip, Mom?" Holden asked while he unloaded ingredients from the huge stainless-steel refrigerator.

Catherine's face lit up as she rattled off details to Holden in another language. To my surprise, he replied to her as well.

"Holden, you speak Chinese?" I asked, realizing how little I knew about the man I shared a bed with.

"Since I was six," Holden said, grinning at his mom.

"If you want to learn, I can teach you," Catherine offered as she removed a large wooden salad bowl from the cabinet above her head. This was a quick change from the woman who had quizzed me about birth control minutes ago. Maybe she was dialing it down since Holden was in the room with us.

"Wow, that's kind of you. I'm not sure I'd ever use it. I've always wanted to learn to speak French, though. Not that I need it either, but the language sounds so beautiful." I smiled at her, hoping that I was selling myself as someone who wished to get to know her.

Over the next half hour, Holden, Catherine, and I chatted about college classes and future plans. The more we talked, the more I liked her. Maybe Holden was right. Catherine definitely seemed more relaxed and friendly.

I set the table while Holden finished the garlic bread. He'd used a broiler so I could put the lasagna back into the oven on warm. Since I had no idea that his parents would be home, I hadn't been able to time the food appropriately. I hoped like hell it tasted good.

Tim joined us and the conversation continued. My hair hung down and covered the side of my face. I used the opportunity to peek at him, and each time I wished I hadn't. I wasn't sure if Catherine was paying attention to Tim, but he certainly wasn't making any effort to hide his appreciation for my boobs.

I rounded my shoulders enough to make my chest not so obvious. Holden never let go of my fingers beneath the table, which told me that he'd noticed his father's behavior as well.

I tapped Holden's Apple Watch on his wrist and looked at the time. I couldn't wait to get the hell out of here. Not only did I need to speak to Holden, but I wanted to talk to Brynn. The first night we met, she mentioned that Holden's parents weren't the greatest, and I was desperate to understand what she meant. Maybe Brynn had some insight that Holden didn't just because he was too close to the situation.

Chapter Twenty-Nine

Fear seeped into my bones, weighing me down. I paced the length of the conference room in Holden's club, wringing my hands while I attempted to put the pieces together. What I did know was that Tim Alastair was a rotten bastard. He hadn't even tried to hide the way he eye-fucked me in front of his wife and son.

I groaned and sat on the top of the live edge table and chewed my thumbnail as I waited for Holden. One wall was floor-to-ceiling windows, and I focused on the city below me. The downtown Spokane lights twinkled in the darkness, and I'd fallen in love with the rush of the Spokane River. If I shut my eyes, I could almost hear and smell the fresh water.

"I'm back, babe." Holden closed the door behind him, then set a tray of snacks and drinks on the table for us.

"Thanks." I joined him and grabbed one of the tall, brown-colored drinks. "What's this?" I tasted it, my eye winking uncontrollably. "Holy shit that's sour."

Holden laughed, then picked up the can of soda and added some to my glass. "It's a Long Island, but I made it on the sour side. It's easier to add Coke than take it out." He took a drink of his, then sat down in one of the Italian brown leather executive chairs.

He frowned as he ran his fingers through his dark hair. Concern flashed in his brown eyes as his gaze landed on me. "I'm worried, River. I didn't like how my father looked at you. It took everything inside of me not to fly over the table and pound the motherfucker." Disgust weaved through Holden's features. "Who the hell looks at their son's girlfriend like that?"

Relief flooded over me. Since Holden and I hadn't been through this situation before, I wasn't sure he would mention it. Admitting that a parent is a slimy piece of shit was hard.

"Your mom didn't say a word, Holden. Does she not care?" His parents were puzzling me more and more.

Holden's gaze dropped to the light-colored wood floors, then back to me. "She has the ability to tune unpleasant things out. Honestly, I don't think they're married because they love each other. I think it's only business. I know one thing. I never want a marriage like theirs. When they're home they avoid each other like the plague."

I reached for his hand and sank into the seat next to him. "I'm guessing that a divorce at this point ... Well, the financials would be a bitch to deal with."

"Yeah, plus it's cheaper to file your taxes married."

I shifted in the chair, my attention landing on him.

Holden leaned back and laced his fingers behind his head. "You never talk about your mom. What happened to her?"

I ran my thumb over the condensation on my glass, watching the droplet of water run down the side. "I don't have a lot of memories. I was almost four when I landed at Dan's." I shifted in my seat, uncomfortable with the topic, but Holden had a right to know. My stomach twisted into painful knots as I decided to tell him the truth. He wasn't the only one that had lost someone.

"I was three ..." A lump formed in my throat, and tears pricked my eyes, but I refused to let them fall. It was in the past. I sighed, then looked at Holden. "Mom had a bad habit of disappearing. I was too young to be able to read the clock, but it seemed like it was for days."

"You were alone?" Holden nearly shot out of his chair, his expression showcasing his horror at the idea.

"Yup." I stirred my drink with my straw, then took a long pull. "The last time I wasn't alone, though. I had a baby brother ..."

"River." Holden slid to his knees and gently cupped my cheeks. "You don't have to tell me."

A tear streamed down my face. "I've never told anyone the details before. Other than the police, Department of Child Services, and Dan, no one else even knows." I turned away and closed my eyes, trying to contain the geyser of grief that had welled up inside of me.

"My brother's name was Alan. He was six months old at the time. I don't have any idea where Mom went, but when Alan got hungry ... I used a kitchen chair and scoured the cabinets and refrigerator for food, but I only found a few cans. Guess who didn't know how to use a can opener?" I offered him a weak smile, guilt swirling inside my gut like a tornado gaining momentum.

"The social worker said the police found me curled around Alan in his crib. He—"

I sank my teeth into my bottom lip, inviting the physical sting to relieve the gut-wrenching emotional pain. "He died next to me with his little fingers wrapped around mine." My body trembled violently, and Holden removed my drink from my hands. Bile swam up to my throat, and I gripped the arms of the chair, my mind reliving those dark moments. "Later I was told that there were claw marks at the door where I'd tried to escape. I didn't understand that it was locked." I hiccupped through my tears, my heart shattering into a million pieces. "I couldn't save us, Holden." I folded over, hiding my face from him as an anguished cry escaped me and I came undone.

"Jesus." Holden pulled me into his lap and rocked me as I sobbed against his shoulder. "I'm so sorry, River. Oh, babe. I'm so sorry." He kissed my cheek.

My tears eventually slowed, and my body shuddered as I

inhaled a deep breath. "I understand your need for redemption more than you realize. When you told me about Hannah, I overreacted because it was like you reached inside me and reminded me of my own failure to protect someone I loved." Closing my eyes, I tried to regain my composure. I'd never cried like this in front of anyone.

"When I was old enough to understand what happened, I swore I would never be vulnerable or unable to take care of myself again." I lifted my head and glanced at him through my damp eyelashes. "After I broke my leg, I didn't stay because I needed you to baby me. I stayed because of you. I was already falling for you. I was just lying to myself about it."

Holden placed his soft lips against mine, cementing me in the present moment where I was safe and loved.

"What happened to your mom?" He smoothed my hair, then twisted a strand around his finger.

I gave him a half shrug. "They never found her. Dan thinks she overdosed and fell in a lake or got lost in the woods. Her body was never recovered, but she used heavily, according to people that knew her. It explained why she would disappear."

"I love you, River. You'll never be alone. I know you're strong and can defend yourself against assholes, but I want to make your world a better place. A place where you'll never find yourself in a situation like that again."

Holden's words were a healing salve to my broken soul. "Then what are we going to do about your dad?"

"First, I need to figure out how long he's going to be home. Most of the time it's only for a week. While he's here, I won't leave you alone at the house with him. I'll skip school tomorrow. It's Friday and I only have two classes. I can work on the assignments at home, though."

"I'm not crazy about the idea of you missing class, but if I went to the campus with you, I'd just follow you around like a lost little puppy." I smiled and kissed him gently.

"If things get any worse, I'll send you to Brynn's. She has plenty of room and her parents are in Greece right now."

"I like backup plans." I placed my palm over his heart, the steady rhythm calming my nerves.

"Why don't I see if Brynn can take you shopping tomorrow afternoon? I think some girl time would do you good. Besides, you need more clothes now that your cast is off."

"I feel like you're my sugar daddy. I don't like it, Holden. I'm healing and I want to be a partner in this relationship. I want my own money and independence."

He smoothed my hair. "Do you want a job at 4 Play?"

I jerked my head up. "Umm, what kind of job?"

Holden's laugh filled the room. "Nothing with the clients, babe. I need someone in the back office. You can wear jeans and a T-shirt for all I care. You won't deal with the public."

I chewed on the inside of my cheek, debating if this might be a good fit and allow me to get some additional experience.

"River, you're smart as hell. You also have great instincts. You'll be trained well. I would much rather have a person that I trust than someone I don't know at all, especially in this position."

My forehead wrinkled in question. "Are you sure?"

"Yeah. I wouldn't have brought it up if I weren't. It's a part time position, but once you get the hang of it, and if you like it, there's easily more hours available. I also need a backup for inventory at the bar, and I know you won't drink it all when you're counting it."

"People just drink your liquor?" I asked, unable to disguise the surprise in my voice.

"Every damned day." A hint of exasperation laced Holden's tone.

"Sounds like you need to clean house, then. If I were you, that's exactly where I would start: getting rid of the people that aren't respecting your business and the bottom line." I stood and sat in the chair again, wiping the remaining tears from my face. "If it's a perk, then that's one thing." I crossed my legs and grinned at him. "Not having a cast on... I can cross my fucking legs!" I threw my head back and laughed. It was funny how I'd taken that fundamental movement for granted.

"Keep talking, babe."

"Huh?" I shot him a quizzical look.

"Perks. What were you saying?" Holden grabbed my ankles and lifted them into his lap. He gently massaged my calf.

"Well, are bottles walking off or do you have an idea who it is?"

"Both. Liquor is where we make our money," he explained.

I drummed my fingers on the table, my brain kicking into gear. "If you don't know how the alcohol is disappearing, it sounds like you need to update your camera system as well as security. It would really depend on how much money you're losing and if you would regain it by paying additional employees. If not, then security doesn't make sense."

A smile spread across Holden's features. "How do I stop it?"

"Employee perks. For every one thousand dollars in sales, they get a free bottle of mid shelf alcohol, or some shit like that. Reward your good people, and the ones who are mediocre, allow them to earn rewards. Cash bonuses or their choice of alcohol."

"I like it. A lot." He gently moved my pant leg up and massaged my calf.

My eyes rolled into the back of my head. "Oh my God, that feels amazing." I allowed myself a minute, then I remembered what I was going to say. "I have a question for you, though."

"What's that?" A spark of intrigue flickered over his handsome features.

"You bought the club and turned it around in a year, so why do you have an employee problem? I mean there are assholes everywhere, I get that. But you're business smart, so why are you asking me when you already know what to do?" I tilted my chin up, waiting for his response.

"I only found out about it a few days ago and I haven't had time to figure out what I want to do."

"Gotcha. So, do you think my suggestion could work?" I wiggled my foot as the massage shot tingles through me.

"I do. I'm going to look over the financials and compare the cost of hiring security versus the loss due to theft. It might be worth it for a while regardless. I definitely like the incentive idea. But ..." He pursed his lips. "Your business sense is impressive. Maybe I should hire you to consult and help me fix some things that I haven't had time to do. We would work together."

I narrowed my eyes at him in disbelief. "Really?"

"Why not? You just helped potentially solve a situation in five minutes. I'm pretty sure we can do more. Forget the back office. Work with me, River. I pay well." A wicked grin spread across his face, and he wiggled his brows at me. "Very well."

I giggled, loving what he was implying. Nearly giddy, I nodded and let out a little squeal. "Oh my god. I'm so excited to be on the inside of this business. The clubs, membership ... It's fascinating."

Holden leaned over, his heated gaze falling on my mouth, then rising to my eyes. "You're fascinating, River Collins and I'm the luckiest man alive to have you by my side."

The sound of my heart melting reached my ears, and I blushed. "And to think I could have slept in someone else's recycling bin."

We sat in silence, grinning at each other like lovestruck teenagers.

Holden straightened his long legs in front of him, his jeans hugging his muscular thighs. "I know we have a small plan for my dad, but I don't know if I feel better."

"Just find out when he's leaving. Worst case scenario, I'll stay with Brynn." I patted his arm, attempting to reassure him. But it was difficult when I didn't feel comfortable with the situation either.

"I don't like the idea of being away from you at night, though. I should ..." A mischievous glint flashed to life in his expression. "What if we moved in together?"

Chapter Thirty

I shot him a questioning look. "We live together already."

Holden laced his fingers behind his head, a cocky smile spreading across his face. "There's space on the floor above this conference room. It's huge. I've always wanted to make it my penthouse. I even have the architectural plans for what I want. What if we go over it and you tell me if you'd like to see changes? You can add anything you want, then we can start on construction. Once it's done, we'll move in upstairs."

My mouth fell open. "We'd have our own space. Just us?" I asked, excitement rushing through me.

"Just us, babe. It's set up for four bedrooms and an office. It's about thirty-five-hundred square feet, so we'll have plenty of room. You can entertain, too."

I threw my head back and laughed. "Holden, I don't know anyone other than you, Brynn, Jace, and Chance. It would be a really small party." I held my thumb slightly apart from my first finger for emphasis.

"With work, you'll branch out and make more friends. But ...

what do you say?" Eagerness and hope flickered to life in his handsome features.

I drummed my fingers against the table. "I need to pay half the bills. I want to be your partner and not your indentured servant."

"River, you are my equal and I don't see you any other way. You know I can cover all the bills, but if that's what you need in order to feel comfortable, then okay."

One thing that I loved so much about Holden was that he understood and respected my need for independence. My heart pounded in my chest. "I would love to move in with you, Holden Alastair."

Holden gently placed my feet on the floor and rose from his chair. He gripped the arms of my seat and leaned over me. "You're seriously turning me on right now."

"Are we going to consummate the penthouse and new job? Seal the deal with the boss?" I batted my eyelashes at him. "If I mess up at work, are you going to spank me?" I reached for the waistband of his jeans and gave it a playful tug. "Or handcuff me?"

Holden stood and scrubbed his face with both hands. "Holy shit. Just imagining you blindfolded and cuffed ..."

"I'm game." I stood. "Is anyone in the Master's Playroom?"

"I don't think so. I can check. Why?" He peered at me quizzically as he took his phone from his back pocket. "I'll pull up the schedule to see if it's in use. We have to sign in and out," he explained. He grew quiet and tapped his screen. "It looks like it's all ours."

"Good. I can finally take a peek around with the lights on and see what goodies you have." I grinned at him.

"This night is turning out so much better than I thought it would." Holden grabbed our drinks, then opened the conference door for me.

"I agree. I have a job." If I hadn't had my cane, I would have done a little happy dance right there in the hallway.

* * *

The Master's Playroom appeared a bit different with the lights on. I eyed the couches, wondering how often they were cleaned. After all, I assumed people fucked like bunnies on every surface in the room.

When I asked, Holden said they were sterilized after every use. He explained the rules to me as I walked around looking at the toys. Restraints hung from the wall, and I remembered how Brynn was spread eagle on the wheel. I wondered what it would be like to be with two men at once, but I wasn't going to bring it up to Holden. I wasn't sure I'd really be up for it, but maybe down the road.

"There are several unopened toys available. We obviously don't reuse them."

"Eww." I scrunched up my nose in disgust. "The thought alone makes my stomach churn." I joined him by the back wall that had several built-in drawers. I pulled one open, my attention immediately landing on an assortment of vibrators, cock rings, nipple clamps, and other items I didn't have a name for.

I tossed a glance over my shoulder, the wheel of sex calling to me. Holden strolled over and gave it a gentle spin. "Whoever is strapped down is the recipient. Anything goes, from getting your pussy licked to anal beads, two guys, two girls, etc.

"How many times have you been on there?" I pointed to the wheel, imagining him naked and strapped down. My G-string grew wetter by the minute.

"A lot." He gave me a sheepish smile. "As I said, though, I haven't been a member for almost nine months now."

"If we play and I'm not up for trying something, is that okay? I mean, I'm not sure about some of the ..."

Holden closed the gap between us and peered down at me. "No way is another guy touching you. You're mine."

I leaned into him and fumbled with the button and zipper of his jeans. "That answered one of my questions, but I'm not interested in another girl either."

"I would never ask you to do anything you didn't want to, babe. Never." He leaned down and kissed me, dominating my mouth with his. "How about we forget the wheel. You mentioned handcuffs earlier. Why don't we start off with a blindfold and cuffs?"

My core throbbed, and I was pretty sure if he touched my clit, I would come.

"Okay. I'm in." I smiled shyly at him, then an alarming thought occurred to me. "What if the other members walk in on us?"

"They can't. I changed the code on the scanner so no one else can access the room, and I texted them it was closed for cleaning. I've got it all taken care of. I promise."

"Oh, thank God." My hand fluttered to my chest.

Holden kissed me, then backed up and turned away from me. He opened a drawer and produced a package with new handcuffs and a black blindfold. I watched as he tore it open, then held up the cuffs on his pointer finger. "I want to show you how to get out of these on your own. There's a safety feature."

After he explained it to me, I practiced a few times. Once I was comfortable, Holden and I undressed, his gaze never leaving me as I tossed my jeans, shirt, bra, and G-string into a heap on the floor.

His erection bobbed free, and I resisted the urge to drop to my knees and suck him dry.

Holden slipped my blindfold into place, then secured my hands behind my back. He guided me to the couch, and I waited for what was next, my anticipation building by the second.

Holden turned me around, then pushed gently on my shoulders. "Sit down and spread your legs," he said gruffly.

I leaned against the cool leather and waited. A gasp escaped me as Holden slid an unfamiliar object into me.

"I thought we'd start with some HULA Beads." He parted my legs more. My back arched off the couch as the toy started to move inside me, and Holden's tongue swirled around my clit. He nipped at it with his teeth, then sucked it.

Not being able to see but only feel what he was doing to me was exciting as hell. I lifted my hips, grinding them against his mouth as the HULA Beads swirled and vibrated.

"Holden," I panted. "Jesus! What are you doing to me?"

He chuckled, then bit the inside of my thigh. Pleasure and pain shot through me. My nipples felt pressure and a tug as he positioned the nipple clamps on me. "Harder," I begged.

"No talking," Holden said.

I sucked on my bottom lip, my body vibrating with sensation as I neared the brink of a mind-blowing release. Holden removed the toy from my pussy, and I whimpered.

"Stand up."

I scooted to the edge of the couch, then stood. Holden turned me around and bent me over. My head rested on the back of the piece of furniture. A sharp sting landed on my left ass cheek, and I screamed. It was more about the surprise than the sting. Another smack landed against my butt, and this time I welcomed it. Holden massaged my sore flesh, then pushed something against my entrance. He rubbed it around my wet folds, then moved it up to my ass. I gasped as he slipped it inside me, then slowly withdrew the toy and eased it back into me again.

"Oh yeah." He growled as he slid his shaft into my pussy while using the toy at the same time. "Your tight little ass is taking that good, baby. I love fucking you like this." He pounded into me, grunting.

Words were beyond me, and my body was on fire as he thrust deeper. I was under his complete control. This was his world, and I loved being a part of it.

My core clenched around him, the heat pooling in my belly.

"That's it, River." He smacked my ass again, and I whimpered.

I wanted to tell him "More," but I had to remember not to talk.

With a hard pinch to my clit, my world exploded, my body begging for him as he slammed into me.

My name rang through the room as Holden came, his body jerking with his climax. Holden pulled out and removed the toy from me quickly. I straightened, and he leaned me back against his body.

His fingers wrapped around my throat as his other hand slipped between my thighs.

"I want you to come again." His breath grazed my cheek while he skillfully played with my bundle of nerves. His hand tightened around my neck, and I tipped my chin up, allowing him access.

"You're sexy as fuck right now." His tone was low and gruff.

My lips parted and I tugged on my cuffs. I wanted to touch him, drag my fingernails down his chest, and stroke his cock. Realizing he was still hard, I managed to shift enough to run my thumb over the tip of his sensitive head.

"As soon as you come, you're going to suck my dick."

I bucked against him. He tightened his grip around my neck, but I could still breathe. I wondered if he would ever push it. Cut off my oxygen while I orgasmed.

A low moan grew into a scream of pleasure as I released.

"That's my girl."

I'd barely regained my senses when he moved from behind me, the leather of the couch making a soft noise.

"Kneel." His hands steadied me as I dropped to the floor. He removed the nipple clamps, then rubbed his cock against my lips. I immediately parted them, then sucked on him while he fisted my hair.

"I could watch you all day. Those beautiful lips wrapped around my dick." Holden lifted his hips, his thrusts short and fast. He pulled my hair, forcing my mouth off him. Warmth landed on my tits as my name left his mouth. Seconds later, he removed my blindfold and kissed me deeply. "Never forget how much I love you, baby."

"I know," I whispered. And I did. No matter how rough we played, I always knew he was my safe place.

Chapter Thirty-One

I was beginning to think that Holden felt guilty after our club sessions. Once again, we'd slipped into his bed, and he made love to me. Maybe it was his way of showing me he was still capable of slow and sweet versus spanking and toys. Regardless, I was perfectly fine with it. I'd quickly learned there were two sides to my sexual appetite.

Afterward, I fell asleep with my head on his chest, the beat of his heart lulling me to sleep. There was no place I would rather be than in his arms.

The following day, I woke up with a smile. Holden and I were going to move. Together. I couldn't wait to see the plans for the penthouse and tell Brynn. Rolling over in the bed, I realized Holden had already gotten up. Hopefully, he left some coffee for me. After our romps last night, I was still tired.

I dressed in shorts and a sweatshirt and tossed my hair up in a messy bun. I staggered out of the bedroom and into the hall, limping. Shit, I forgot my cane. I held onto the doorframe, my leg immediately giving me a big fuck you. I scanned the room, and I finally located it on the floor next to my side of the bed. I hobbled over, then reached for it. An abrupt movement caught my attention. I straightened slowly, then froze.

"Good morning, River." Tim said, leaning on the doorframe with a leer on his face.

"Morning." I squared my shoulders and held eye contact. "I was on my way downstairs to find Holden."

"He's visiting with his mother in the other kitchen."

Shit. Tim must be referencing the kitchen I hadn't seen yet.

"On the opposite side of the house." Tim took a few steps toward me. "Where he can't hear you scream."

With a quick lunge, Tim backed me against the wall, his hand over my mouth. The cane fell to the floor with a thump. My nostrils flared in anger. Holden was home and this stupid fuck was going to ... I wasn't sure, but he wasn't very smart.

"You reek of sex, River. Are you riding Holden every chance you get?" He tugged on the waistband of my shorts, and I screamed against his palm. "Be still, honey. It will be over in a few minutes."

The sound of his zipper filled the room, then he pushed his pants and boxers down.

Hell no. I slammed my eyes closed as I reached for his balls. I wrapped my fingers around them, squeezed, then gave a little twist for good measure. Tim screamed as his hand fell away from my mouth.

"Mr. Alastair. Don't you ever touch me again. Don't eye fuck me, don't make rude gestures, or say a goddammed word to me ever again. Or—" I gave his nuts a firm squeeze. "—you can kiss these goodbye. I've been bullied and hurt by men like you in the past, but it won't ever happen again. Do we understand each other?"

He whimpered and nodded. I let him go, and he collapsed to the floor with a thud. He groaned and curled into a fetal position. "You fucking bitch. You'll pay for that."

"Pay for what?" Holden asked, entering his room and taking note of the situation. He flew around the bed and straight to me. "Are you hurt? Did he?" Fear twisted Holden's features.

"I'm fine. Your father isn't, though." I pulled my shorts up, stepped around Tim, and walked to the bathroom to scrub that disgusting bastard off of me.

"You sorry piece of shit," Holden seethed.

Whack! Whack! Whack!

The sound of crunching bone filled the room, and I hung my head. I knew once Holden realized that his dad's pants were around his ankles, he would deal with it. It wasn't my fight anymore, so I'd quickly moved out of the way. Finally realizing that Holden wasn't going to stop, I ran over to him. Blood pooled on the beige carpet as Holden slammed his fist into his father's face.

"Holden! Holden! Don't kill him. He's not worth it."

Holden's fist hovered in the air, his breathing ragged from exertion. He stood, blood dripping from his busted knuckles. "Get the fuck out. Don't come back until I say you can, or you'll be facing charges for attempted rape. I will destroy your business reputation."

Tim peered at his son through a swollen eye. "Don't threaten me, Holden. This isn't over by a long shot."

My mouth gaped at the audacity. He'd just gotten his ass beat, but he was still threatening his son.

"You disgust me." Holden walked to the bathroom, fury rolling off him in waves. He grabbed a towel and tossed it at Tim, and I took the opportunity to grab my cane. Holden gathered my hand in his, then we left Tim on the bedroom floor sniveling.

"You sure you're, okay?" Holden asked as we hightailed it through the house.

"He didn't hurt me. Tim made the mistake of trying to rape me standing up. When he dropped his pants, I had enough room to grab his balls and twist."

Holden stopped abruptly and cupped my face, his warm palms on my cheeks. "Of course you did." He gave me a lopsided grin, then he kissed me hard. "I love you. I love you so damned much." He embraced me, planting kisses on the top of my head.

And for the first time, I looked up at the man who had set my heart free and said, "I love you, too, Holden."

He looked at me, his brown eyes drinking me in. "Say it again."

"I love you, Holden." I grinned at him. We were the weirdest two people on the planet. His father had just tried to rape me, and here we were standing in the foyer confessing our love for each other.

He kissed me deeply, then continued walking to the other side of the house. "Is your leg okay?"

"It's sore. I walked a little without the cane." I grimaced. "It didn't feel very good."

"Let's get you settled with some ice." Holden slowed down as we walked toward the formal dining room that I'd seen the other day. We went through it, and on the other side of a swinging door was the most beautiful kitchen I'd ever seen. The white-and-tan marble countertops gleamed in the sunlight, and multicolored stones lined the wall over the five-burner stove. I was certain that the refrigerator was the size of two. The tile floor was cool on my bare feet as we approached a small kitchen table in the corner near the row of windows overlooking the neighborhood.

The aroma of freshly ground coffee beans tickled my nose, and I squashed the urge to run over to the coffeepot.

"Mom," Holden said as we reached her.

"Good morning, River. Son, what's wrong with your hands?" Catherine gave me a kind smile, then she took a sip of her steaming coffee, her attention on Holden's knuckles.

"Dad tried to rape River. He's lying on the floor in my bedroom, bleeding."

Catherine spit out her drink, spraying the table and her laptop. "Jesus, Holden. Do you think you could not open communication with such a foul statement?" Catherine stood and adjusted her robe. "Are you okay?" Her gaze traveled over me.

"Yeah. I think he took the most damage."

To my surprise, Catherine patted my back. "Good girl." She

squared her shoulders and gave me a tight-lipped smile. "If you'll excuse me."

I watched her walk away, her long blue robe swishing behind her. She appeared composed, but I noticed her tight fist.

"She believed us?" I asked, frowning.

"She knows I would never lie about something that important." Holden blew out a breath, then walked over to the sink and washed his hands. Crimson dripped off his knuckles and into the water. While we were gathering our thoughts, I grabbed a mug and filled it with coffee.

"That was a hell of a way to wake up," I whispered before I took a sip, the hot liquid scalding the top of my mouth.

Still rattled from the experience with Tim, it took me a minute to realize that Catherine's reaction was extremely calm. If someone told me Holden had tried to rape someone, I'd fucking come unglued, beat his fucking ass, then buried him.

Holden collected his mug, and we sat at the table.

"Holden?" I reached for his hand. "I don't want to admit that your father ..." I shook my head. "But what the hell did he just pull, and why was your mom so calm?"

"She's not, but she won't lose her shit in front of you."

"And fucking stay out!" Catherine's scream echoed through the main floor of the house. The slam of the front door followed, and I cringed.

Holden pinched the bridge of his nose. "We won't see her for the rest of the day. Maybe not until tomorrow." His shoulders slumped in defeat. "My family is seriously fucked up, River." His voice was low and haunted.

"We're all screwed up, Holden. Your family isn't any worse than mine." I'd meant that to help, but I wasn't sure if it had.

Holden took a sip of his coffee, then stared at the floor, appearing lost in thought. "When I was eleven, I heard some strange noises, so I followed them through the house. Finally, I found Dad in the gym. He was beating the hell out of the heavy bag. At first, I didn't think anything about it, but then I noticed several bruises on his back and arm. Dad had a temper. I assumed he had pissed someone off and they'd gone at it. My dad shoots his mouth off when he's mad, so it would make sense that he'd get his ass beat." Holden glanced at me before he continued. "I never asked him about it, but I never forgot it. Over the years he grew more aggressive toward Hannah, Mallory, and me."

"He hit you guys?" I asked softly, my faded bruises burning into my skin with the memory of Dan's fists.

"Only me. After that, he and Mom traveled more. It was clear he didn't want to be around us. Back then ..." Holden tossed his hand up, puzzled. "He's never hurt a girl before."

"He's gone now. Maybe we can hurry up with the plans for penthouse. This is *his* home."

Holden practically snorted. "It's Mom's house and we all know it. If she really kicked him out for good, he won't be coming back."

I remained silent, giving Catherine major kudos. She could have dismissed me and thrown me out on the streets. At least one of Holden's parents liked me.

Chapter Thirty-Two

The next day Holden, Jace, and Chance met for lunch downtown while Brynn and I had made plans to shop. In less than an hour, she arrived at the front door.

"Hey, babe!" Brynn said, slipping her black Dior sunglasses on the top of her head. Her red hair flowed past her shoulders and down her back as she strolled through Holden's foyer like she owned the place. Her light wash blue jeans hugged her curves, and her black boots clicked against the marble floors. She wore an emerald-green blouse and a diamond pendant around her slender neck. She looked so stunning I almost questioned my sexuality.

"Hey babe, yourself." I grinned at her.

She greeted me with a warm hug. "Are you ready to do some damage?" She held up her credit card and winked at me.

"Hell. Yes." I held up my own black American Express card and giggled.

"Holy. Shit." She snatched it from my hand. "Girl, please. He gave you your own card?"

"Yes, but I'm going to pay the bill because I also have a consulting job at 4 Play!" I bounced on my toes, elated that I had my own money.

"What? Oh my God! That's amazing." She hugged me again. "But your man is paying for this trip. Save your money."

"Why? Are we spending a lot?" As soon as the words left my mouth, I knew better. The few times I'd shopped with her, Holden's wallet was ten to fifteen thousand dollars lighter. A few dresses, heels, bras, panties, and spa days will do that, apparently.

"Mimosas and a mani-pedi to begin with, then we're getting your sweet little ass some jeans, tennis shoes, and some shirts. We need to pick you out a few more cocktail dresses, but that doesn't have to be today. Then ..." She sunk her teeth into her lower lip. "Holden wants me to take you to start shopping for the penthouse."

"What?" I asked, gawking at her. "We've not even finalized the plans yet."

She shrugged and grinned. "He wants to know what your style is."

"Well, shit. I don't even know what my style is." I tossed my hand in the air, flustered that I had no idea.

Brynn held her elbow out to me. "Exactly."

I slipped my arm through hers as we strolled through the foyer to the front door.

"There's an amazing art gallery I want to take you to. You need to pick a few pieces out before they're gone."

I scrunched up my nose. "Not sure I'm the art type?"

Brynn opened the door for me. "You are, you just don't know it yet."

Laughing, we walked toward a black Mercedes, then I slowed down. "I thought you drove a Jaguar."

"Yeah, about that." She placed her sunglasses on her face. "Holden wanted us to be accompanied today since ... his dad."

I stopped mid-step and leaned on my cane. "No offense, Brynn, but Holden needs to talk to me about these things, not you." Anger simmered below my somewhat calm exterior.

"I completely agree. It was very last minute. He'd called to see if I had time to take you to the gallery and he filled me in on the highlights of his fucked-up father. I actually suggested we have one of his bodyguards go with us. He agreed. I swear there's nothing more to it."

My phone vibrated in the back pocket of the jeans I'd borrowed from Mallory. I pulled it out to see Holden's name flashing across my screen with a text.

Babe, I'm an ass. I chatted with Brynn, and she thinks you two should have a bodyguard with you today. I agreed, but I wanted to let you know before she got there so it wouldn't freak you out. I'm not sure where Dad is, so I would rather be safe and take care of the one thing in this world I love with all my heart.

"From the look on your face, that's Holden." Brynn's big green eyes softened with understanding.

"Yeah. I feel like a total bitch. I think his text was delayed. I just now got his message." I handed the phone to Brynn.

"It's okay. I won't say a word about the misunderstanding. Your secret's safe with me." She returned my cell, and I texted him a quick reply and that I loved him. I shoved it in my back pocket, then we continued to the car.

"Just a head's up, you might need an extra pair of panties with you."

I narrowed my eyes at her. "Why?"

"Wait until you meet the bodyguard. His name's Vaughn and he has two different colored eyes. Plus ..." Her tongue darted across her bottom lip. "He looks like he could fuck and play hard." She laughed.

I finally focused on the man that was waiting near the car. "Holy shit," I mumbled as we neared him. "You might be right." Vaughn was easily over six feet tall, and his broad shoulders filled his black suit jacket to perfection. His slacks hugged his thick thighs, and I wondered what else was thick. Jerking my attention away from him, I sucked in a breath, attempting to calm my rampaging hormones.

Brynn and I kept the conversation light in the car, but I didn't miss the sidelong glances she gave Vaughn. I'm sure he was used to women drooling over him. Honestly, I didn't blame them. He and Zayne were straight off the cover of a magazine. I wondered if Brynn had been with any of them before. She looked like she was about to hop the seat and straddle Vaughn at any moment.

After our amazing manicures and pedicures, we stopped at Nordstrom. I tried on what felt like a million pairs of jeans before we narrowed it down to eight. I'd grown accustomed to changing clothes in front of Brynn, but there were times I wondered if she liked the show. While trying on a few nice tops, I finally got up the courage to ask her a question.

"Brynn?" I slipped into the royal blue blouse, then started to button it.

"Yeah, babe?" She grinned at me.

"How much did Holden tell you about his dad and me?"

She shook her head. "He's such a piece of shit. Him eye fucking you at the dinner table is disgusting. I'm sorry you had to deal with that."

I pulled my hair out of the back of the top and sighed. "So ... Holden didn't tell you that he tried to rape me yesterday while Holden and Catherine were home?"

Brynn shot out of the chair in the dressing room, her Gucci purse spilling its contents on the floor. She bent over collecting the items, including a purse-sized vibrator. I stifled my giggle. I loved Brynn for being so free and content with her sexuality.

"That fucking piece of shit. I'm going to run over him with my car, back up, then run over that fucker again. Oh my God." She rose, her cheeks red with anger. "Are you okay? Jesus, I should have been worried about you, but my brain immediately went to killing the bastard."

Red hot anger pulsated through my veins and my pulse quickened as images of Tim's attack bombarded my mind. "He made the mistake of trying to rape me standing up. My hands were free, so I grabbed his balls, squeezed, and gave them a twist. Needless to say, he backed off."

"Oh. My. God. You're my hero! That's amazing! You're such a badass, River. This is why we're friends. I need you, not the other way around. You inspire me."

I blushed furiously. "I wouldn't go that far, but I've had practice getting someone off me. Sometimes it worked and sometimes it ... didn't." I wrapped my arms around my waist as though I could stop the rush of anger and hatred I felt for Dan. At least that motherfucker was dead.

"Hey, Dan's gone. It's over. You're strong and took care of Tim yourself. I also know Holden, and once he found out ... wait. You did tell him, right?"

I smiled. "He walked in while Tim was on the floor curled up in a fetal position with his pants and boxers around his ankles."

Brynn screwed up her face. "Eww. I'm sorry you had to see that. Tim is not a good-looking man."

I barked out a laugh. "I know, right?" I turned away from her, admiring the blouse. "What do you think?" I needed a break before I asked if she knew any dirt on the Alastairs.

Brynn's green eyes softened. "You look beautiful," she whispered. Our gazes connected in the mirror. "I can see why Holden loves you so much." She reached up and touched my cheek, then her hand fell to her side as though she realized what she was doing. "If you weren't with him, I'd ... I'd want to be with you." She focused on the floor.

The moment should have felt awkward, but it didn't. I turned to her, my heart pounding in my chest. "I love him."

"I know, and I'd never cross a line with you."

"If I thought you would, we wouldn't be together in the dressing room right now. I'm taking my clothes off in front of you. Believe me, I trust you, Brynn."

She turned away.

"You're my best friend, Brynn. I want to keep it that way. But ..."

She glanced at me over her shoulder, and I continued, "If I ever want to experiment with a girl, I'll ask Holden if he's okay with that girl being you."

Her face lit up. "Oh, yummy." She winked at me, letting me know that the conversation was over.

She'd had a moment, but I was secretly flattered. Brynn was one of the most beautiful women I'd ever seen. I also understood it was just a little crush on the new girl. I had my suspicions about who really owned Brynn's heart, and it wasn't me.

"Besides, I thought you were into Jace or Chance. I mean, you all flirt so much, I assumed there might be something to it other than the club."

Brynn collected the items of clothing from the chair and hung them on the hangers. She'd never done that before. I'd hit a nerve. "They're so much fun. I don't know what I would do without them."

Brynn had just dodged my comment, which made me even more suspicious. I removed my blouse and reached for the tag. "I really like this one. What do you think?"

"Yes, and this one." She held up a teal top.

"I like them both. Do you think I could pull off a look like what you have on?" I pointed at her jeans, boots, and blouse.

"Yes! Do you have any boots?"

"Nope."

"Well, we're shopping for shoes next." She grinned at me as I slipped my sweatshirt back on. It would be nice to have something else to wear other than Mallory's clothes.

Brynn and I filed out of the dressing room. "Brynn, do you remember the night we met?"

"Of course I do. Your face was all busted up and you had the cast on your leg."

I hung the items on the rack that I wasn't interested in. "You said Holden was the black sheep of the family. What did you mean?"

I watched as she folded the jeans. "It's only because he's not warped like his dad."

"What do you mean? Do you know something about him?"

She gently took my arm and led us back into the store. "There are rumors that he works with some seedy characters," she said quietly. "Illegal activities."

"What? What kind of activities?" The mental image of his sneer and palm against my mouth stole my breath, and I stopped mid-step.

"River?" Concern etched into Brynn's features. "Hey, what's wrong?"

Chapter Thirty-Three

I gripped my cane, searching for a place to sit down. "I know I handled Tim, but ..." My panic eased as I spotted Vaughn watching us. "I forgot Vaughn was here." I pressed my palm against my chest.

"River, he's been here the entire time. He just can't be in the dressing room with us unless there's an emergency. Plus, the body-guards hang back a little bit." She squeezed my hand. "As long as he's around, we're safe." She brushed a stray hair from my face and gave me a tight, worried smile. "Let's find a place to grab lunch, then I'll tell you what I know. You really look pale, so some food might help."

I nodded and Brynn led us toward Vaughn.

"We're going to find somewhere to eat. We need a quiet corner," Brynn said.

"I know the perfect place," Vaughn replied while his mismatched eyes landed on me. "Everything all right?"

I gave him a weak smile. "Yeah, my leg is hurting." I hadn't lied, but I didn't tell him I'd just had a flashback concerning Tim, which brought up Logan all over again.

He nodded, then we left the store after making our purchases and went straight to the car.

Half an hour later, we arrived at a restaurant with zero curb appeal. From the outside, it looked like a gray, rectangular box.

"It doesn't look like much, but it's a safe place to talk and the food is fantastic," Vaughn said after he opened the door to the restaurant for us. "This way." Vaughn waved at an older guy who appeared to be in his early fifties. "Ladies." He opened an additional door for us.

"Oh wow!" The room held only a booth and another table. It was small, but there weren't any other customers. Two ceiling fans circulated the air while Brynn and I settled into the leather seats. I admired the gold-and-green wallpaper. I loved a good design. It could really add depth to a room. Large ornate black hand fans hung on the walls. "Chinese actually sounds amazing."

"You won't regret it," Vaughn said. "I'll be right outside the door. No one will come or go unless I allow it. Settle in and enjoy your lunch."

With that, Vaughn strolled to the door, power rippling off him with every step.

"It should be against the law to be that gorgeous," Brynn said the second he'd left us alone.

"No shit." I fanned myself and laughed.

Our waiter entered with a few glasses of water and took our drink order. Since Vaughn was driving, Brynn and I had agreed that we would indulge in some fun day drinking. We ordered a few mimosas, and I hoped they were as yummy as the ones we'd had at the salon. I held my fingers up, appreciating my dark red nails.

"Now that we're alone, spill." I took a sip of water.

Brynn leaned back, her gaze narrowing in on me. "You can't repeat what I'm about to tell you."

I frowned. "Not even to Holden?"

She shook her head. "If it's true, it would put him in danger."

"Shit. You're serious, aren't you?" I wrung my hands in my lap. I wondered if it was too late to revoke the question.

"As I said, I'm not a hundred percent sure that this information is true, but I tend to believe the person who told me about it."

I nodded, holding my breath while I waited for her to continue.

Brynn leaned forward, and her green eyes darted around to make sure we were alone. "Tim doesn't make his money from financials. He's an illegal weapons dealer and he's extremely dangerous." Her voice was so soft I almost didn't hear her.

I leaned against the edge of the table, my mind swimming from what she'd said. "How sure are you, Brynn? Who told you?"

The door opened again, and our waiter dropped off our mimosas. "Thanks." I immediately picked up mine and downed half of it. "I'll need another one."

I grinned sheepishly at the waiter, who suppressed a chuckle and said, "You got it."

As soon as the door closed, I returned my attention to Brynn.

For the first time since I'd met her, she looked terrified. Dammit. This was way more serious than I thought. Thank God Catherine kicked that monster out of her house. She was safer without him. Catherine and Holden definitely deserved better than that piece of shit. The other part of me reeled in my heavy judgment. I'd always tried to base my opinion on fact and not hearsay. What I knew for a fact was that Tim was a sleazy bastard who had attempted to rape me. But a weapons dealer was on an entirely different level.

Brynn's face paled and she took a drink of her mimosa. "My father told me."

I froze. "Do Tim and your dad run in the same circles?"

"Sometimes. They play golf and attend the same get togethers, fundraisers, and that type of thing, but they don't hang out as friends anymore. Things changed about five years ago."

"Do you have any idea what happened between them?"

Brynn drained her drink, then wiped her mouth. *Oh shit, this is going to be big.*

"I'll tell you, but please don't repeat any of this. I swore I would take this to my grave."

I reached across the table and took Brynn's hand in mine. "I swear."

"I caught my father and Tim Alastair together. As in, naked together."

My mouth hit the floor, and I released her, smacking my forehead with my palm. "That is *not* what I thought you were going to say!"

"Yeah, well, it wasn't what I had expected to see either."

"So, no one else knows?" I tucked my dark hair behind my ear as I studied her expression. Pain, loneliness, fear. I wanted to hug her and tell her everything would be okay, but I couldn't say that to her when I didn't believe it myself.

"No. Not my mom, not Catherine, and definitely not Holden. It would ruin our families, River." Tears welled in her eyes.

"I'm so sorry. That's a really lonely place to be."

The waiter entered the room again with more drinks, and we placed our food order. Even though we were talking privately, I appreciated the waiter interrupting. We needed a break from the intensity of the conversation.

"Now that I've had a nanosecond to process what you said, did your dad tell you before or after you caught them?" Her answer would tip the scale for me in one direction or the other. Rumor or most likely the truth.

"After, which made me wonder if Dad was just angry with Tim, or if he was warning me. When I caught them, I agreed not to tell their wives but only if they didn't see each other again. I have no idea if they did or not, but I felt like I needed to say something that might make it too risky for them to be together."

She raised her hand in the air and said, "For the record, I don't care if they're in love or just lovers, but they're married and have families. That's what I have a problem with. If you're single, then do what the hell you want."

"Yeah, I'm the same way. No cheating allowed." I drummed my fingernails against the tabletop. "Well, shit. I'm really trying to figure out if what your dad said was out of spite or if it's legit." I closed my eyes and shook my head before I opened them again. "I'm so sorry, Brynn. I just accused your father of being a liar and I didn't mean to."

She waved me off. "He is. I mean, he was having an affair with Tim. Dad is a lot of things, including a cheater and liar. But this time I believe him."

A sharp ache stabbed me and spread through my chest. I'd always wanted parents. At this rate, I wouldn't be close to Holden's parents either. If I were in Catherine's shoes, I wouldn't ever want to see the girl my husband had tried to rape, much less live with her.

"Are you leaning one way or the other that Tim really isn't who he says he is?" My mind was spinning out of control. How would I keep this from Holden, and was it worth putting him in jeopardy and losing Brynn as my best friend? I already knew the answer. It was a big hell no. I would have to protect Holden without him knowing what was going on.

"When Dad sat down to talk to me, he knew that Tim had just arrived home from a business trip. I'm not sure why my father had him followed, but Tim said he was going to Australia, and that was a lie. He went to Monte Carlo where he met with one of the most dangerous men in the world. They were seen laughing and sharing drinks, so from that information it was assumed that he's in business with them. Dad didn't give me names in order to protect me."

My stomach dropped to my toes like a lead ball. "That's not a rumor, Brynn. It's not normal to hang out with men like that unless you're involved, too."

"Exactly, but Holden and I have grown up together. I know Tim and Catherine well, so I struggled to believe it was real." Brynn examined her fresh French tips. She'd opted for the French manicure this time.

"That's what you meant about Holden being the good guy in the family!" I slapped my hand against the table, finally putting it all together.

"Yeah. Holden thinks I'm teasing him. I am, but he has no idea how serious I am behind the joking. Holden certainly doesn't take after Tim. Or even after Catherine, for that matter. She can be the sweetest person to you, then turn on a dime and tear you to pieces. She was practically bi-polar with Hannah way before Hannah took off, but that's another story for another day."

A heavy silence hung in the air. "Brynn, I have one more question, then let's try to enjoy our day together."

"All right." She tapped her fingers against her glass, obviously stressed.

"Why are you telling me all of this? Why not keep your mouth closed and pretend nothing happened? I don't understand."

Brynn removed the straw from her water and stirred her mimosa. "I haven't had a genuine female friend in a really long time. My best friends are guys. That's part of it, but when you told me what happened with Tim, it scared the shit out of me. I'm afraid you're in danger. If you're in danger, so is Holden."

The waiter entered again with our food and my stomach growled in response.

"I understand." I moved my napkin and silverware over so the server could place the plate of Mongolian beef in front of me.

Over the next half hour, we kept the conversation more upbeat, but my mind was running in frantic circles. The more Brynn had shared, the harder it was for me to dispute that Tim was involved in some serious shit. I wasn't able to tell Holden about it, but I could insist on extra safety measures. After all, I'd just handed Tim's nuts to him and made it clear he'd better not mess with me. Then Catherine threw him out of the house. An eerie shudder traveled through me. *Son of a bitch.* I'd made myself a fucking target again. First Logan and now Tim. Even after the new information, I couldn't shake the feeling that Logan and Tim might be working together.

Chapter Thirty-Four

After lunch, Vaughn drove us to Brynn's favorite art gallery. My leg felt better after our break, and I was looking forward to learning what expensive pictures I liked. More than that, I was eager to work on the penthouse. At least there I would be out of Tim's line of sight.

Vaughn held the door open, and we entered. It was busier than I'd anticipated, and I eyed the people mulling around with champagne glasses in their hands.

"Brynn, darling. How wonderful to see you." A tall, lean man approached us. His black hair was slicked back, and his pale blue eyes sparkled as his gaze roamed the length of Brynn's body, then back to her face. His bright green suit was tailored perfectly to his shoulders and his fitted slacks tapered off at the ankle. His smile was striking.

"Ah, Pierre." Brynn kissed him on his cheek, then squeezed his bicep. "How are you?"

"Wonderful. I've been busy buying art and working with galleries around the globe. I've finally made myself a name in the world of art, sex, and drugs." He chuckled. "Speaking of sex ..."

Brynn raised her eyebrow, and Pierre had the decency not to finish his statement. "Pierre, I'd love for you to meet Holden's girlfriend, River."

Pierre assessed me harder than he had Brynn. "Holden Alastair?"

"Yeah." I gave him a little wave, feeling horribly self-conscious.

"Damn, girl. You must be something else to make the Pacific Northwest's most eligible bachelor settle down."

"Pierre, you're embarrassing her." She winked at him.

"Did you meet Holden at 4 Play?" Pierre asked.

Shit. How was I going to explain how we met?

"No, she didn't meet him there. They met through a mutual friend."

Relief washed over me, and I mentally thanked Brynn for saving me from sharing personal details with someone I didn't know.

"Well, River, if Holden breaks your heart, just let me know. Maybe I can talk you and Brynn into getting a room together on the lower floor."

I choked and turned away quickly. *What the fuck?* This guy was seriously forward. He was obviously a member at 4 Play, too.

"Behave, Pierre," Brynn scolded.

Pierre chuckled, then Brynn got down to business and had Pierre give us a tour of the new pieces that had arrived. Vaughn walked quietly behind us, and I constantly checked over my shoulder for Tim.

"River," Vaughn softly said from over my shoulder. "I'll make sure no one messes with you, including him." He gave a discreet nod in Pierre's direction. "You're safe."

I released a breath I hadn't realized I was holding. "Thanks," I replied in a hushed tone. "I appreciate it."

Once Vaughn had reassured me, I was able to relax and enjoy the rest of the afternoon. Some of the art pieces were seriously strange, but one in particular grabbed my attention. A faceless woman stood naked, her palms covering her breasts. Red, yellows, and blues dripped down her skin, mixing together. The complexity of who she was, her feelings, and the depth to her many layers struck a chord inside me.

I slipped my arm through Brynn's. "This is amazing." I remained still, admiring the painting and the emotions it evoked.

"You like it?" Brynn glanced at me, then back to the piece of art.

"Yeah, and the longer I stand here looking at it, the more I love it," I confessed.

"Pierre, are there any additional pieces to this one?" She patted my hand.

"There are four total. They can be sold separately or together. In my opinion, it would be a shame to separate them. The girl has different poses and colors in each. Would you like to see the others?"

"I would," I chimed in. Pierre took us to the back of the gallery, where the other three pieces graced the wall. In two of the paintings, the girl had a face and was crying. In the additional one, she was faceless.

"What do you think?" Brynn asked me. "They're gorgeous, if you want my opinion. If you and Holden don't get them, I will." Brynn grinned at me.

"Hands off, lady." I giggled, then took my phone from my back pocket. "Pierre, can I take a few pictures and send them to Holden? I would like his thoughts as well since they'll be in our new home."

The color drained from Pierre's features. Maybe he didn't think Brynn was serious when she explained that I was Holden's girlfriend, but it seemed as though he understood now.

"Turn your flash off." He stepped away and gave us some privacy. I snapped the pictures of the pieces individually, then together.

Hey, babe. What do you think of these for the penthouse?

My phone buzzed almost immediately.

They're fantastic. Buy them, and we'll store them until our place is ready. On second thought, I'd like to strip you down and paint you. He added a smiley emoji.

I laughed as my fingers danced across the screen with my response. *I love you too. I'll let Pierre know we want them.*

Excellent, meet me at 4 Play when you and Brynn are done. Let Brynn know the guys are here as well.

I replied with a heart and an eggplant.

LMAO. Get your ass over here. I miss you.

"Pierre, we'd like the set, please." I grinned at Brynn. "Holden likes them, too."

"Of course, he does. You picked them out." She gently nudged me with her elbow and winked at me. "Tell Pierre to put the art on Holden's account."

I blanched. "He buys here a lot?"

"Next time you're on the top floor of the club, look around. A lot of expensive, seductive art."

"And how would you like to pay for this today?" Pierre asked, rubbing his hands together. "The total cost is five hundred thousand dollars. We take credit card—"

I smiled, then interrupted him. "Please put it on Holden's account." Proud of myself that I didn't pass out cold on the floor from the price tag, I offered him a confident smile.

"I'll need his authorization. You understand."

I did, but the tone in Pierre's voice was condescending and I didn't appreciate it.

I tapped Holden's number on the screen and held it up to my ear.

"Hey, babe," Holden answered. "Does he want to make sure that I sent you in there to buy something?"

I couldn't help but grin. "Yeah. I'll let you speak to him." I offered Pierre my cell, then studied his face while he spoke to Holden.

"Yes, of course. Anything you want. Absolutely." Pierre nodded enthusiastically, then said goodbye. He gave my phone back to me.

"Are you still there?" I asked Holden.

Holden's deep chuckle rumbled through the speaker. "You can shop there anytime you want. I gave you authorization to buy the entire store and threatened his job if he laid a hand on you."

"What?" I slapped Brynn's arm, my eyes widening. "Why?"

"I know Pierre, and he'd either try to sleep with you or he'd treat you like the scum of the earth unless I let him know how it would play out for him," Holden explained.

"He's a member," I whispered. "He already—"

Brynn jabbed me in the side and shook her head.

"Already what?" Holden's tone was clipped.

"He already mentioned that he knew you from there." I bit my lower lip, hoping I saved us from unnecessary drama. I could handle Pierre, but I would prefer to stop running into men that were absolute pigs.

"All right. Let me know if there's ever a problem, though."

"I will. Brynn and I should be there shortly."

"Good. I miss you." I could hear Holden smile through the phone. "Love you."

"Love you, too." I disconnected the call and leaned on my cane.

"That's all I need. I'll contact you or Holden to schedule the delivery," Pierre said, his voice warm and friendly.

"Thanks for your help."

Once we were outside the gallery, I glanced at Brynn. "I feel like I need a shower after being around him. Eww. He's hot but an absolute asshole."

"Now you know why I adore Holden so much. This world is filled with disgusting men that don't respect women. You've got a good one."

I inwardly swooned a little. Holden was one of the good ones. "Oh, the guys are at the club. Holden said to come on up." I peeked at the time on my phone before I shoved it into my pocket. "I'd like to change into some of my new clothes first. Ya know, get his first impression."

"Oh, great idea." Brynn slipped her sunglasses into place as we arrived at the Mercedes in the parking garage. "Wear your Sevens, black boots, and that burgundy blouse. While we're at Holden's, grab the necklace."

My stomach shook and I wondered if Tim might show up. "Vaughn, are you able to accompany us inside Holden's house?"

"I will if you need me too."

"Please." I grabbed Brynn's hand, wondering if Tim had come back home.

Chapter Thirty-Five

Brynn and I strolled through the club at a little after eight. The party hadn't even started. I self-consciously ran my fingertips over my necklace, loving what the H stood for. Maybe I should wear it all the time. If Pierre had seen it, he'd have understood not to offer himself to Brynn and me.

I tucked my new dark wash jeans into my black boots and left my blouse unbuttoned to show a little cleavage, but not too much. It had been Brynn's idea, and since I was with her and Vaughn, I felt comfortable enough to leave a few of the buttons undone. Plus, we were going up to the fourth floor without stopping.

We were flooded with attention as we walked through the main floor and to the elevator. I pushed the button, and the doors whooshed closed. "He said to meet them in the party room."

Brynn rolled her eyes. "The guys are here so much they set up a pool table, television, PlayStation, and Xbox upstairs. That's the party room." She grinned. "Holden's been known to sleep here on occasion after a late night."

I almost asked with who, but I caught myself before I stuck my foot in my mouth. Holden hadn't ever tried to hide the fact that he'd been a player, but I didn't want to know about it.

The elevator stopped, and we stepped into the same hallway as the conference room. Brynn made a left, and I followed her. "Here we are." She turned the handle and opened the door. Vaughn remained outside in the hall. I bet his job was boring as hell sometimes.

"Dayummm." Jace stood, his eyes on Brynn and me.

"Back up, man." Holden playfully smacked Jace on the chest, then approached me.

"You. Look. Sexy. As. Fuck." Holden slipped his arms around my waist and planted a searing kiss on my mouth.

A low whistle filled the man cave, then laughter. I peeked around my boyfriend, my attention landing on Chance.

"You two are steaming up the room. I'm not going to be able to see the game if you don't stop." Chance leaned to the right, his fingers flying over the controller.

Brynn laughed and sat on the arm of the couch near Chance.

"Did you have a good day?" Holden whispered against my ear.

"I did. It was really good." I peered up at him through my eyelashes, heat stirring deep inside of me.

"Excellent. I have something to show you." He kissed my forehead and took my hand. "See you all in a bit."

The guys just grunted at us as we slipped out of the room. Holden led us to the elevator. "Vaughn, we're going to the penthouse. We'll be back in a few."

"Sir." Vaughn nodded, acknowledging Holden's request.

"I wanted to show you the space."

"I'm excited. Hopefully the new art pieces will work well with it." Anxiety hummed beneath my skin as Brynn's earlier conversation played in my mind again. I'd promised not to tell Holden, but now that I was with him, I wasn't sure if it was the right thing to do. My conscience flipped around faster than a weathervane in a tornado. Either way, there would be consequences.

The elevator doors pinged and slid open. We strolled down the hall, then to a door. Holden removed a key from his jeans pocket and unlocked it. I chewed on my lip. That had to change. We needed an eye scanner here as well. I made a mental note to talk to him about what security upgrades we would have.

"Damn," I said, my attention shifting as I scanned the huge space. My boots scuffed across the clean concrete floors as I walked around.

"This includes the kitchen, dining area, and living room. I was thinking about an open concept. What do you think? We can make any changes you want to."

I nodded in agreement. "It will be perfect. Plus, the view is stunning. I would prefer not to have walls in the way." I strolled over to the windows.

"You can see for miles and miles." Holden joined me and slipped his arm around my waist. "I can't wait to wake up here with you every day, River." He glanced down at me, and my heart raced in response.

"Me, too." We stood in silence, reveling in the peace and beauty that surrounded us.

"Are you ready to see the master? Well, what will become the bedroom?"

I nodded, grinning like a little girl on Christmas morning as we strolled to our future hideaway.

"Wow." I hurried to the middle of the room and spun around. "This is way bigger than the one we're currently in at your mom's place."

Holden chuckled. "Yeah, I guess a big-ass bedroom and huge bathroom are perks of owning it."

I laughed, loving the idea of our own home.

"Do you know what I love the most?" Holden approached me, his brown eyes flashing with mischievousness.

"What's that?"

"You never have to wear clothes at home again."

My mouth formed a big O. "Oh my God. We can walk around

naked and fuck on every surface available." I grinned and did a happy dance the best I could with the cane.

"I like the way you think." Holden placed his finger beneath my chin and tilted it up. "I love you, River."

"I love you, too." I leaned into him, then pressed my lips against his.

Holden showed me the rest of the space, and we made some decisions about the design. One of my favorite things about the penthouse was the windows on two sides. The view of the Spokane River warmed my heart.

"Hey, I have a question," I said, standing in the middle of the last guest bedroom and tapping my chin with my finger. "Is there enough room to have our own ... playroom?"

Holden's features lit up. "Like the Master's Playroom, but for us?"

I nodded. "For when we want privacy."

Holden's heated gaze landed on mine. "Is there a time we don't want privacy?"

I gave him a half shrug. "I've toyed with the idea of someone watching us."

Holden scrubbed his face with his hands and blew out a breath. His bulge was evident in his jeans, and I resisted the urge to free his thick cock while we talked. "We would be safer in the Master's Playroom, but our friends would be the ones watching there."

Oh shit. I liked that idea way too much. "I'm getting wet just talking about it." I bit my lower lip and placed my palm against his chest. "I know you all have watched each other before, but I'm the new player. Are you sure you're okay with that?"

"It would be dark, so they'd see our outlines, but babe, they would be busy playing on the other couches."

"So we'd be watching them too?" I asked, heady with anticipation. "Can I trust them? In some ways a stranger would seem safer."

"If we use the Voyeur Room, they'll see us, River. Not only your body, but your face. I can't have men stalking you in the club or while you're at work."

"You're not worried about Jace, Chance, or Brynn?"

"No. They understand the rules. This doesn't have to happen, babe. The only reason I'm agreeing is because you're exploring what you like. I know what I like. We don't need any toys, whips, hand-cuffs, or anything else. I love being with you, connecting on a heart-to-heart level."

"Brynn admitted she likes me." I mentally kicked myself for blurting that out.

"I know." Holden rubbed my cheek with the pad of his thumb. "She asked if we might be able to share." A slow grin eased across his face. "I told her hell no."

I blushed furiously. "I told her I loved you, but if I ever wanted to try it with a girl, I would see if you'd be all right with it."

Holden's mouth opened and closed before he spoke. "Are you saying ..."

"Nope. Don't get your hopes up." I patted his arm. "I love Brynn, but I'm not interested in a physical relationship. All I meant was that if I ever wanted to try it, I would feel safe with her."

"Damn, I was hoping."

"Holden Alastair!" I smacked him on the chest.

"Babe, I'm asking for your honesty, so I've got to give you mine as well. I've lived that life. Yes, I like to play and play hard, but with you, not anyone else. I do trust the guys, but I won't lie. I don't like the idea of them or anyone watching us."

I loved him even more for being honest with me. "Then let's table the thought. Holden, you've opened a brand-new world for me, but I never want to hurt you. Please promise me that you'll continue to tell me when you're not okay with an idea. The communication goes both ways." I slipped my arms around his waist and dipped my hands into the back pockets of his jeans.

"You're right. I want to give you everything you want, babe. I want to show you that the world isn't all bad, and I want to protect you. Once the clothes are off in front of someone else, people look at you differently."

I completely understood what he was saying. It took me a while to adjust after my first visit to the Master's Playroom.

Holden kissed me gently. "I have one more thing I want to show you."

"Yeah?" I was finally realizing that Holden's surprises were good ones. Growing up, they never were. My heart twisted painfully in my chest as Dan's sneer appeared in my mind. I grabbed Holden's arm and squeezed it.

"Are you all right?" he asked as we walked to the elevator.

"Yeah, it's just that sometimes memories pop up." I couldn't force myself to tell Holden that Dan had stolen my virginity. It wouldn't have done any good to talk about it. Dan was dead. Gone. Wild animals most likely ate his flesh, and only the bones were left. I'd heard that seeking revenge usually ended up badly, but I found great satisfaction in recalling that Dan had gotten what he deserved.

"You're safe, babe." Holden placed his hand on my back, the warmth of his palm comforting me.

The elevator doors slid closed, and within a few seconds, we were exiting again on the third floor. Instead of heading to the conference room, we went in the opposite direction. Holden stood in front of the eye scanner. The door clicked, then he opened it. An overhead light turned on as soon as he stepped inside.

"This is my office."

A large cherrywood desk sat in front of the row of windows. Three dark brown leather chairs lined the wall, and I assumed those were for potential clients. The far-left wall was lined with built-in bookcases directly above a couch.

"It's gorgeous." I strolled to the other side, admiring the city lights below us.

"This door ..." He opened it, and I followed him into the next room. "This is your office, River."

I gawked as my attention bounced around. It was as big as his and already furnished with matching furniture, except that I had a black couch and chairs instead of brown.

"I'll add you to the retina scanner for both offices."

I nodded, too overwhelmed with the idea that I had my own space at the club. Not a closet or basement office, but a gorgeous office with a row of windows behind the cherrywood desk.

"What do you think?" Holden shoved his hands in his pockets as I slowly took it all in, touching every surface with my fingertips.

"I love it. I'm blown away, but I love it." I strolled over to him, pushed up on my tiptoes, and pressed my lips against his. "When do I start?"

"We'll review the contract with legal tomorrow. They'll answer any questions and if you need something else, then they can write it in."

"Makes sense." I kissed him again. "Does anyone else have access to the offices other than us?" I tugged at the waistband of his jeans.

"No." His response was husky.

"Good." I fumbled with his button and zipper, then reached into his boxer briefs and wrapped my fingers around his thick cock. I stroked him as our kisses grew needy and desperate.

Holden grabbed my waist, then lifted me off the floor and onto my desk. I set my cane down, then leaned back and propped myself up on my elbows, watching as he removed my boots, jeans, and G-string. The cool air brushed against my bare legs, and I shivered.

He knelt and gently spread me apart. "Perfection." He eased two fingers inside of me, then swirled his tongue around my bundle of nerves.

I was on fire. Every part of me hummed with expectation and need while I watched as he devoured me, licking, sucking, and fucking me with his mouth. My head fell back, and my eyes closed as I tilted my hips. Desire licked through every inch of my sensitive skin.

"Holden," I panted.

He gripped my thighs, and I tipped over the edge into oblivion. I leaned against the desk, then Holden crawled on top of me. I giggled as I realized we were going to break in my office properly.

"Every time I look at this desk, I'm going to remember this moment." I placed my palm against his cheek and smiled.

"I hope so." He gently pushed himself inside of me and pressed his mouth against mine.

My lips parted, our tongues tangling as he found his rhythm. He placed his palms on either side of me and moved his hips in a circular motion, massaging my clit as he made love to me.

"Jesus, River, you feel so goddammed good."

I slipped my hands beneath his shirt and scraped my nails along his sensitive skin. He nipped at my ear and picked up the pace. Our bodies rocked in unison and nothing else existed except for us. I could stay forever in this safe bubble with him, ignoring all the bad in the world.

A soft whimper escaped me, the delicious feeling swelling in the pit of my stomach. The sweet and warm orgasm unfurled and claimed the rest of my body. He released a low growl, gripped the backs of my thighs, and plowed into me. His body shuddered as he came.

He dotted my face with kisses and smiled at me. "Are you happy, River?"

Confused, I frowned at him. "Of course, I am baby. Why would you ask me that? I'm the happiest I've ever been."

Holden stood and pulled up his pants. "I just wanted to make sure." He sank onto the couch, his expression turning grim.

After I buttoned my jeans again, I grabbed my cane and hopped off the desk. "Hey, what's wrong?"

Chapter Thirty-Six

Guilt clung to Holden's features as he took my hand in his. "While you and Brynn were out shopping today, I poked around where I shouldn't have."

I laughed softly. "Holden, I don't care if you looked through my belongings. I don't have much, and I certainly don't have any secrets to hide." I leaned over and kissed his cheek, touched that he was worried I'd be upset with him.

Holden gave me a weak smile. "It wasn't your stuff, babe. For whatever reason, Dad's office wasn't locked. I'm guessing it's because he got thrown out on his ass and didn't have time to lock up."

The hair on the back of my neck bristled. "What did you find?" Brynn's words returned to me, and I wondered if Holden had found any information backing up Brynn's accusation of Tim being involved as an illegal weapons dealer.

"Mom had left for a while, so I had the house to myself. For some reason I gave his office doorknob a turn and it opened. His laptop was open, and papers were on his desk. After what he pulled with you, I had a sinking feeling that he wasn't the man he pretended to be."

Anxiety descended over me. "What did you find?" I stroked the back of his hand with my thumb, encouraging him to continue.

"Nothing at first. It was all encrypted. I reached out to Jace and he connected me with some genius computer guru named Sutton. Apparently, she's the wife of Pierce Westbrook, who owns the security company I use. Sutton promised me full confidentiality. I've met Pierce a few times, and he always has great men working for him, so I trusted them already. I paid her to help me. Within a few hours, I was able to read every word."

He leaned against the couch, a faraway expression clouding his face. "We can't go back, River. The information that Sutton found puts us in grave danger. Plus, Dad's pissed that you brought him to his knees, and Mom kicked him out. He has a key to the house ..." He gulped. "I can't take a chance. I can't risk anything happening to you." Tears welled in his eyes. "I don't want to tell you any specifics. It would put you at an even greater risk."

I pursed my lips together, trying not to tell him what Brynn had shared with me earlier. There was no way I would break her trust, but that didn't mean I couldn't encourage Holden and Brynn to discuss what they each knew.

"Growing up, I learned the most powerful people are always the most corrupt. Their need for control is deep-rooted and often requires a darker outlet. Tim Alastair is no different." Holden's features grew stormy. "I want to hunt him down and slam my fist through his perfect teeth." Fury rolled off him in waves. I sat still and waited for him to continue. "Names, contacts, money, shell companies, and offshore accounts. From what I can tell, Mom doesn't have any idea that Dad is dealing illegal firearms."

Even though Brynn had said the same to me, this was different. There was proof, and Holden's words sat in my gut like sour milk.

"I'm too selfish to give you up, River. But I'll admit that I considered it. You're in danger if you stay."

My breath stuttered and I clasped his face in my palms. "You know I'm in just as much danger, if not more, if I go. I would much rather be with you, Holden. Our odds are better together." I brushed my lips against his. "I love you." I looked into his sad eyes.

"There was one more thing." His whole body was rigid and strained. "There was a name ... Logan Huntington. Is that the same one as the Logan in the picture with my family?" His brow lifted in question.

I attempted to still my racing heart, but I couldn't. "Yes," I choked out. "And thanks to Shirley and Ed, he knows exactly where I'm sleeping at night." Fury sizzled beneath the surface, battling with sorrow and disappointment over Shirley and Ed's betrayal.

A simmering rage lurked inside Holden's eyes. "I'll kill anyone that tries to hurt you." He lifted my hand to his mouth and kissed my knuckles.

"Do you trust me, Holden?"

"If I didn't, I wouldn't have told you what I'd learned about Tim."

Holden was flipping between referring to his father as Tim or Dad. He was torn and conflicted, and I wanted to kiss his pain away and make it all disappear.

I raised my hip off the couch and slid my phone from my back pocket. My fingers flew over the screen, and seconds later, it vibrated.

I need you to talk to someone.

Holden leaned over and rested his elbows against his knees, his head hanging down. "If I'd known, I would have never brought you into my home. I was supposed to protect you, River and I've only let you down." His voice sounded haunted. Devastated. Alone.

The ache that never stopped throbbing in my chest intensified to an earth-shattering roar. "It's not your fault. You can't think like that. I was running from Logan and his men when I landed in your yard. We were already connected, just in a way neither of us anticipated."

A soft knock at the door interrupted our conversation. "I've got it." I stood and crossed the room with my heart beating wildly against my chest. I knew who was on the other side of the wall. I slipped into the hallway and held my finger to my lips, indicating we had to whisper.

"Are you all right? You look like you've seen a ghost." Brynn hugged me and I swallowed my tears. I was so grateful for her friendship.

Pulling away, I cleared my throat. "I gave you my word that I wouldn't say anything to Holden about Tim, and I haven't." My eyes pleaded with her to help me. "You need to tell him, Brynn, and Holden needs to tell you what he learned today."

"What happened?" she whispered.

"It's not my place to tell you his story any more than it's my place to share yours. From what I've learned so far, he doesn't know about the affair." I couldn't say another word without betraying Holden's trust.

"Okay. I'll talk to him," Brynn said.

I squeezed her hand in appreciation, then led us into my new office.

"Babe, you need to tell Brynn." I stood rooted to the floor as his head snapped my way, eyes open wide and filled with caution.

He pinned me with troubled eyes. "River, I trusted you not to repeat—"

"This girl is tight-lipped as hell, Holden. Calm down. This has to do with what I shared with her earlier today."

Holden's attention bounced between us. I sat at my new desk while Brynn remained near the door.

"I don't know what you said to River," she continued, "but I told her Tim wasn't who he said he was. From the information I heard, it seems like he's a very dangerous illegal arms dealer."

Respect for Brynn's courage welled up inside of me. She took me at face value and trusted me during a difficult situation.

Holden's mouth gaped. "You know? River, why didn't you tell me when I brought it up?"

"I made River swear she would take that information to her grave, but I also wanted her to be able to protect you both," Brynn explained.

"I'm sorry. It was a fucked-up situation to be in," I added. "Two people I love more than anything in this world confided in me, making me promise I wouldn't talk. Holden, once you told me about Tim tonight, I knew I had to bring Brynn in. Maybe we can figure this out together."

"That had to have been tough, babe." Holden's gentle gaze landed on me.

"I want to protect you, Holden. I'll do anything necessary." We stared at each other in silence, communicating how much we loved each other.

Brynn smoothed her boyfriend jeans, then sat down in a chair, appearing less stressed. "Are you willing to tell me what you shared with River?" She crossed her legs, then swung one slightly.

I listened as Holden shared what he'd learned with Brynn.

"Where's his computer now?" she asked.

"It's where I found it. All I did was send Sutton the files. That way if he came home to get his laptop, there wouldn't be any suspicions."

I slumped back into my chair, relieved.

"And that's what we have to do as well," I said.

Holden shot me a questioning look. "What do you mean?"

"If we change anything or sleep somewhere else, it will indicate that we know something. We'll raise suspicions with your mom and at some point, she and Tim will have to talk. Plus, he's going to want his shit back. Tim knows what's on his computer."

"Goddammit." Holden massaged his neck. "You're right. I can't leave Mom on her own, either. Not until I make sure the house is secure. She's not safe from that monster, but I can't tell her what I know. She'll go straight to him."

"I'll help as much as I can, but please keep me out of it," Brynn said.

"Brynn, I would never betray you like that. You trusted us, and I'll make sure you're not pulled into it."

"Thanks."

Holden stood, his attention landing on me. "We should get back home. I want to talk to Mom first thing in the morning about updating the security system. I'll also install an eye scanner on our room. If he comes home in the middle of the night, you'll be safe. I'll call Pierce tomorrow and see if he can assign Zayne and Vaughn to us full time. That way you're free to leave the house and club whenever you wish."

If the situation hadn't been so serious, I would have wiggled my brows at Brynn, but it wasn't a matter to be taken lightly. At least we could enjoy the eye candy more often.

"River, I have an extra taser and mace, but you should start carrying a purse," Brynn said.

"I agree," Holden added. "I need to know that you have the tools to defend yourself."

"I can pick up a knife holster to strap on my leg too." Thinking about how I got my knife, my brain played tug-of-war with my emotions. Why would Ed give me a weapon and then put a tracker on my phone, or did Shirley act on her own?

"Brynn, we'll see you tomorrow." Holden crossed the room, leaned down, and placed a kiss on the top of her head.

"We'll be fine. As long as we stick together, we'll make it through this," Brynn assured us.

Maybe she was right, but I couldn't ignore the pang her words created. They echoed through my chest like a whisper, telling me that we were missing something.

Chapter Thirty-Seven

The next morning, I quietly descended the stairs, then made my way toward the smell of coffee. My heart stuttered as my eyes landed on Holden and his mom at the kitchen table. He spoke in a hushed tone and held her hands in his.

Unwilling to disturb them, I crept backward with the help of my cane.

"River," Catherine flashed me a warm smile. "Join us. Please."

I glanced at Holden, and he nodded.

"I'm sorry to interrupt." I stifled a yawn and headed for the coffeepot. Removing a cup from the cabinet, I poured the hot brown liquid into it.

"Nonsense. Holden was just telling me that you two will finish and move into the penthouse. Are you excited?" Catherine crossed her legs, her cream-colored slippers matching her robe.

It shouldn't have surprised me that he'd mentioned this to his mom so early in the planning stages, but she should know what our plans were. Hell, I hoped we could bury any bad feelings about Tim's behavior, and she'd join us for dinner on occasion.

"I am." I smiled at them as I sank into the chair next to Holden.

"Morning," he said, then gave me a sweet kiss.

"Morning." I beamed at him. Life was a fucked-up mess at the moment, but as long as Holden was with me, I had faith that everything would be all right.

"River, I hope that you're not rushing plans because of what my husband did." She smoothed her hair, her French-manicured nails flashing in the light. "It wasn't your fault, and I don't blame you in any way. Tim ..." She pulled nervously on the opening of her robe, clutching it closer to her chest. "Our marriage has been over for a few years. It's time that I move on."

I sucked in a gasp. "Was ... was I the final straw?" I choked out.

Compassion flashed in her brown eyes. "No. I'd planned on breaking the news to him while we were home this week. It just came a few days earlier than planned."

Internally, I sighed with relief. I couldn't handle the guilt of breaking up a marriage, even if it was a shitty one. "I'm sorry. I can't imagine how difficult this has been for you."

Holden squeezed my hand under the table.

"I'm ready to get off this crazy train, hon. I've built a highly successful financial business and I have no shame in being alone. Hell, I'll probably enjoy it. Of course, I'll have to split the company with him, but he has his clients and I have mine, so it shouldn't be too difficult. I've been working with a wonderful attorney over the last several months. I had to make sure I had all of my affairs in order before I delivered the news to my ... soon to be ex-husband."

I secretly hoped that Catherine got everything she wanted in the divorce. If she only knew what a horrible man Tim really was, she wouldn't give him a single penny.

"I'll make sure he doesn't bother you, Mom. We'll have the locks changed today and the security system upgraded. I think you should consider hiring a bodyguard as well."

My heart warmed at Holden's protectiveness toward Catherine.

"I love you for your concern, Holden, but I don't need security following my every move. I've managed your father for almost thirty years."

But you don't know who he really is. That would eventually be a conversation between Holden and Catherine. For now, I needed to keep my mouth shut.

Over the next hour, we shared our morning together and drank coffee. It was refreshing to wake up without worrying Tim was there, although I would feel a shit ton better after the security was upgraded.

Finally, Holden stood, and I followed. "I'm going to make some calls, Mom. Are you going to be around most of the day?"

"Yes. I have to make some calls of my own. I'll work in your father's office."

I literally felt the color drain from my face, and I turned away from her, my attention landing on my boyfriend.

"Let me know if you need anything," Holden said while remaining calm.

We walked through the house and up the stairs leading to our bedroom in silence. The moment we were alone, he swore. "If Mom sees any of the papers that's on Dad's desk ..." His expression twisted with worry.

"Can you get down to the office and hide them before she goes in there? I mean, maybe it's still unlocked."

Holden sprung off the door, then flung it open and darted out of the room. My heart pounded in my chest like a jackhammer while I begged and pleaded with the universe that he wouldn't be caught.

I sat at the desk and counted to a hundred as slowly as possible without losing my mind.

A few minutes later, heavy footsteps reached my ears, and I shot out of the chair and poked my head into the hallway.

Holden made a beeline to me, his face pale.

I pulled him into the room and shut the door. "What happened?" I whispered, my gaze raking over him for any signs that he was hurt.

"It's gone. His computer, the papers—everything in his desk is gone."

My pulse stuttered against my wrist as I witnessed Holden's anxiety climb the walls. "Let's get the locks changed now, babe. He can't come back in without a key unless he wants to break in and get arrested." I didn't say it out loud, but I liked the idea of him landing his sorry ass in jail.

"He must have come in while we were all asleep." Holden's expression fell, worry taking over his features. "He could have hurt you in the middle of the night."

I placed my finger on Holden's lips. "We can't waste our time and energy with what could have happened. Let's stay on track, baby." I stretched up and pressed a kiss against his mouth. "I love you. Now let's show this fucker what we're made of."

* * *

The rest of the day was a blur as all the locks in the house were changed, additional cameras were placed on the outside of the home, and Holden installed a retina scan for our bedroom door. It was odd at first, but I knew it was the safest option.

At three in the afternoon, we met with the lawyer, and I finalized my employment agreement with Holden at 4 Play. I was officially employed and being paid generously. Not only would I consult with Holden, but I would be involved in the financials and oversee the bar employees and security. I wouldn't have anything to do with the lower-level membership and clients. It was also in my contract that I would wear the necklace with the H on it. Holden said he would have a few more made for me, and I could choose the color of the stones. Under no circumstances would I be at the club without it on.

Afterward, Holden took me to the bank, and I set up my first savings and checking accounts with the signing bonus he'd given me. I didn't want to take it, but he said it was a common practice. I just wondered if it was common to have a bonus of a hundred thousand dollars. After arguing with myself, I decided to accept it just in case I had to take off and run again. At least I would have money to live on and I could stretch the shit out of a hundred grand. Plus, I could buy him something special for his twenty-second birthday in May. March had already snuck up on me, and now that I would be filling my days with work, I needed to plan ahead. I would definitely need Brynn, Chance, and Jace's help. I had no idea what to give a man that could buy himself anything he wanted.

Our last errand of the day was to Nordstrom, where I bought a new purse. Holden helped me choose one that would be large enough to house the taser and mace. Twenty-five hundred dollars later, we strolled out of the mall with my new handbag and wallet safely wrapped and in a Nordstrom bag that Holden insisted he carried for me. I'd expressed my concern about being a target, but he assured me it wouldn't be an issue.

"You'll get used to carrying an expensive purse, babe." Holden opened the car door of his navy BMW i8, then handed my new purchase to me. I stretched my jean-clad legs in front of me and placed my cane between them. Since I'd been attending all of my physical therapy sessions, I was hoping to be able to ditch it soon.

Holden started the car and eased out of the underground parking space when his phone rang. He clicked a button on the steering wheel and winked at me.

"This is Holden Alastair," he answered.

"Holden, Pierce Westbrook. I apologize for not getting back to you sooner."

It took a moment for me to realize it was Pierce with the seriously hot bodyguards.

"I was wondering if Zayne and Vaughn would be available on a full-time basis for a while. My girlfriend and I need some additional security."

"Let me take a look at their assignments. I know you've used them over the last several months on an occasional basis, but since it's always been in the evening, I assigned them to other jobs as well."

These guys work around the clock. When the hell do they sleep?

"I understand. They're my first choices since I know them."

"When would you need to switch to full-time?" Pierce asked, the clicking of the computer keys filling the phone line.

"Immediately." Holden glanced at me, then squeezed my knee.

"Give me just a minute," Pierce replied.

"Babe?" a girl's voice said in the background.

"Sutton, Holden Alastair is on speaker," Pierce explained.

"I'm sorry. I didn't realize. Hi, Holden, how are you doing?" Sutton asked.

"I could be better but thank you again for your help." Holden flipped on his turn signal, then took a right onto Division Street.

"It's what I do. Let me know if you need anything else. I'll let you and Pierce discuss business. Have a good evening."

I hadn't even seen Sutton Westbrook, but I immediately liked her. Not only was she smart, but she sounded like a person you could hang out with, down to earth and fun.

"Holden, I think I can move my men around for you. I need to make some calls, then I'll reach out when I know more. It might be late, but I'm assuming you'll be awake since you own a club." You could hear the smile in Pierce's voice.

"You can call me at three in the morning if you need to. And Pierce, if the guys aren't available, that's fine. I need someone no later than tomorrow around ten."

I peeked at Holden, and he smiled at me. "You have work," he mouthed.

"You bet. I'll make it happen. Talk to you soon," Pierce said and disconnected the phone.

Holden's headlights landed on one of the garages of his house, cutting through the darkness as the door slowly opened.

"Babe?" I grabbed Holden's arm, dread knotting my stomach. "I have a bad feeling."

Holden hesitated, his gaze sweeping the area in front of us.

"Fuck!" Holden gripped the steering wheel. "Stay here. Call the cops if any shit starts to go down."

Chapter Thirty-Eight

Anxiety twisted my insides as I watched Holden exit the car and enter the garage. Fortunately, I could see him and Tim as they faced off.

I wasn't sure if it was a blessing in disguise that I couldn't hear what they were saying, or not. Tim's hands were fisted, but he never raised one to his son. Holden's muffled words carried through the windows, and I strained to listen. Surely, he wouldn't admit to seeing the papers on his desk. I hoped like hell Holden didn't get so angry that he slipped and told Tim that Sutton had cracked the encryption.

My name reached my ears, and I held my breath. I hoped the yelling match was about me rather than the truth.

Tim got in Holden's face, his cheeks burning red with fury, then he stomped off. He shot me a debilitating glare as he stormed away. My gaze followed him as he walked down the driveway and to a dark green Jaguar parked at the curb.

Holden climbed back into his car and eased it into his parking space. The door closed behind us, and I turned to him.

"What happened and what in the hell was he doing in here?" I asked, nervously twisting the hem of my shirt.

Frustration and anger twisted his handsome features. "I'd forgotten to change the garage code, so he waited for me." Holden ran his fingers through his hair. "I need to make sure Mom is all right. He said he couldn't get in, but I don't trust a fucking word he says."

I exited the car and grabbed my Nordstrom bag before he could finish his sentence. Although it sounded like Tim didn't get into the house, seeing that Catherine was safe would soothe my jumpy nerves.

Before we reached the door, Holden's phone rang. He took it from his pocket, and we stepped into the mudroom that connected to the kitchen.

"Holden Alastair," he said in a hushed tone.

I walked ahead of him and checked to see if anyone was near us on the main floor. I shook my head no.

"Excellent. I'll be expecting them soon. Thanks a ton, Pierce." Holden disconnected the call. "Zayne and Vaughn will be here within the hour. While we're home, they'll keep an eye on the property. I know you won't be crazy about it, but they'll also be with us at work."

"I understand. If I stay in my office though, the only people that can get in are you and me, right? If you need one of them elsewhere, then that can happen."

"I know you'd be safe in our offices, but I don't want you to feel as though you're caged in, either." Worry lines creased his forehead. "I think I'll add another retina scanner to the fourth level. After the penthouse is finished, we'll add one at the front door as well."

"I like that idea. Then we don't have to have security all the time. Save your money. Add me, Chance, Jace, Brynn, and the bodyguards to the scanner."

"That will work. No one needs to reach that floor unless they're accompanied by either you or me anyway. I occasionally have meetings in the conference room, but that's easy enough to manage."

Holden kissed me gently.

"I think this will be better. Maybe you can have a bodyguard for your mom part of the time. I'll be spending my days at 4 Play. Hell, I can even work on my classes there in peace." I flashed a smile at him, suddenly exhausted. "When do we need to be at the club tomorrow?"

"I don't have classes on Monday, so around nine." He took my hand and we strolled through the kitchen and formal dining room. Holden paused in the foyer. "Why don't you head upstairs, and I'll see if I can find Mom. I'm not sure if she's here."

"Sounds good." I was excited to fill my purse and wallet while I waited for Holden to join me. Next on my to-do list would be a Washington State driver's license instead of the one from Montana. With each day, I was building a new life with Holden and my new friends. Everything was perfect, *except for Tim.*

Anger reared its head inside of me. First, I had to deal with Dan, and now I had another sorry bastard to take care of.

Reaching the bedroom, I stood still for the retina scanner, then proceeded into our room. My leg ached like a son of a bitch. I sat down and removed my Nikes. Unless I was at the club, I preferred comfy tennis shoes, especially while I was healing.

I flopped back on the bed, sinking into the mattress. The doorbell rang, and I grabbed my cane and hurried down the hall in case Holden hadn't heard it.

When I reached the top of the stairs, I smiled. Holden peered through the peephole, then opened the door. He stepped aside, inviting Vaughn and Zayne into the house.

I descended the steps and joined the group of men in the foyer.

"Hey guys," I said to Zayne and Vaughn as I cozied up to Holden and slid my arm around his waist.

"River," Vaughn said, nodding in my direction. His mismatched eyes held an element of seriousness, and I wondered what the men's backgrounds were. The way they presented themselves and their posture made me guess military. My attention landed on their hands, but no wedding bands were in sight. I would have to let Brynn know.

Zayne greeted me as well, his stoic expression in place. They both wore black slacks and black Westbrook Security coats.

"Babe, they're going to patrol the perimeter tonight, then they'll drive us to the club in the morning."

"Thank you both. I really appreciate it."

"Our pleasure," Zayne responded.

"I'll let you guys finish." I gave Holden a quick peck on the lips, then left them to discuss any additional business.

I returned to our room and undressed, exhaustion seeping into my bones. Since we now had a retina scanner at the door and no one could just waltz in, I slipped beneath the covers naked. Before my head hit the pillow, my eyes fluttered closed, and I sank into a fitful sleep.

* * *

Holden's alarm woke me the next morning and I reached for him. I wasn't sure what time he'd crawled into bed, but he'd wrapped me in his arms when he had. I gave him a kiss, then bounded out of bed, nearly giddy about my first day at work.

After my shower, I dressed in skinny jeans, my black boots, and navy blouse. Holden had slipped on a blue button-down shirt and jeans that hung low on his hips, hugging every muscular curve in his ass and thighs. I was tempted to take them off, but it would have to wait.

I held my long, dark hair up so Holden could slip the necklace around my neck.

"I love you, babe. I have to admit I get horny as hell when I see this on you." His fingers lightly danced over my skin while he slipped the necklace around my neck and fastened the clasp. A soft moan escaped me as his hands slowly glided down my body. "We have time for a quickie." He nipped at my ear, and I laughed.

I faced him and slid my arms around his waist. "How about on top of *your* desk when we take a lunch break?"

Holden groaned. "I wish I could. After I show you what to do for the day, I have to be upstairs with the contractors. I hired construction around the clock. There will be a few hours in-between shifts, but I want this up as fast as humanly possible. I'm ready to carry you through the door of our new place and straight to our bed."

"I love the sound of that." I kissed him slowly while I slid my hand down his chest and stomach. He sharply inhaled as I cupped his hard dick through his jeans. Normally, I saw Holden in suits that cost thousands of dollars while at 4 Play, but he would be in the middle of a construction zone.

"You're not playing fair." Holden chuckled and leaned his forehead against mine.

"Nope. But at least you'll think about me all day." I winked at him and sighed. My mind ran through my to-do list. "I have to catch up on my classes after work."

"Me too. I have one tomorrow as well, so I won't be in until later. You can call or text if you need me, though."

I'd already decided that next semester I would take business courses. If Holden was taking a chance on me, then I wanted to show up for him the best way that I could. I owed him everything. Not just because he'd taken me in, but because he'd saved my life and taught me to love.

The day flew by as I reviewed problem areas concerning the bar and security. Holden also shared some of the financials with me so I could see where he was losing money. My brain kicked into high gear as I started to play with other options to bring in more profit. Problem-solving was one of my gifts and an area I'd excelled at in high school.

Holden had considered my idea of not having a bodyguard while at the club, but when I opened my office door to take a break, Zayne scared the shit out of me.

My hand fluttered over my heart. "I didn't know you were there."

His green eyes assessed me, then he spoke. "The retina scanners won't be installed for a few days, so you're stuck with me."

I cracked a grin even though he didn't. "Can I ask a personal question?"

"You can ask anything you want. I just might not answer." He folded his hands in front of his waist.

"That's fair. I've noticed that you don't wear a wedding band. Are you in a relationship?"

Zayne's brow arched slightly. "I don't have time."

"I get that. It sounds like you stay busy with work." I tapped my chin with my finger. "Well, if you need some stress release, my best friend Brynn would be happy to help." Before he could respond, I turned away and started to walk down the hall to the elevator with a huge-ass grin on my face. Zayne might not reach out to Brynn, but I had at least planted the seed.

I pulled my phone from my back pocket and typed out a text to her.

Zayne is single, doesn't have time for a relationship, but that doesn't mean he doesn't have time to play. I let him know if he wanted to relieve some stress to reach out to you.

The elevator arrived, and Zayne and I entered, then I punched the button for the penthouse floor. My cell vibrated with a message.

Helllzzz yes! Thanks, babe.

I glanced at Zayne from the corner of my eye and stifled my laugh. The dude was seriously uptight. Brynn might be exactly what he needed.

Sixty seconds later, I entered the construction zone and immediately spotted Holden with a gray hard hat on. Although walls were now roughed in, I could still see through them, but it was definitely taking shape. A table was the only furniture in the wide-open area, and Holden and another guy were focused on papers spread out across the surface.

I started to approach them when Zayne gently grabbed my shoulder. "Wait here. It's not safe."

Even though he was my bodyguard, I felt that he'd just gone the extra mile to take care of me.

I hung back, watching as Zayne strolled up to the men. Holden's head popped up, then a wide grin split his face. He said something to the guy he was with, but I couldn't hear over all the hammers and saws.

Holden hurried over, then wrapped me in a warm embrace. "I've missed you." He pressed his mouth to mine, and my heart melted.

"I've missed you too. How's it going?" My gaze swept over the busy room. Men were working in every area.

"It's only the first day, but we're already ahead of schedule. John and I were reviewing the plans and making some minor changes. You and I will need to pick out the floors and furnishings. Hell, we need to do it for each room." He beamed at me and smoothed my hair.

"I'm excited." I stretched up and gave him a lingering kiss.

"Me too. You're the only girl I've lived with, and now we're picking out the details for our first home together."

"The first one?" Confused, I frowned.

"First." He kissed my forehead. "Then we'll have vacation homes, and maybe someday we'll move from Spokane. Until then, we can fly in from anywhere in the country, and stay for a week. I'll have Chance oversee the daily responsibilities here in Spokane and take care of the rest remotely. Chance does a lot of that already, so it won't be a problem."

"Really?" I was surprised to learn about his plans. For some reason, I'd never considered our future past where we were, but apparently, Holden had. Not only that, but I was in his life down the road.

"I love you so much." I slipped my arms around his neck and laid my head against his chest, the beat of his heart against my ear.

"Let's meet after work for drinks and you can tell me all about your day."

"I can't wait," I replied.

Holden kissed me goodbye, then I watched him walk away, admiring his jeans hugging his ass and muscular thighs.

I'm not sure Holden could deliver better news than that the penthouse was already ahead of schedule. Even though we had a retina scanner and updated security at Holden's house, I wasn't sleeping well. The minute I closed my eyes, Tim's sneer filled my mind. Holden had enough on his plate, so I hadn't mentioned it to him. A part of me whispered that we'd never be safe from Tim. My stomach clenched and twisted into knots. Little did I know how accurate my instincts were.

Chapter Thirty-Nine

The next few months flew by, and we finally had a firm move-in date. The floors, sinks, counters, cabinets, and other details had all been selected and had arrived. I was nearly giddy as I witnessed all of the details and hard work fall into place. Catherine had also chimed in when we asked her opinion. She had fabulous taste, and I was happy that she wanted to help.

Catherine and I had grown closer, and Holden and I supported her as she began divorce proceedings. Tim claimed he was overseas working, but he would return in two weeks. Thank God we'd be moving then, and I could easily avoid him since I'd be busy at our new home.

Holden only had a few classes left to take, then he would graduate. I'd decided to continue classes over the summer as well. I was behind schedule and wanted to get caught up before the fall.

The day I was able to ditch the cane, Holden took me dancing. Brynn, Chance, and Jace went with us to a few other clubs, then back to 4 Play. It was interesting to see how 4 Play was steps above the others we'd seen, but that night had also sparked some ideas.

Holden and I worked well together. He listened to my

suggestions, and I never took it personally when he said no. He'd done a hell of a job with the club before I ever came along. At the same time, it did feel pretty amazing when he did make the changes I'd suggested.

Shuffling through papers at my desk, I was suddenly overwhelmed with nausea. The closer we got to Tim arriving, the more my stress was showing up physically.

I took a sip of water, but it wasn't working. Sweat dotted my forehead as my stomach churned. I jumped out of my office chair and ran to the bathroom, barely reaching the toilet in time before I unloaded my lunch. My leg strap sheath poked me, and I took comfort knowing my knife was there. The weapon would be easier to reach than rummaging through my purse for the taser or mace.

Shaking, I stood and leaned against the counter. I turned on the cold water, the creak of the faucet annoying me. I hated when I was sick. Every noise and smell made me feel like shit. I washed my face and pulled out the toothbrush and toothpaste Holden and I had stashed in our office bathroom. As soon as the mint hit my tongue, I hurled again. Grateful it was over the sink and not on the floor, I rinsed my mouth out and placed my hand against the wall for support.

I needed to go home, but I would be alone. Catherine had left two days ago for a business trip. Maybe Zayne could be inside the house with me. I would have to ask Holden where Zayne was since I no longer needed a bodyguard while at work.

I carefully made my way back to my desk and opened the drawer. I'd finally gotten used to carrying a purse, and most of the time, I left my phone inside of it. I grabbed my cell and typed Holden a text. Since he was in meetings, I wasn't sure how soon he would respond. Unwilling to wait, I messaged Brynn.

I'm sick, and I need to go home, but I'm nervous about being alone. Maybe Zayne could join us at the house later, but for now, I needed my bed.

Brynn's name flashed across my screen. *Can you drive yourself there?*

No. Zayne drove me, and I have no idea where he is. Holden's in meetings and not answering his messages.

My phone vibrated with her reply. *I'm on my way. Hang tight. Do you need anything from the store?"*

Crackers and 7 Up would be wonderful.

Little black dots flickered on my screen. *Oh shit, babe. Do you have a stomach bug?*

I think it's just stress with everything going on.

I waited for her response.

Stress is a bitch. On the bright side, Catherine keeps a stash of saltines and soda at the house. I know where they are. I'm almost to 4 Play. Hang tight.

I tapped out a message for Holden, letting him know that Brynn was picking me up and taking me home.

I gathered my purse and laptop and waited for Brynn to arrive. Fifteen minutes later, the sound of a soft knock at the door filled the room. Still shaky, I made my way over to it and looked through the peephole. Even though it was an office, Holden never wanted to be caught off guard. I didn't either.

Brynn waited in the hallway, and I let her in, my head spinning.

"Fuck! Girl, you look like shit."

I leaned against the doorframe, hoping I wasn't going to puke again. "Thanks. I feel like shit, too."

"I've got you covered. I grabbed a barf bag and put it in the car just in case. My little sister had her wisdom teeth removed and they sent her home with a few. She's all healed now, so I figured she wouldn't miss them."

"Thanks." I locked my office behind me and hugged the wall as we made it to the elevator.

"When did you start feeling bad?" Brynn wrapped my arm around her waist as we walked, steadying me.

"I've been nauseous off and on for a few weeks. The closer it gets to Tim arriving, the sicker I've gotten."

"Have you told Holden?" Brynn pushed the button for the main floor.

"No. He's dealing with enough. Most of the time it's only for an hour, and I've never hurled."

Brynn remained quiet as she stared at me. "Let's get you home and see if we can get you feeling better." She placed the back of her hand against my forehead. "No fever."

I gave her an apologetic smile. "I'm sorry I interrupted your day, but I love you for keeping me company."

"Girl, please. It's what family does for each other." She winked at me as the elevator arrived.

Somehow, I managed to not blow chunks all over Brynn's red Jaguar, but the minute we were home, I puked until I dry heaved.

Brynn was an amazing nurse and helped me get settled on the couch downstairs in the basement. She gave me a little 7 Up in a glass and ensured I didn't gulp it. She also grabbed a trash bag and laid it on the floor next to me, along with a plastic trash can. There was no way I had anything left in my stomach, but the last thing I wanted to do was puke all over the gorgeous rug.

I groaned as Brynn sat at the opposite end of the couch, and I curled up on my side, clutching the pillow she'd brought me.

"Will it bother you if I turn on the TV quietly?" She rubbed my leg, concern etched into her gorgeous face.

"No, it will be a good distraction." I sipped my soda, the carbonated bubbles tickling my nostrils.

"Hopefully you can fall asleep for a while." She opened her purse and fished out her phone. "I'll text Holden again."

I nodded, my eyelids drooping. "Thanks, Brynn. Love ya tons."

"I know, babe. I know."

* * *

I woke to the soft sound of voices and a sharp pain in my neck. Sitting up, I searched the room, my gaze landing on Holden and Brynn talking in the kitchen.

"There she is." Holden smiled warmly at me and approached the couch. "How are you feeling?" He kissed my forehead.

"I want to kiss you, but I might be contagious." I rubbed my stomach, suddenly hungry. "I'd like to try some 7 Up and crackers." I pulled my knees up and propped my chin up. "I'm feeling okay at the moment."

"If you can't keep soda down by tomorrow, we need to get you to the doctor. As much as you puked, I don't want you to get dehydrated." Holden smoothed my hair, worry flashing in his brown eyes.

"I'm sure it's just a twenty-four-hour bug."

Brynn brought over a plate with a few crackers on it.

"You're an awesome nurse." I grinned at her and accepted my dinner. I nibbled around the edge of one, then swung my legs in front of me so I could sit up better and not choke.

"I have younger siblings. It's part of the gig." She sat down near my feet again, and Holden grabbed a chair from the table and brought it over.

I wanted to put my head in his lap, but if I puked, I would be really embarrassed.

I glanced at Holden. "Do you have meetings again tomorrow?" Although I realized they were necessary, I didn't like the fact I hadn't been able to reach him.

"Yeah. Babe, I'm so sorry I didn't receive the texts on time. I added you to my favorites list, and from now on you can text and call even if I have the do not disturb on. I have no excuse except that my brain was on the meeting, and I fucked up." He took my hand and kissed my palm.

"It's okay. Brynn came to my rescue." I offered him a queasy smile.

"She's going to stay with you tomorrow. I don't like leaving you here by yourself when you're not feeling well."

Tears pricked my eyes. "Thank you both. I've never had anyone give a shit before." My focus bounced from Holden to Brynn, my heart full of gratitude and love for my new family.

After I realized the crackers and soda were settling well, I ate a few more. It was a little after midnight before I felt it was safe to go to bed.

"River, I'll be over around nine tomorrow morning. It seems like you're turning the corner, but it will be good to hang out."

"Sounds awesome. Thanks again." I waved at Brynn as Holden walked her upstairs and to the door.

I leaned forward and stood slowly. Although my stomach felt better, I was still a little dizzy.

"Hang on, babe," Holden said, hurrying down the stairs.

Not listening to him, I took a few steps toward him. He chuckled. "Always the stubborn and independent one." Before I was able to reply, he scooped me up into his muscular arms. "I've missed carrying you around, so I'm taking advantage of the situation."

"Sometimes I miss it, too." I leaned my head against his shoulder as he carried me to our room.

Once inside, he set me down on our bed, grabbed the trashcan and a towel from the bathroom, then placed them on the floor next to me. "Just in case." He stood, scanning the space. "I'm going to grab you some crackers and soda. I'll be right back."

I slipped out of my jeans and hung them on Holden's desk chair. Every time I looked at the desk, Tim and Logan's faces flashed before me. My stomach rolled again, proving my point that I was stressed out about the two men.

"Here ya go," Holden said, joining me. He set a plate and drink on the nightstand.

I crawled into bed still wearing my T-shirt and flopped over on my back.

"You're beautiful even when you're sick." Holden climbed in next to me and pressed a sweet kiss to my forehead. "Hopefully you'll be better in the morning, then you can rest."

I burrowed under the covers and glanced up at him. "How was the meeting?" I stifled a yawn, exhausted again.

"Good. Well, I thought so, but you'll need to let me know what you think."

My curiosity was piqued. "Oh? Do tell." I placed my hand over his and propped my head up with my other arm underneath me.

"What would you think about taking over another club? We would set it up similar to 4 Play."

"Wow, that's the business opportunity you were talking about?" I sat up, giving him my full attention. "Where's it located?"

Holden ran his fingers through his hair and glanced away. "That's the thing ..."

Chapter Forty

I stared at Holden, waiting for him to drop the bomb, my heart pounding against my chest.

"It's in New York."

My mouth hit the floor. "Holy Shit. Are you serious?"

"Very. We would travel back and forth." He paused, pinning me with his stare. "I'd love to do it, but I can't without you."

"Of course, you can, Holden. You built 4 Play before we ever met."

He grabbed my hand. "You don't understand, babe. Home is where you are. If it's here, or New York, or California ... The where doesn't matter to me as long as you're by my side."

"But you love what you do. I can't hold you back from that, and I —I." My eyes narrowed. "I'm selfish, Holden. I'm not okay with a part-time boyfriend, especially with Tim coming to Spokane."

"I'm not either, River. Where you are is where I'll be. If the New York club doesn't pan out, it's not the end of the world. I'll have other opportunities. *We* will have other opportunities. I'm not opposed to growing our business at 4 Play. After another year, you'll have more experience and I'll have graduated. The only reason I'm entertaining the possibility is because it knocked on my door. And it would give us some space from Tim." His words hitched, and I finally fully understood why he was toying with the idea. *Tim.*

"When do you have to have an answer?"

"Next week. We have time to talk it through." He stood and undressed, grinning at me. "You might be sick, but I can still be your eye candy."

I barked out a laugh. "Yes, you can." I appreciated him for lightening the moment. The information was overwhelming, and I wasn't at a hundred percent mental capacity yet.

Holden slipped beneath the blankets, and I snuggled up to him. He rubbed my back and turned on the television quietly. Minutes later, I drifted off to sleep.

* * *

I slept through the rest of the night, but at six in the morning, I was hugging the toilet again.

"I don't like this, babe." Holden held my hair for me as I puked.

"Oh God, this sucks ass." I propped the side of my head against the wall while he located a washcloth and wet it with cold water.

He wrung it out, then knelt beside me and placed it on my forehead. "How does that feel?"

I nodded and held it into place. "It still might just be a twenty-four-hour bug. I didn't start feeling like shit until after lunch."

Concern flashed in Holden's eyes. "I hope so. I'm glad Brynn will be over. It helps me not worry as much."

The washcloth fell off and landed on the tiles with a plop. Holden picked it up and grabbed a new one, wetting it with cold water again. "Do you think you can go back to bed?"

"Yeah. I think I'm okay now." Holden helped me off the floor and tucked me in.

* * *

My vision adjusted to the thin stream of light that had snuck its way into the bedroom. I blinked several times, attempting to clear the sleep from my eyes. The numbers on Holden's alarm clock glowed red and alerted me that it was after ten in the morning. Holden would have left when Brynn arrived.

I sat up, slowly swung my feet off the mattress, and rested them on the floor. My stomach didn't give me a big fuck you, at least. I took my time, then stood and changed into a pair of gray sweatpants, picked up my cell phone, then made my way downstairs to find Brynn.

"Hey, you have more color in your cheeks." She set her cup of coffee on the table and scooted to the end of the couch.

"Did Holden tell you I got sick early this morning?" I set my cell down near her mug, then plunked down on the other side of the sofa and grabbed my pillow from the night before. I clutched it to my stomach and eyed the steam rolling off her drink. "I don't even want coffee. Pretty sad, huh?" I offered her a weak smile.

"Holden's panicked, babe. He's not good with people being sick." She turned and faced me on the couch and tucked her legs beneath her.

"I'll be fine."

Brynn's lips pursed. "He wants me to message him at noon and if you're not making significant changes, then he asked me to take you to my doctor. She'll squeeze you in if I call."

I rolled my eyes at her. "He's overreacting, but I have a feeling I have no say in it, do I?"

Brynn grinned at me. "You're a fast learner. And it won't hurt anything. She can look you over, then pat you on the back and explain that you have the flu. She'll tell you to grab some Gatorade and rest. As long as you're not dehydrated, you're fine, but that's the tricky part."

Once I thought about it, I hadn't been able to keep any 7 Up down yet. "I'll get some soda and see how it works this morning." I stood and wobbled.

"Oh, fuck no. Sit down, babe. Holden will kill me if you hurt yourself." She hopped up and ran to the kitchen before I could object.

"Oh, God. What the hell is wrong with me?" I groaned and rubbed my face with my hands.

"Stress can manifest in strange ways, River. I'm sure you'll be running around tomorrow, good as new." She gave me the glass and I took a small sip.

Brynn sat down again, her green eyes searching me.

"What? Do I have puke in my hair?" I smoothed the back of my head, frowning.

"River, when was—"

My phone rang, interrupting her. I scooped it off the coffee table and answered with a smile. "Hey, how's your day going?"

"Fine, but I can't stop worrying about you," Holden said, fear dripping off his words.

"I'm drinking some soda now. Brynn said you've ordered her to throw me in her car and rush me to the doctor's if I'm not doing better by this afternoon." I stole a glance at Brynn. Her green eyes were wide.

She leaned forward, grinning. "I never said that."

We all laughed. "See, I'm even joking around. I'll be fine, babe. Please don't worry. As soon as I'm good to go, I'll be back at the club, then we can have lunch together."

"Mmhm," Brynn said under her breath, and I tossed my pillow at her.

"Brynn wants to eat Zayne for lunch." I shot her an ornery grin as Holden's laughter filled the phone.

"I can't deny the truth." She tossed up her hands in surrender.

"It sounds like you're doing better but keep me posted. I won't be able to get home until later this evening. On the positive side, the penthouse is looking damn good. I want to bring you up as soon as possible. It's just the finishing touches now. We're almost there." His voice was low, sending little delightful shivers through me.

"I can't wait. When will the furniture be delivered?" I chewed my lip, unable to contain my grin.

"Tomorrow. The truck will park at the unloading dock near the bar. They'll take the service elevator to the penthouse. If you're up to it, maybe you can check everything out before it comes up."

"Plan on it." Excitement coursed through me, and I took a big gulp of my 7 Up, feeling better by the minute.

"I've got to get back to work, but I'll call you later. I love you, River."

"Love you too, babe." My heart flip-flopped with happiness. "We're moving tomorrow." I bounced in my seat and squealed like a little kid.

"He's excited, too." Brynn grabbed her mug and took a drink of her coffee.

Over the next several hours, we talked about 4 Play, moving, and made plans to have a big housewarming party. Apparently, Brynn knew the entire city of Spokane. The more we planned, the better I felt. I was still tired and finally dozed off for a nap. By the time Holden arrived home around eight that evening, I was almost back to normal. Other than an occasional bout of mild nausea, I felt like myself.

Brynn hugged us both and left shortly after. She had to have been bored babysitting me. As soon as I had a chance, I wanted to buy her something special. I'd never had a best friend other than Addison, and she needed to know I loved and valued her.

"I'm so happy to see you feeling better," Holden said once we were settled into bed. He kissed me gently and I slid my fingers over the muscled planes of his stomach and into his boxer briefs.

"Show me," I said against his lips.

Holden rolled me over and brushed his mouth against mine. He drank from my lips and stroked my tongue with his. I melted into him, savoring each touch and caress as he made love to me. There was no doubt in my mind that this man was giving me all of himself. With every whisper and every slow thrust, he poured himself into me, and I held the special moment in my hands, then locked it safely away in my heart.

Chapter Forty-One

The following day, I groaned at the sound of Holden's alarm, then I realized I was excited. We were about to start a new chapter together. I rolled on top of him and peppered his face with kisses. "Wake up, babe. It's moving day." I giggled and nipped at his ear.

He wrapped his arms around me and moaned as he pressed his erection into my stomach.

"Lunch break, babe. I have to get cleaned up and get ready for the day." I attempted to get up, but he pinned me down and chuckled. "How about we shower together?"

"Only if I can soap you up." I giggled as he practically threw me off him and onto my side of the bed.

He took off running for the bathroom, his laughter filling the room.

"Cheater!" I yelled after him, jumping out of bed and standing near the doorway.

Holden turned the hot water on and grinned at me. "I have to pee, but you're welcome to stay if you want."

My brows shot up to my hairline. "Only if I have no other

choice. I'm the kind of girl that believes in privacy while using the bathroom, but ..." I danced around as I realized I needed to pee as well. "Let me know when you're finished." I backed away and turned in the other direction since Holden hadn't bothered to close the door.

"Finished. I'll be in the shower."

"No peeking!" I practically ran to the toilet, sat down, and relieved myself. I flushed the commode, then joined Holden under the spray. I leaned in, allowing the water to cascade over my body, rinsing my past down the drain along with it. Today I was taking my life back. Holden and I were starting a new phase together. My heart swelled with excitement. Five months ago, I would have never imagined that I would be on such a different path.

Holden pressed his lips against mine, pulling me away from my thoughts.

"Why don't you wash your hair and I'll take care of this?" He knelt and carefully placed one of my legs over his shoulder. Holden didn't waste any time as he sucked my sensitive flesh. I flattened my palms against the walls in order to steady myself.

"I'm so glad we have a seat in the new shower," I whimpered.

Holden moved my leg, then ordered me to turn around and bend over. He continued to worship my throbbing pussy until I yelled out his name with my release.

He stood and I grunted as he shoved himself into me.

"What do you want, baby? Fast and hard or slow?" He cupped my right breast as he asked.

"Hard."

Holden plowed into me furiously. Since no one could hear us, we moaned and panted loudly.

I glanced at him over my shoulder "Fuck me, Holden."

A low, throaty growl escaped him, and he picked up the pace, our bodies slapping together as we released in unison.

"Oh God, that was good." I laughed. "Told you we would be late."

"You're worth it." Holden pulled out of me, then turned me to face him. "I love you, River. Don't ever forget that."

He pressed his mouth against mine, and I wrapped my arms around him. "I love you, too, baby."

We soaped each other up and shared how excited we were about spending our first night in the penthouse.

Twenty minutes later, we stepped out of the shower, grinning like lovesick puppies. I dried off, then blew my hair dry while Holden dressed in jeans and a black polo shirt. His shirt was tight across his chest and arms, revealing his sculpted muscles. My tongue darted out over my bottom lip, and if we weren't already running late, I would've jump him again.

Holden poked his head into the bathroom. "I'm going to grab us some coffee to take with us."

"Perfect. Thanks." I applied a light amount of makeup and put my hair in a ponytail. I'd chosen a pair of light wash boyfriend jeans and a purple polo shirt. After I dressed, I fastened the necklace around my neck. I grabbed my phone off the nightstand and picked my handbag up from the floor. I unzipped the bag and froze. With trembling hands, I reached for the box with a sticky note on it.

Take it, then call me. Love you, Brynn.

Goddammit. She must have slipped the pregnancy test into my purse while I was asleep yesterday. There was no way that I was pregnant. I'd just had a stomach flu. *Fuck.* The possibility hadn't even crossed my mind since I was on the pill. I stared at the box, unwilling to touch it. Anxiety hummed beneath my skin. I narrowed my eyes, gathering my determination to prove her wrong.

At least Holden didn't know about her suspicions. I peeked at the instructions. Results took five minutes. There was no way that I could take the stupid test here. Holden would find out. I would have to take it at the club in our private bathroom. I rolled my eyes at Brynn. I loved her, but sometimes she jumped to the worst conclusions right out of the gate. I felt great this morning, plus I was on the pill.

I shoved the box deeper into my purse and placed my phone on top of it. Holden would freak the fuck out if he saw it, and today was our day. Nothing would ruin it.

After a final sweep over the room, I had everything I needed. The rest of our belongings would be packed and moved for us, which was a relief. Not that I had much, but Holden did.

I mentally told Holden's bedroom goodbye, then pulled the door closed. A pang of sadness filled me as I walked down the hall and descended the stairs. I'd fallen in love with Holden in this house. Our first memories were here, but on the other hand, I was ready to create new ones with him ... in New York. He was right, home was where I was, and all I wanted was to be with him. Flying back and forth wouldn't be a big deal. Besides, I'd always wanted to visit New York, and now I could support Holden with his dream.

Elated with my decision, I hurried through the house and to the kitchen. I halted when I laid my eyes on him. He took a drink of his coffee, his attention on his phone.

"Holden?"

He glanced up, a beautiful smile on his face.

"Yes," I said, my voice bubbling over with excitement.

He shoved his cell in his back pocket and set his cup on the counter. "Yes?"

"Yes to you. Yes to New York. Yes to the club."

"Are you sure, River? We'll be busy as fuck between the two clubs."

I walked toward him. "Do you promise to put me first? Make time for us? Because I will promise you the same. You'll always be my top priority. But you're right, we'll be super busy, and I need more than a quick kiss and fuck before we fall asleep each night. I need *all* of you." I placed my palm against his chest.

"The easiest thing I've ever done is put you first, River. I'll hire a manager immediately so we can have time for ourselves. I want to take you on a carriage ride in Central Park. I want to pick out a new place to live there. I want to spoil you rotten with dinner and Broadway." He kissed me. "I'm saying yes to *you*, River."

Holden's phone buzzed, but he ignored it.

"Then let's do it." I grinned at him so hard my face hurt.

Holden threw his head back and released a loud whoop as he picked me up, my toes no longer on the floor.

He set me down and laid a searing kiss on my mouth. "I love you so much."

"Love you too, babe." I placed my palm on his cheek and peered into his eyes, lost in all of the beauty that was him. Lost in us. I finally had the love of my life and a safe future beside him.

Holden's phone rang again, and he snatched it off the counter and answered it. "We're on the way. Excellent. Be there in twenty." He hung up and patted his back pocket. "The furniture is waiting for us. Wallet, cell, and the car key. I've got everything." A boyish grin eased across his features. He fished around in his jeans pocket, then produced the key. "You don't need it since I'll be with you, but ..." He reached for my hand and placed it in my palm. "Why don't you drive us to work, babe?"

My mouth hit the floor. "Are you sure? What if I mess up your baby?" My pitch rose with each word.

"As long as you're all right. It's just a car. Have fun."

I nodded and put the key in the front pocket of my purse, my mind wandering to what was waiting for me once we arrived at 4 Play.

I practically skipped to his car, giggling like a little kid on her birthday. If someone had told me five months ago that I would be living with the wealthiest man in the Pacific Northwest and driving his i8, I'd have laughed until I peed myself.

The drive to the 4 Play was like floating on a cloud. The car handled like a dream. One I'd never had before. Holden was calmer than I was, but once I got a feel for it, I relaxed. I pulled into the garage at the club before I was ready to. Then I remembered the delivery truck was there. Zayne and Vaughn eased into a parking space next to us.

We all hurried to the unloading dock, and I ran up the steps in front of Holden.

"We're here," Holden announced to the guys sitting on the ramp waiting for us.

Over the next few hours, we inspected and signed off on the furniture, then it was moved upstairs. I'd been so wrapped up in how amazing everything looked I forgot that I was supposed to pee for Brynn.

"Hey, I need to go to the bathroom. I'll be right back."

Since Holden didn't tell me to take Vaughn or Zayne, I figured he assumed I would use the restroom on this floor, but I needed some privacy.

I kissed him on the cheek and hurried to the elevator. I jabbed the button with my finger, then slipped in. The doors started to close, but an arm shot between them and the side, blocking them from shutting.

"Where are we going?" Zayne asked.

"No. No. Out." I pointed at the hallway, but he pretended as though he hadn't heard me. I glared at him. "Fine." I wasn't a foot-stomper or a girl to throw a tantrum, but for some reason, my temper went from zero to sixty in seconds.

The moment the doors opened, I flew down the hall to my office. Since no one else was on the floor and I wasn't inviting Zayne in, he took his time.

I stood still for the scanner, then hurried inside. My anger simmered below the surface as I slung my purse on the bathroom counter. I removed the pregnancy test, read the directions, then sat down to pee on the stupid stick. Once I was finished, I placed it on top of a few paper towels near the sink, then I set my phone timer for five minutes. While I waited, I typed a text to Brynn that the results were negative, but I didn't hit send yet.

I paced Holden's office, waiting for the silliness to be over with. I should be in the penthouse right now, directing the men where to place the new furniture.

My timer went off and I practically ran to the sink. I picked it up, ready to snap a picture for Brynn to prove she was wrong. Instead, I gawked at the result, then dropped it on the floor.

"Fuck!" I screamed to no one. "No!" I knelt and scooped up the positive pregnancy test. Tears streamed down my face. This couldn't be happening. I erased Brynn's message and took a picture to send to her later. I couldn't tell her that I was pregnant until after I talked to Holden. And I knew myself. If I didn't tell him now, then I would take matters into my own hands and not tell him at all. I couldn't do that. I'm sure he'd be on board with terminating the pregnancy. I didn't want kids yet, and maybe never would.

I choked on my tears. How in the hell would I be able to take care of a baby when I hadn't even been able to keep my brother alive? My anguished cry tore through me. There was no way I was keeping this kid. I wanted to finally live my life and be happy, but what if Holden didn't feel the same?

Clutching the edge of the sink, I pulled myself off the floor, then splashed my face with cold water. I shoved the test into a Ziplock baggie I kept for my toothbrush and secured it in my purse. I placed the phone next to it in the zippered compartment of the bag. My heart pounded in my ears as I rushed to the door.

I nearly knocked Zayne over as I darted into the hallway, then ran to the elevator. I had to lose him. I wanted to have just one goddamn minute to myself.

The doors opened, and I hopped inside and pushed the button. This time Zayne didn't make it. I barked out a laugh, imagining how pissed he was right about now. But I needed to find Holden and have a private conversation.

Once it stopped, I hit every button, delaying the return of the elevator to Zayne. I made a mad dash to the loading dock, determined I was going to tell Holden before I chickened out. I refused to have a relationship with secrets.

I stopped short when I arrived at the empty delivery truck. No one was there. *Dammit, they must all be in the penthouse.* I gazed into the massive space, trying to calm my racing heart. Footsteps approached me from behind, and I sighed. Zayne had caught up to me. I placed my fists on my hips, ready to explain why I'd ditched him.

I turned slowly when I felt a sharp sting in my neck before a bag was slipped over my head. Then a meaty hand covered my mouth as my attacker flung my body forward. I landed on a hard floor, my knees taking the brunt of the impact. Then I heard a door slide down. Bile swam up to my throat as I tore the bag off, gasping for air. My vision blurred in and out as the large vehicle lurched forward.

"Holden," I cried out. "Holden!" I crawled across the floor and banged on the wall. With a turn of the vehicle, I rolled and slammed against the side. Fat tears fell down my cheeks as I faded into oblivion.

* * *

My eyes shot open as I woke with a start to bone-chilling water all around me. Panic seized me as I recalled the needle in my neck and being tossed into the back of the truck like a rag doll before I'd passed out.

Forcing myself not to take a breath, I struggled against the hands that pinned my shoulders underwater. Fear ripped through me as I stared into savage eyes lurking above the surface. Savage eyes that I recognized well.

Holden's beautiful smile flashed across my mind and fueled a flicker of optimism that I could survive. I had to. I had to reach him. Holden needed to know the truth. I had to protect him.

With an extra boost of adrenaline, I wedged my thumb between the two ligaments of my attacker's wrist, then pushed into the soft flesh as hard as I could. This had to work. My energy was dwindling, and fast.

Suddenly, my head popped up, and I gulped in much-needed air as I gazed into the twisted and depraved face of a monster.

Whack. A scream tore from my throat as the impact rendered me helpless. Stars danced in front of my eyes as I started to slip away from reality. If this was it, I had one thing to say to my captor before I left this screwed-up world.

"Fuck ... you ..." The darkness beckoned to me, urging me to give in as she welcomed me into her arms.

* * *

Drip.
Drip.
Drip.

The steady sound reached my ears, and I struggled to open my eyes against the pounding in my head. Holy shit, I was alive. Hope bloomed in my chest. I had to find Holden. He was in danger.

A thin ray of light filtered through a crack in the ceiling, and I sat up slowly, attempting to make out my surroundings. A shiver ran up my spine, and I rubbed my arms as my gaze swept the nearly dark space.

"What the fuck?" My words fell flat, and I jumped to my feet as I searched the small room: dirt ceiling and dirt floors. I banged against the wall with my fist, pain shooting through my arm. *Where the hell was I?* My toes dug into the soil, the shock of my environment finally sinking in. *No! No! No!* I struggled to breathe, and the smell of the fresh earth tickled my nose.

I was trapped. Underground. Naked.

I pushed up on my tiptoes and tried to reach the cellar door, but it was no use. I frantically searched the space for any stairs or tools, but it had been stripped clean.

"Help! Someone please help me!" My head pounded while I waited for a response. Nothing.

Images rushed through my mind as I recalled nearly drowning and remembered the two additional people who were in the room other than the person attempting to kill me, watching as I struggled to survive.

A cold sweat rippled over me, and my pulse hammered, making me feel like I was going to pass out. How the hell had I made such a stupid, emotional decision to ditch Zayne? The horror of my mistake glared at me, and I placed a hand over my stomach. *Oh God, the baby.*

"Holden," I whimpered. "Holden! I'm so sorry!" Panic swelled up inside me, my chest aching. My knees buckled, and I sank to the cold floor, sobs wracking my body. I sucked in a deep breath, then screamed. It tore from my lungs, scraped through my throat, and shattered my soul.

* * *

Holden's search for River leads to dark, evil secrets, and heart wrenching moments.
Beautifully Broken is coming February 2022
Preorder it here!

* * *

Turn the page for a sneak peek of Beautifully Broken.

Beautifully Broken Sample

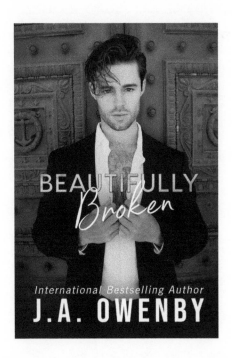

I didn't plan to fall in love with her, but she was my salvation.

When I found her—scared and abused, I knew I'd stop at nothing to protect her.

I grew up a billionaire and she grew up with nothing.

We're from completely different worlds, but that didn't stop me from falling.

She's feisty and smart—everything I never knew I needed.

Loving her gave me peace from the darkness that hides inside me.

Someone took her from me.

I won't stop until I find her and get her back.

But if there's one thing I know—the past doesn't stay buried forever.

Follow Holden as he searches for River and dives deeper into a world full of corruption and deceit, learning about the dark, buried secrets that torment him.

Turn the page for the Beautifully Broken Sample!

Prologue

The sunlight glinted off River's brown hair as she stood, her hands framing her slender hips. Excitement rippled in the air as our penthouse's first pieces of furniture were unloaded from the delivery truck.

I was ecstatic, not only because our place was finally ready, but because River had agreed to go to New York with me and turn an existing club into another 4 Play. At one time, I'd been thrilled about expanding, but honestly, as long as she was by my side, I'd be happy anywhere. She was my future.

"What do you think?" I slipped my arm around her waist as we eyed the black Italian leather couch that the men had unloaded in front of us on the loading dock. The walnut dining table caught my attention. I was counting the minutes until I could pick her up, place her on the edge, and eat River for dinner.

"It's all beautiful." She grinned at me, and my heart jumped. "You're beautiful."

"This is just the beginning, babe." I leaned down and pressed my mouth against hers. "I can't wait to make love to you in our bed. Then

I'm going to bend you over and fuck you on every possible surface of our new home," I whispered against her ear.

River discreetly grabbed my ass, and I nearly moaned as her tongue darted over her lower lip.

"What if I'm a bad girl?" She peered at me through her eyelashes, and my cock pushed against my jeans, ready to be freed and buried deep inside her. I could almost taste her sweet pussy on my lips and tongue.

"I hope you are. I have a surprise for you later."

A flicker of regret danced across her features, then morphed into relief. "Surprises used to suck, but I love yours." River leaned against me, and I pulled her closer.

She placed her hand on my chest and smiled. "Holden, I need to go to the bathroom. I'll be right back."

"Okay, babe."

She kissed me on the cheek and walked away, my gaze landing on the soft sway of her hips and the curve of her ass. Not only was River physically beautiful, but I loved her heart. Her mind. Her fight. And I was the lucky son of a bitch she slept next to at night.

This moment marked a new chapter for us—a new beginning. River finally had her fresh start. I briefly closed my eyes and imprinted this memory on my brain for eternity, promising myself that I'd never take her for granted.

* * *

Chapter 1

I clutched the little black velvet box in my hand, nerves tingling up my arm as my heart hammered against my chest. Maybe spending so much time together had bonded us faster, but I knew without a shadow of a doubt that I wanted to ask River to marry me. It was rushing things with River, but I'd had more sex than most men would in their lifetime, drank more booze, used more drugs, owned a successful club, and shared secrets that I'd take to my grave. I'd lived a full life already at the age of twenty-two. River's presence made me a better man, and I wanted to wake up next to her for the rest of my days.

With a smile on my face and love bubbling inside of me, I sat on the edge of our brand-new bed. The sheets, blankets, and light blue and white comforter were still in bags, resting on top of our dresser. *Our* dresser. It was funny how furniture could make me feel so connected to River.

I gazed out of the bedroom windows, overlooking the city of Spokane. River had fallen in love with the gorgeous view of the rushing water of the river. Maybe we could get married on a boat, or at least honeymoon on one. The mental image of River in a skimpy bikini made my dick instantly hard. I couldn't wait to fuck her on every surface of our new home.

A pop of lightning split the sky as stormy, blue-grey clouds rolled in. Plump raindrops splattered against the glass. I was grateful the weather had held off until we'd moved the furniture.

Flipping the lid of the box open, I stared at the two-carat diamond surrounded by emeralds on the engagement ring. It was one of a kind. I'd had it designed with Brynn's help. While River and Brynn shopped, Brynn would peruse the jewelry stores, collecting information for me on River's tastes. And tonight, surrounded by our friends, I planned on dropping to one knee and popping the question. I sighed with contentment. Even though I wanted River to have the wedding of her dreams, I wasn't opposed to marrying her tomorrow. The moment I'd found her sleeping in my recycling bin, I realized there was something different about her. Something fierce and beautiful. My life had drastically changed over the last five months. She'd taught me to live again, to love again. My heart had opened up, and instead of running from it, I ran to her.

I gently closed the box as my mind reeled. Pierce had informed me that my father, Tim, was back in Spokane, and shivers of disgust tiptoed up and down my spine. Once I'd learned more about who he really was, I referred to him as Tim. In my mind, he was no longer my dad. The sorry son of a bitch had tried to rape River, but she'd put him in his place. If he were smart, he'd stay the hell away from us.

My hand balled into a tight fist. While he was in town, I'd make sure that River had security with her twenty-four seven. I couldn't take any chances. If Tim was tangled up in illegal weapons, then the men he associated with were as dangerous as he was, if not more. The hairs on the back of my neck bristled at the mere idea that Tim might hire someone to come after River. It was my responsibility to keep her safe. Guilt twisted my gut into knots as memories of Hannah's smile haunted me. I hadn't kept her from harm, but I wouldn't fail this time.

Hopping up, I busied myself with opening the package of the Frette Bold sheet set. I couldn't wait to bring River home that night. This was our bed, not one that I'd had other women in, including Becky. I was still in shock about Becky's behavior toward River. I'd known Becky for several years, and if anyone had mentioned to me that she would hold a knife to someone's throat, I would have told them they were fucking crazy. Man, had I missed that one.

I quickly fluffed our pillows and tucked the blankets into neat corners under the mattress. I was ready to give Tim, Logan, and Becky a swift kick in the ass and file them and their shitty behavior in the past. Since Dan had died owing Logan a ton of money, Logan was willing to take River for payment, and that shit didn't fly with me. From what River had mentioned, Logan was a meth dealer and bad news. I didn't want him anywhere near her. River and I were off to New York soon. We had a new and exciting future in front of us, and that's what I wanted to focus on.

My cell buzzed in my back pocket, and I removed it. Zayne's number illuminated the screen.

"This is Holden."

"Is River with you?" Zayne asked, his voice thick with tension.

Goosebumps pebbled my arms. "No. Isn't she with you?"

Silence filled the line for the length of a heartbeat.

"She ditched me." There was no way that I could ignore the seriousness in Zayne's tone.

Anxiety punched me in the stomach. "Where are you?" My palms grew sweaty, and I wiped one against my jeaned thighs.

"At the loading dock," Zayne responded.

I didn't even bother telling him I was on my way. I just hung up and dialed River's number. No answer. I tried again, but it went straight to voicemail.

Opening the new nightstand drawer, I placed the ring in the back where River wouldn't find it. Then I bolted out of the penthouse, my mind clamoring with possibilities of where she might be. The first stop was our office.

I called River three more times as I searched for her everywhere on the third floor, including the conference room. Nothing. Absolutely no sign that she'd even been there.

I swore under my breath as I paced in front of the elevator, willing it to hurry the hell up. My brain told me there was a logical explanation for why she would ditch Zayne, but a storm was brewing in my heart. Had Logan found her? Had Tim done something to her? Fear wrapped its cold fingers around my chest, and I rubbed my sternum. Surely, she was okay, and this was all a misunderstanding.

The doors whooshed open, and I hurried inside, selecting the main floor. As soon as I reached my destination, I darted out and ran to the loading area. Vaughn had joined Zayne, concern flashing in his mismatched gaze.

"What the hell is going on?" I asked, placing my hands on my hips, remaining beneath the overhang with Vaughn and Zayne.

Zayne turned slowly, and my stomach plummeted to my toes when I realized he was holding River's purse. Time stood still. The sound of my heart drowned out the rolling thunder and sheets of rain slamming against the side of the building.

"This was left here on the loading dock." Zayne's voice was low, his expression grim. "They'll take prints, so if you want to look through it before the police, then I'd grab some gloves."

Nearly stumbling backward from what Zayne was implying, I whirled around and headed inside for the bar. Someone had taken River. Frantically, I rummaged beneath the sink until I found what I needed. I shook out a white pair of latex gloves, then returned to Zayne. He handed me her purse, and I cringed. I'd never gone through her belongings unless she'd given me permission, but this was different. I swallowed, my throat thick with fear.

Without pause, I opened her bag. "Fuck. Her phone is here." I glanced at the men, then pocketed her cell. If the cops found out, I'd get in trouble for withholding evidence, but I didn't give a shit. If she was really missing, I needed to know what the hell was going on. I offered a silent prayer to the universe as I unzipped the middle compartment. I could hardly breathe when my attention landed on a clear, zip-top baggie. Its only content was a little white stick—a white stick with two blue lines and the word "positive."

My heart rate exploded into a frenzied gallop. I couldn't catch a breath. Sheer terror coiled in my chest.

Reality seeped into my soul as I slowly dropped to my knees. River was pregnant ... with my baby. I was going to be a father. Shock clouded my mind briefly, then I rose to my feet.

Tears blurred my vision. "River is pregnant. We have to find her. Now!" Anger churned beneath the surface as it dawned on me that Zayne hadn't kept up with her. I replaced the test into her purse, then set her bag down. My hands clenched and unclenched, itching to slam my fist into his face. "How the hell did you lose her? This is why I fucking hired you! You're supposed to be keeping her safe!"

Zayne straightened and met my furious gaze, which made me crazy. He was going to be a man and own his fuck-up.

"She ran out of her office and down the hall. The elevator must have been on our floor already because she was on it before I reached her. I ran back to the opposite end to take the stairs, but the door was locked from the other side." Zayne's green eyes narrowed. "River didn't want me to follow her, Holden. I don't know why, but something had her spooked pretty badly. It took almost five minutes before the elevator returned. I could see that it had stopped on every floor. By the time I got here ... all I saw was her purse. I called her, searched this area, and had Vaughn search the other floors." Zayne swallowed visibly. "Maybe she's with Brynn?"

"I don't understand why the door to the stairwell was locked. It never is. I use the stairs every day. Did you let River out of your sight long enough for her to lock the stairwell?"

"No. We went straight to the third floor. She went into her office for a few minutes, then flew past me to the elevator. Unless you have access from one of the offices directly to the stairs, it's not possible. The only other person she was with this morning was you, then me," Zayne said.

I scrambled for his explanation to make sense, but Zayne was right. River had eyes on her all morning. Something wasn't settling right inside my gut. "Zayne, call Chance. Vaughn, if you'll reach out to Jace, I'll contact Brynn."

I grabbed River's purse, entered the club, and sat at the bar. I tapped the green icon on my iPhone and pulled up Brynn's number in my favorites.

"Hey," she answered.

"Is River with you?" I asked, cutting out the pleasantries.

"No, I haven't seen her today."

My pulse skyrocketed. Sweat broke out over my skin as fresh anger coursed through my body.

"Holden?"

How had I let this happen?

"Holden, what's wrong?" Brynn pleaded, concern bleeding into her normally perky tone.

"Have you talked to her? Texted or anything?" I mentally begged River to come home ... to be safe.

"No. We were all meeting at your penthouse this evening, but I haven't talked to her yet." Brynn paused. "What's going on, Holden?"

I hung my head and ran my fingers through my dark hair as foreboding iced my skin. "River's missing, Brynn. She was able to ditch

Zayne, and now we can't find her. Her purse was on the loading dock, along with her phone and ..." Did I tell Brynn that River was pregnant? I chose to wait in case River waltzed through the door at any second.

"Fuck. Holden, that's not good." Panic seized Brynn's voice. "I'm on my way to the club. Have you called the guys to see if they've talked to her?"

I could hear Brynn moving in the background, and I imagined she was running through her kitchen and to her garage.

I glanced up, eyeing Vaughn and Zayne, who were now inside standing next to me. "I had the bodyguards reach out, but by the sound of it, no one has seen her." My stomach lurched, and bile swam up to my throat. "I think someone took her, Brynn." I nearly choked on my words.

"No. She has to be all right. We have to stay positive. I'm in my car. See you in a few minutes. Please let me know the second you find her." Brynn disconnected the call, and I placed my phone on the bar top.

"Holden," Zayne said. "You need to file a police report, but I'd like to reach out to my bosses. Pierce and Sutton can help before the cops can. We can keep it quiet and move faster."

My nostrils flared. If Zayne had kept up with River, then she wouldn't be missing in the first goddamned place. I turned slowly, and my fingers clenched. In one quick movement, I hopped off the barstool and closed the gap between us. "This is your fault," I spat.

Regret coasted over his face, followed by a shadow of conflict. "I know," Zayne said, not denying my accusation. I backed away, wrapping my fury into a neat little package, and shoving it down like I always did.

Vaughn stepped in front of Zayne and blocked me. "I understand that you're upset, but handle it later, man. We need to find River and we're wasting valuable time."

My anger simmered down long enough for me to realize that he had a valid point. I'd deal with Zayne later.

Over the next half hour, I called the cops and reported River as a missing person. It helped that I had a few connections with the police, but there wasn't much they could do yet. Zayne was right. I needed Pierce and Sutton's help.

"I'm here!" Brynn said, running toward me. "Have you found her?" She halted in front of me, her hands trembling. Brynn's long, red hair was piled into a messy bun. She must have been in a hurry because her face was free of makeup and her white shirt was untucked.

My heart galloped. I shook my head and pulled her into a hug. "We think someone took her." I grabbed Brynn's hand and led her away from the bodyguards. We'd stay where they could see us, but I needed Brynn's help and didn't want Zayne and Vaughn to know.

I removed River's phone from my back pocket and the pregnancy test from her purse. "I don't want the cops to have these." I turned Brynn's palm up and placed the life-altering contents in her hand, the plastic crinkling beneath my fingers.

"Holy shit." She paled, then glanced up at me. "This is why she has been so sick." Tears moistened her eyes.

"I need you to hide those. I'd rather have Sutton help with River's cell than turn it over to the authorities." I hesitated. "If we get caught tampering with evidence ..."

Our conversation was interrupted by a few officers arriving. Brynn discreetly shoved the items into her handbag. "I've got your back, Holden. You're not alone." She squeezed my shoulder and remained next to me as the cops approached.

Jace and Chance arrived at 4 Play half an hour later and practically ran to me. Chance's expression was grim as he approached. "What can we do to help?" He shoved his fingers through his blonde hair and blew out a breath. Chance was clearly frazzled but remained calm. He'd slipped on black dress shoes with his designer jeans and a white rumpled shirt.

"I don't understand," Jace said, placing his hands on his hips, worry flickering to life in his blue-grey eyes. "How did this happen?"

Jace rubbed his chin, most likely analyzing the situation in order to find a missing piece. He kicked the toe of his tennis shoe against the wood floor and bowed his head. "What can I do?" He shoved his hands into his jean pockets, his bulging triceps peeking out beneath his basic black T-shirt.

"I'm not sure yet. Let me talk to the authorities and I'll know more here in a few." I patted them each on the back, grateful that my best friends were with me.

For the next several hours, the police searched the club and delivery area for any signs of a struggle, then reviewed the security footage. I swore a blue streak when I realized there was a blind spot at the loading dock. The camera hadn't picked up shit.

They asked all of us questions concerning the furniture company, names, descriptions of the employees, and who else was on site. Since I'd been in the penthouse, I wasn't sure if anyone had shown up after the men had unloaded our belongings.

The longer we searched, and the longer River didn't show up, hope began to fade away. I'd denied the nudge of my instincts, but I couldn't anymore. The harsh reality had been shoved down my throat until I fucking choked on it.

River was gone.

Order Beautifully Broken on Amazon!

Also by J.A. Owenby

BOOKS BY INTERNATIONAL BESTSELLING J.A. OWENBY

Bestselling Romance

The Love & Ruin Series

Love & Ruin

Love & Deception

Love & Redemption

Love & Consequences, a standalone novel

Love & Corruption, a standalone novel

Love & Revelations, a novella

Love & Seduction, a standalone novel

Love & Vengeance

Love & Retaliation

The Wicked Intentions Series

Dark Intentions

Fractured Intentions

The Torn Series, inspired by True Events

Fading into Her, a prequel novella

Torn

Captured

Freed

Standalone Novels

Where I'll Find You

About the Author

International bestselling author J.A. Owenby grew up in a small backwoods town in Arkansas where she learned how to swear like a sailor and spot water moccasins skimming across the lake.

She finally ditched the south and headed to Oregon. The first winter there, she was literally blown away a few times by ninety mile an hour winds and storms that rolled in off the ocean.

Eventually, she longed for quiet and headed up to snowier pastures. She now resides in Washington state with her hot nerdy husband and cat, Chloe (who frequently encourages her to drink). She spends her days coming up with ways to torture characters in a way that either makes you want to throw your book down a flight of stairs or sob hysterically into a pillow.

J.A. Owenby writes new adult and romantic thriller novels. Her books ooze with emotion, angst, and twists that will leave you breathless. Having battled her own demons, she's not afraid to tackle the secrets women are forced to hide. After all, the road to love is paved in the dark.

Her friends describe her as delightfully twisted. She loves fan mail and wine. Please send her all the wine.

You can follow the progress of her upcoming novel on Facebook at Author J.A. Owenby and on Twitter @jaowenby.

Sign up for J.A. Owenby's Newsletter: BookHip.com/CTZMWZ

A note from the author:

Dear Readers,
If you have experienced sexual assault or physical abuse,
there is free, confidential help. Please visit:
Website: https://www.rainn.org/
Phone: 800-656-4673

This book may contain sensitive material for some readers. River and
Holden's story is considered a dark romance with language, sex, and
violence.

Lightning Source UK Ltd.
Milton Keynes UK
UKHW010119010222
398006UK00002B/42